D1798927

Little Fingers!

Little Fingers!

Tim Roux

Copyright © 2007 by Tim Roux.

ISBN: Softcover   978-1-4257-4513-4

"Little Fingers!" was first published by Night Publishing, a trading name of Valley Strategies Ltd., a UK-registered private limited-liability company, registration number 5796186. Valley Strategies Ltd. can be contacted at http://www. valleystrategies.com .

"Little Fingers!" is the copyright of the author. All rights are reserved.

The cover image is based on the painting "Sheherazade" by Sharon Hudson, and is the copyright of Sharon Hudson, 1992. All rights are reserved. Sharon Hudson can be contacted at http://www.byhudson.com .

With the exception of Su and David Erhardt of the El Almendro Hotel & Restaurant, and the Molino Santa Ana, Cacin, all characters are fictional, and any resemblance to anyone living or dead is incidental.

This book was printed in the United States of America.

To order additional copies of this book, contact:
Xlibris Corporation
1-888-795-4274
www.Xlibris.com
Orders@Xlibris.com
36221

This book is dedicated, with all my love, to Ralette, who is a constant inspiration.

Chapter 1

"I know you know the answer. I am absolutely bloody convinced of it. I can taste it."

You leant forward towards me over your beer, Inspector, and your brown alcohol fumes plumed around my nose. Ten years earlier, you would have been smoking. You used to smoke forty a day, you told me.

You were looking sad and troubled, and defiant, as usual. Determined in the face of habitual defeat. In your world, no outcome is ever good, but you are driven to get there by the shortest route anyway. That is what makes you a policeman. You have the mind of a drill bit.

"You don't know you know the answer, Julia, not yet. You may have a lurking suspicion. You may even have it all worked out subconsciously. We have to unlock your brain to solve this mystery. There is a serial killer out there. He is living in that brain of yours as an unrecognised memory, a shadowy computation, and he must be stopped. You can stop him. You have to concentrate, but on something else, to get there. These repressed truths have to be approached obliquely. What do you do to relax?"

Your voice sounded earnest and professional, but your thoughts were sliding up my thighs. They went all the way. I always know what you are thinking. A few hours in the sack with me, and you might have both a climax and a result. I wasn't prepared to try it then. It was not that I wanted to deny you, only that I could not face losing Mary. She is so fragile, and so honest. I cannot hurt her.

Do you remember the first time we met, when you arrested me for Tom Willows' murder? You came to my front door and knocked. My first glimpse of you was as a frosted shadow through the glass door panelling, swaying slightly. I opened the door, and you turned to me, a grey, pock-marked face, grey eyes, grey hair curling greasily and untidily—someone I would normally not have noticed with any sense of appreciation.

"Are you Miss Julia Blackburn?"

"Yes, I am."

"May I come in?"

"You may have to say who you are first."

"Apologies, Miss Blackburn." You showed your police identity. It could have been almost any piece of identity, except for the stock exchange security badge, which I would have recognised. "Police."

"Police?"

"Yes, Miss Blackburn. I would like to have a word with you, if I may."

I was thinking "Police? Police? Driving offence? Dog licence? Being a nuisance to the neighbours, but I am as quiet as a ghost. Why the police?"

You instinctively seemed to know where the sitting room was (left into the hallway, and left again). Or perhaps you already knew the house.

"Please sit down, Officer."

"Inspector," you corrected me. I do not know the difference between an officer and an inspector. Isn't an inspector an officer? It seemed to matter to you.

"Inspector John Frampton."

"Pleased to meet you, Inspector." I know that it is always wise to be polite to the police.

"Miss Blackburn . . . ."

"Yes."

"I have just come from Tom Willows' house on the green. I believe that you know Tom Willows."

It was less than a loaded question.

"Indeed, I have just come from there myself. Well, an hour ago. Maybe two. One-and-a-half."

"You saw Mr. Willows this afternoon?"

What was this? When I had left Tom, he was lazily dissolving into a satiated sleep.

"Were you at Tom Willows' house around two hours ago?" you repeated. Beyond those nondescript grey eyes I could detect a killer instinct lurking. Well, it was nothing to do with me. I was innocent in relation to this line of questioning.

"Yes."

"You are sure."

"I am absolutely sure."

"In that case, Miss Blackburn, I must ask you to accompany me to the police station and warn you that anything you say may be taken down, and may be used as evidence at your trial."

"Inspector, I do not have a fucking clue what you are talking about." The use of the swear word startled you momentarily.

"I arrest you for the murder of Tom Willows this afternoon."

I fainted.

When I came to, I was still in my house, lying on the sofa with you, Inspector John, and two uniformed policemen hovering over me.

You said something, but I could not immediately lock into your speech patterns. Then you were helping me to sit up against a pile of my red super-sized, soft cushions, and you had placed a mug of sweetened tea into my hands. I assume that you were doing this by First Aid numbers. When a suspect faints, lay her out flat, and make sure that all the air passages are clear. Monitor her pulse. When she comes to, encourage her to drink a cup of warm sugared tea, except that you made it a mug. In my limited experience of the police, everything is done by numbers and according to procedure. How can you live that way? Does it make you feel re-assured to be free from any degree of discretion, other than to shock me into a head-crunching faint with the starkly-delivered news that the man I had left in great contentment two hours beforehand was dead, and that I was to be charged with his murder?

I noticed some fluff on the carpet, and traces of peanut shells. A larger ball of fluff, and a smaller trailing one, crumbs of white outer-shell interspersed with red speckles. Why does it take the presence of strangers to make me to want to clean the house?

You did not apologise for your clumsiness. You stood there patiently for me to become sufficiently compos mentis to be driven down to the police station. Gargoyle threw his small sausage body on top of me, and lay looking at me from the comfort of my stomach.

I heard one policeman say to the other "That must be the ugliest dog I have ever seen." The man passing this judgment was several barrels of beer overweight, and otherwise undersized and sweaty. I laughed. Gargoyle looked round to scrutinise him, and turned back towards me.

In your mind, Inspector, I could hear many thoughts churning and fluttering, declaring that you were no longer sure of yourself. You had walked through the door with a betting certainty, and now the evidence was sifting away. You were watching my every move and expression, and I was watching your grey, dead eyes. You were like a fish staring into an aquarium. I was a human being drowning inside it. We were both fighting for breath.

After about ten minutes, you led me to the car. There were several bystanders loitering in asymmetrical groups. I did not know any, except by sight. "What shall we do about your dog?" you asked me.

"You can come and feed him here, morning and night," I replied.

"I do not believe that we offer a dog sitting service in this police force," you remarked sardonically.

"You don't offer much of a police service, either," I responded. "If you were doing your job properly, I would not need a dog sitter." I had given up on being polite to the police.

"Don't you have a neighbour you could ask?"

"If you had given me more notice, quite possibly. Should I wander around the village asking some friends?"

"OK, we will deal with it."

"I hope that you will put more effort into it than that. Gargoyle is a very good friend, and does not deserve to be worried. He must be given the impression that all is well."

It is strange how, even in the most adverse circumstances, even when every gun in the room is trained upon you, you can take control. I was so angry with you, that I was determined to make your life hell.

I attacked you all that evening, and over the next day, until you were convinced of my innocence. I was not afraid of you. I wanted to rip your throat out. One might have assumed that this insight into my aggressive nature could have reinforced your belief in my guilt. After all, you had arrested me for murder, and who more likely to have committed that murder than a hot-tempered person who had left the victim's house only minutes before he was killed? Instead, it convinced you of my innocence. You work at an emotional logical level, not at a rational one. Truly intelligent people do.

So, after twenty hours, alternately inquisitioned and abandoned in that bare, tatty, third-world police station, I was released back to my home. I did not reach for the whisky bottle. I drank warm, sweet tea, and reflected on why police stations are so scary. I decided that it is because they are so devoid of care and attention that you get the terrifying impression that if that is the way they treat their environment, how will they treat you?

✳   ✳   ✳

Over the months, we became not quite friends, but at least regular acquaintances and conspirators. Mary no more comes to the pub with me than she does with Frank, and I like lunchtime pubs, at least once a week. So, we sat down together as apparent outsiders to the village, and we talked, and watched the indigenous of Hanburgh discussing us.

I became an insider to your thoughts, more so than you ever realised, because I can hear so much of what you are thinking.

Frankly, we were both lost. Events were unravelling around us, and we could not individuate the causes. We knew whom we liked and disliked. We loathed Mary Knightly and her father, Dr. Berringer. We loved Mary (Maloney) of course, and Brenda behind the bar. We suspected George Knightly, and were devastated when he died, and our only hunch was blown apart. Tony James was a contender, but we never really believed in him.

One day, you placed your empty pint glass carefully onto the beer mat, leant back in your chair with your hands up around the back of your head, arms out like wings, and declared "The way things are going, Julia, it is either you or me. And it isn't me."

"And it isn't me."

That is when you leant forward towards me and said "Julia, I know you know the answer. I am absolutely bloody convinced of it. I can taste it."

Following your hunch, you consulted a psychologist to find out how best I could be helped to surface my subconscious understanding of events in the village. She suggested that I be encouraged to describe these events in a stream of consciousness. If I could be persuaded to write a book . . . .

So, you asked me to sit down and write out everything I know about Hanburgh village from when I first arrived there until after the latest murder took place. There may have been more by now; we have been out of reach down here.

I cannot work out whether you really think that I know the answer, or whether you were just hoping to spend intimate time with me. I don't know because you don't know. You are attracted to me, and you are following a hunch. You are an intuitive man. All the arrows point in the same direction. That is enough for you.

I hope that you do not suspect me of having any part in the murders (I don't). Two of those who died were very special to me. The third was not, but he was my uncle, I suppose.

You say that I must write absolutely everything that I remember, exactly as I remember it. Ideally, I should write about each memory as if it were happening now, and view it from all angles—from my own point of view, but also from those of others.

I should give my every thought, no matter how embarrassing or libellous or hurtful it would be to anyone. I must pour out a stream of consciousness. My mental editor must be locked up in a broom cupboard, and not allowed out. She will bang on the door and try to kick it down, like a drug addict undergoing cold turkey. I must resist. You want everything.

I agreed. I know that I shall never rest until I have gained access to, and pieced together, all the clues that I have subconsciously gathered along the way. And, anyway, I have always wanted to write a story, so this is a great opportunity. God has given me the script, so now all I have to do is to discover what it is, and to write it down.

You see, I agree with you, Inspector. I too believe that there are things that I have picked up, stray conversations, observations, intuitions, that, when moulded together either by you or by me (or by both of us together) will lead us to the murderer(s). It will be fun to solve these crimes, won't it, as well as a relief. You are the professional policeman. Now what we need is the gifted amateur sleuth to come up with the goods, and I would love it if that were me.

So I am going to write, and to write, and to write, until "bang!" the truth will explode out of me. I am looking forward to it. I have never done anything like this before. It is an adventure, and I shall emerge triumphant, and with a book on how I did it. A true life murder mystery—it could be a best seller. I don't need the money, but I fancy the fame.

I am not planning on suffering while I do it. No white walls to stare at in some dingy northern town like Wigan for me. I have set myself up near Béziers in southern France. That may have upset you. You will not be able to sit around for hours on end discussing every nuance of my mind. There is something of a torturer-victim relationship going between us. I don't object to it—they say that the victims become quite dependent on their torturers after a time—but it gets in the way of my task, to find out who murdered all those people.

You may think that I am running away, but what from? I have nothing to hide. I have nothing to fear. Things are hidden from me, fearful things, but with time and application I will force them out into my consciousness. I am nothing if not determined.

Mary is accompanying me on this sombre, if exciting, voyage of discovery. Well, sort of. She gets to go and lie on the beach and generally laze about, while I do all this writing in the garden, listening to the cigales, smelling the rosemary, and squinting in the sun.

Mary has agreed not to read this, which means that there will be one huge and growing secret between us, but that is her choice. She does not want to inhibit me, and she feels that her catching up on what I have written on a daily basis will inevitably release that editor from the cupboard.

I love Mary. She is so extraordinary, and compassionate, and gentle, and a warm presence at all times, first thing in the morning, last thing at night, when we are relaxed, even when we are stressed, when we are dressed and when we are naked. Mary, I repeat even though you will not be reading this for a long time yet, I love you. I love you. Thank you for everything. You deserve the full thirty minute Oscar speech all to yourself!

There you are, Inspector, I am getting into the flow already, and I haven't really started yet. Mary and I have just been into Béziers to stock up with all the things I need to liberate my mind. We adore Béziers, it is still unspoilt, it has beautiful churches including that huge cathedral on the hill. There is a rather dishevelled broad promenade in the centre, lined with trees and cafés, and with great potential. There are streets of smart boutiques. We have bought wine, we have bought cheese, we have bought bread, we have bought tomatoes, and we have bought loads of chocolates from that charming couple at the Jeff de Bruges franchise who have recently abandoned their office jobs in the north to make a go of it here.

So, with this idyllic backdrop of lavish gastronomy, the undiscovered version of Aix-en-Provence, the pitch-perfect love and companionship of my "wife", let's kick this baby into action.

I promise you, Inspector, you are going to be shocked. I have heard a lot. I will not hold back, not on what I know you were thinking about me, not on what I was thinking about you, not on any random thoughts I had at the time, however dirty, or violent, or shameful. You have asked for it warts and all, so here it is, warts, shit, unbridled passion and all.

I hope it leads us to your murderer. I'll re-phrase that. I hope it leads us to the murderer(s) you are determined to catch. I hope we become famous. I hope this technique becomes standard police practice for use with talented and insightful witnesses who happen to want to write a book (the "Blackburn-Frampton" technique). I hope that it will continue to be as riotous as it feels now, starting out.

Hang onto what little hair you have left, Inspector. Here goes!

Mary is here to defend me from the murderer when I discover him, although at the moment she is looking about as threatening and as protective as a Labrador, curled up reading her Côté Sud homes and décor magazine. And if the murderer turns out to be her, I'm a gonner! Yikes, Scooby!

❋   ❋   ❋

I was going to start the story on a new page, but after two days, I am still skirting round the clear open space.

Well, that is not strictly true. I have typed a few lines many times and deleted them again. So, I am faced with a clean new white sheet in the centre of my computer each time.

Finally, I have become impatient with myself. This is ridiculous. Just get on with it, girl (I always laugh at that). I have to surprise myself into starting.

It is weird this nervousness of mine. I am not habitually a nervous person. I am used to taking massive risks, both with other people's money and once with my entire way of life. Why should it matter whether I type a few things that nobody will ever see, unless I choose to let them? If my thoughts are complete rubbish, I can simply throw them away as we simply throw away nearly all our thoughts in our lives. Every day we have a million thoughts that are stupid, banal, mean, or absurd, and of those million perhaps we remember one, and then only fleetingly. Only about once in every five years have I had a thought that embarrasses me regularly, that rears up like a skeleton out of a graveyard to shame me as I pass. And that is invariably when I have placed that thought out into the open.

The last time, I was in a room talking to some people, and I was commenting on how seldom people notice the supremely obvious. I turned to Richard and said

"You know, Richard, you could be sitting next to somebody most of the evening, and you would never notice that they were bald. Somebody would comment that your neighbour was bald, and you would say, oh, I never noticed." There was a slight hush around me, and Richard looked rather embarrassed, and it was only then that I realised that the person sitting next to him was indeed bald. He took it in good part, but I spent the next three weeks intensively wishing my faux pas back inside my head.

I have decided to begin with the car crash.

I acknowledge that the crash is not the start of the story, but it is why I decided to live in Hanburgh. The real start of the story is my mother, who was brought up there. However I would never had bothered to go there if it weren't for the accident.

I was coming down a mountain in the Alps, south of Grenoble. It was a stunning mountainscape morning. I had been driving for hours, only stopping to fill up with petrol, to drink coffee and to buy baguette sandwiches (gruyère, salami and ham in that open sweetened bread, as you ask). Actually, I did also sleep for about an hour in the car as I was feeling exhausted. You may know that feeling too, when you are so tired at the wheel that you begin to miss moments of your life, and you think "Was I asleep?" On a motorway there is a reasonable chance that the rat-a-ta-ta of the studs protecting the hard shoulder may protect you. On a mountainside you are unlikely to be so fortunate.

As I was saying, I was driving this old left hand drive Mercedes 250 over the mountain. It was 22 years old, and I had not had it checked over. It had been pitch dark when I woke up, and then the skies were lightening, and finally it was like the most beautiful dawn I have ever seen, in late November, the fresh air layered over the open meadows surrounding me. Heaven beckoned me. The sun came up, and I put on my sunglasses.

I started to descend the mountains, breaking carefully on each turn because I was not used to driving up there. I was wondering whether I could fill up with petrol shortly. The gauge had gone on the car, and I feared I might be approaching empty. I had a spare 5 litres of petrol in the boot, but a Mercedes 250 is a big car and chokes through the fuel, especially with an out-of-condition engine.

Cars occasionally crossed me from the other direction, their occupants feeling their way around the bends as much as I was. We were none of us going fast.

Then, round one bend, there were no more brakes. There was no warning. I pushed my foot down on the brake peddle and it went flat to the floor. No pressure; no resistance.

This is a problem in any car, but an especial problem in a Mercedes 250 as there is no handbrake as such, only a fourth pedal that ratchets on the parking brake. The trouble is that this is one of the few makes of car to be fitted with such a system, so applying it in an emergency is not second nature. I eventually remembered it when I found myself in mid air sailing over the bend and down about 200 feet into a village below, when of course it is no longer of any great benefit.

It was at that moment that I experienced peace. Gliding through the air, silence, calm, the sun bouncing off the bonnet, the village clear below me, beautiful, chalets with their long swept roofs, a spired church with a cross. It did not feel that there was a fearsome distance between the car I was sitting in and the village. I saw everything arching very slowly. I let go of the steering wheel. In mid air it is of no more use than the handbrake. I looked around. I was probably going to die. Maybe I would live. I did not anticipate being hurt, perhaps being a quadriplegic for the rest of my life. I just thought that there was a straight choice—and not my choice—between living and dying.

I was in a coma for three months after that. Sometimes such decisions take time.

Chapter 2

After the accident, and back on the streets, so to speak, everything was shocking. I was numbed. I could not stand up without feeling faint. I was continuously anxious and afraid.

In the hospital, I had been protected. I had been given six weeks of psychiatric help and psychological coaching by leading experts in their field (after all, I was something of an experiment). I felt really confident about returning to the world, impatient.

Then, released out into that world, all of my expectations were turned upside down. It was like viewing a hotel from the kitchens and backstairs when you are used to being a guest. My automatic reactions were of no value. Worse, they were dangerous. They would lead me into exactly the wrong direction. I was repeatedly battered over the head with the difference from my previous life. I was running down a red carpet that someone was pulling out from under me, and I was barely keeping my balance.

During the first few weeks, I would discover people staring at me.

However, within three months, I had acclimatised.

I went back to work in the City. That could have taken some explaining. I imagined trying to explain it, and I found that I couldn't. I foresaw the complete lack of comprehension, and to be honest avoidance, in the eyes of the people I would try to tell that the old me had died, and that the new me had come back all the hungrier after my near-death experience, and I knew that any explanation would just take up too many sentences for anyone to listen to, and demand too much attention and courage, and that if they did listen and react, it would be for all the wrong reasons. I would be labelled a freak, never to work again. So, after fifteen seconds of rehearsal, I stopped and resolved not to restart.

I let Mark Findlay in on the secret, and he gave me a second chance. He also surreptitiously cleared up on the old me.

I did well. Exceptionally well. Better than before in fact, so Mark did not lose out. Far from it, he made a killing. And he had a secret. Mark loves secrets.

The strangest experiences I had during those first few months took place in City bars. They were recurring nightmares. This is a scene (only the name of the man changes) . . . .

I am sitting opposite a considerably older man. He is not attractive. He has just slipped his wedding ring into his pocket.

He asks me why money is such a terrible burden.

"You may not believe this, Julia, but having too much money is a curse. I feel cursed. It would be so much easier to be poor".

That's funny, I reflect. I can bring to mind one hell of a lot of people who believe that having a great deal more money would answer all of their problems instantaneously. I should bring these guys together for a spot of match-making, and pocket the commission.

It wouldn't work. While old floppy jaws would be only too delighted to give away his money, it can only be to someone who already has lots of money and is trying to get rid of it himself. Those who do not have all the money they can dream of simply do not deserve it. Those who are not already trying to give it away lack a moral perspective, and so don't deserve it either. So he is lumbered with it, which is of course what he wants to be, plus inside my knickers.

The other development I had to come to terms with during that period was a newly acquired gift for unsolicited telepathy. I do not know where it came from, but it turned up with a flourish, and it stayed. However much a burden having too much money is, being on the wrong end of unsolicited telepathy is much worse, I promise you.

Thoughts come from everywhere constantly. Not only thoughts—visions.

The first time it happened, there was suddenly this enormous great **Kerblamm!** I leapt four foot in the air, and screamed.

Everyone in the bar turned round on me and asked each other what was going on. I didn't have a clue. All I had was **Kerblamm!**, a blinding flash and a roaring monster in my ear. And such fear! Not only my fear, but someone else's fear underneath it.

I searched all the faces around me trying to work out where the sound came from. Everyone was looking at me. There were no clues. I only saw what I saw, a huge explosion that someone else had witnessed, God knows where.

And what I am picking up from this man opposite is that he would like to see all the girls in the bar naked, at least all the pretty ones. The uglier, fatter ones get to stay as they are. Men spend a lot of time thinking about sex. It is almost constant. I have now honed my technique, and I can track down to the square metre who is thinking what, but it doesn't matter because all men are obsessed by sex. The fantasies are interchangeable.

I suppose that any attractive girl guesses that men want to peer down her front and slide their hands up her dress, but to know it absolutely and relentlessly is something else. It is like being dowsed in a carwash of lustful speculation. It is not a light drizzle to be quietly endured. It is a raging torrent to force you into the doorway and beg for a passing of the cloudburst. Imagine being caught in a downpour forever.

I'm sorry if I am frustrating you, Inspector. I am just letting you know how it is. It is boring. I want other thoughts. I want stimulation. And all I ever get are the same thoughts in different voices.

Well, the man opposite me has worked up the courage to ask me out for a meal. Is it true that in America, if you accept the third date, it is like the third match, you're skewered? No third date for him then, nor even a second.

"Sorry, David. I must go back to do my hair. I have to work tomorrow, and I am seeing Suzie in the evening."

So many non-sequiturs in one statement.

❁   ❁   ❁

The air is cool outside. It gets me away from all these fetid thoughts.

The truth is that I am turning cynical from everything I experience, and I am becoming excoriated—I am losing my heart.

I have noticed it in nurses and policemen, such as yourself. You see so much bloodshed, so many people at their worst, so many injustices, so many cruelties, so much stupidity.

In the end you give up caring. You are employed for a special responsibility that you undertook because these things really mattered to you, and you become gradually overwhelmed by it.

You have done better than us, me anyway. You have cared in the first place. You answered to your vocation. Sorry, Inspector, you have lost. I can see it in your eyes as we talk, in your whole demeanour. You are no longer trying to save the world. You are trying to solve a case for pride and professionalism's sake.

With my now heightened understanding of the world, born of privileged glimpses, I am in danger of becoming lost too. That is perhaps what we recognise in each other. We are the damned as we sit at our table talking.

I did not volunteer for this. I did not approach any humanitarian employer with a bleeding heart anxious to shed my blood. I had insight thrust upon me virtue of one God Almighty bang to the head, and who is to say that it was not He who arranged it. I must have been a prime target, the way I was living my life at the time. Maybe he decided to make me privy to what was really happening in the world, to see where I would jump. Would I turn my head away, or would I address the real world?

I cannot turn my head away. Turning my head away does not tune down the voices, the fears, the joys, the passions, the anger, the affliction. Turning my head away does not allow me to escape for one second what I admit I should have been paying more attention to many years ago. If I had paid attention then, perhaps I would not be deafened now. Deafened without the hope of becoming deaf. All man's suffering is landing on my plate as a main course, with Death-by-Chocolate scratched from the menu.

I did not choose this. Probably it was not chosen for me either. I survived, and this is my price, not for survival, but for surviving. It is the package I picked up on the way, and will never put down.

It is all humanity screaming for something, and against something else.

Imagine you were surrounded by a billion cabbies demanding justice and their fare. That is where I stand, God love me. And he probably does, not least for giving him the night off.

Every time I think of God I think of a man (because I am a traditionalist) who made the world by mistake.

I have no specific "in" on this, so your guess is as good as mine, but that is what I imagine.

God is a man who was absentmindedly rubbing some quarks together, and two quarks made a quawk. He examined it a bit, and He started rubbing the quawk, and it made a super-quawk. With a lot more rubbing He gained an atom, and from an atom eventually He got a molecule, and from a molecule a cell. Then everything was way out of His hands.

So I doubt that He did it deliberately. I do not picture Him getting out His pens and His papers, muttering "Let's get to the drawing board", and intentionally inventing life.

Nearly all great inventions come about by accident. True, the inventors often had something in mind, but often not the same something as they got.

I am not at all sure that God was after anything at all. He was just fidgeting.

Then this thing grew bigger and bigger, like expanding foam except that it was intelligent expanding foam. It learnt things, and it adapted.

God watched all this in awe. It gradually dawned on Him that one day this tumescent soup would be capable of rocket science and cloning.

He got very excited. Well, you would be. Something He had created (His fidgeting was now reframed as a deliberate act) was taking on a life of its own. Think about it. Man has been desperate for centuries to create a new life form, and God had achieved it in the palm of His hand on an eternity morning while mulling over what to do that day.

Show any child a patch of ground, and sprinkle seeds onto it. Take the child back to the same spot a few weeks later, and there are seeds growing. The child jumps up and down with glee.

So God jumped up and down too. He was beside Himself with pleasure at His new creation. He spent all the hours that He had (so all the hours) watching it develop. And it got bigger, and bigger, and bigger.

He lost himself in time while it grew, and it grew, and it grew.

Then something alarming happened. It grew differently. It stepped out of the framework it had started with, and diversified. God bent down and watched, fascinated. This was even more exciting, this dysfunctional aberration. Then the aberrations got aberrational, and out of those by now multitudinous aberrations, life was formed. Imagine your first sight of life, man or God.

At some point He must have asked himself "How do I control this?", and then He thought "Let's put it off for a few centuries. Let's leave it be and see what happens."

And what happened happened quite quickly, at terrifying speed over millions of years, which wasn't long for God. And the more it happened the more He let it happen because it was so fascinating, so many ramifications and speculations. He tried to work out what was going on. He became a philosopher. He became a mathematician. He became a scientist.

He gave things a little nudge from time to time, and provoked new outcomes. Was He interfering for the better or for the worse? For good or for evil? What was good and what was evil? It started out as what He liked and what He disliked; what He wanted to see happen and what He did not. After a while God, as a philosopher, examined His own motivations and decided that they were not enough. There had to be an objective basis for good and evil. So He travelled the path all later philosophers travelled down. It is difficult to entertain a thought that God has not pondered with great seriousness first. Except that He took a much wider view. He was concerned for the well-being of all creation, all materials, all formations, all substances, all life. Each element of His universe got a vote. He had some complex calculations to make. Did the benefit of 1,000,000 beings that lasted no more than a day outweigh the interests of 100 beings that lived 100 years? How does a life equate to a square metre of earth?

To answer this He decided that He had to create an objective for His universe, a vision (He did not bother to tangle himself up in too many definitions, worrying Himself over the differences between visions, missions, goals and objectives. He took an empirical view—was it over here or over there that we should be striving to attain? He did not allocate random timelines, milestones and deadlines either. When He first heard people using these terms with great earnestness, He roared with laughter because no corporate plan ever laid down that such and such an objective would be achieved in a million years, which was often about its realistic timescale. People laid down tiny timescales—next week, two weeks' time, next month, by the end of the year, in five years' time—then randomly hit them or missed them. However, He did notice that applying these timescales motivated people to do more than they otherwise would have done. Was that "more" for the better or for the worse? He could not answer that without His vision).

And this is where He got stuck. The world was created without a vision. It had no original purpose. It was a fidget. God tried to superimpose a purpose. He considered that good was whatever was in the best interest of the continuation of the universe. You could ask why the universe should continue, that was a valid question, but unanswerable. It had to be considered a given. Now He got to the calculation. How do you calculate whether a tiny activity over here (say an ant's breath) benefits or not the continuation of the entire universe in some sustainable fertile form? When you think that there are more stars in the sky than grains of sand on a beach, you begin to grapple with the enormity of the problem.

So God gave up, and decided that He would just try to keep the volume down instead. There were all these cries coming up from everywhere in the universe—cries of happiness, of sadness, of distress, of exultation, of agony. They were making a huge eternal booming wave of a noise (as arrives in my head nowadays on a much smaller scale), and God decided that they were seriously interfering with His enjoyment of the universe.

So He created another human being, whom He called His son, to at least try to sort out human beings, who were disproportionately responsible for the distress God was suffering because they were so articulate. Christ came down to earth and delivered his message well—"Love God, and love your neighbour as yourself (and therefore quieten down a little—you are making far too much noise!)". Unfortunately, the humans started shouting and clapping when he announced the first two sections, and so never quite heard the third message in brackets. Human beings have selective hearing.

Christ said "God is listening to you (there is no need to shout)." They missed the second bit out of their excitement over the first.

Christ on the cross cried out "Father, oh father, where art Thou now in my time of need?"

God said "Human, all too human."

When Christ ascended back into heaven he looked downcast and said "Father, I have failed you. I have not stopped them, and I have started shouting myself."

God said "Catchy little so-and-sos, aren't they? Do not distress yourself. We are all doomed to failure. It is an inevitability of the universe. I understand that now. I shall no longer interfere in the universe's affairs, except for fun. I am not going to have the universe deny me some fun. I want to see the smile of children when they are given their favourite toy. I want to rejoice with the mother who has given birth to her child. I want to feel the exhilaration of men who achieve great feats at the limit of their capacities. I want to share the breathtaking beauty of landscapes, sunsets and of all creatures. I now declare that good is everything that is joyous and generous, and that evil is the opposite. Now all I need to work out is how to judge it. It is an intractable problem."

❈   ❈   ❈

Chapter 3

My sister, Louise, died at the age of six of leukaemia.

I was ten at the time, so I can remember her well.

She was the nicest of children, and I talk as a rival for affection. Well, less a rival than a loser. Everyone doted over Louise because she was blonde and pretty, and smiled easily. At the time I was dark and plain-looking, and inclined to sulk.

Children grow different ways. While in my case my transformation came at the end of a surgeon's knife, I have seen many girls (and especially those wearing glasses) shock all those around them by seemingly overnight switching from pug-ugly not-a-chance-in-hell-of-getting-laid types into slinky-legged sizzling sex objects. You can always tell these types by the startled look on their faces when it becomes obvious that the most handsome man in the room fancies them.

Equally, I have seen very pretty little girls bulk out into ordinary looking adults with four kids, a pushchair, and a best friend they moan to as they walk along the pavement. Maybe Louise would have become one of these, but at the time of her death she was still beautiful.

Beautiful but ethereal. For two years we all fought to keep her, and the medical profession did everything it possibly could for, or arguably against, her. The holy hope is first of all the bone marrow match, then the transplant. I would certainly have given my bones to help her, even my entire body, but I was not a match. Appeals went out around the country as her surgeon sharpened his scalpels for a spot of heroic surgery.

We were told throughout that the odds were good, that most recovered from childhood leukaemia. A match would be found, the chemo and radiation therapy would work, and she would "soon be clambering back on board the raft of life". You may think that was my analogy, but you should be able to tell from the clunk it gave that the words came directly from a euphemism-wielding medical professional.

Hope started low, leapt high in the air, followed by progress, regress, and finally digress. By the end we were consulting anyone at all no matter how unlikely their treatment régimes. Louise was an innocent child led by the hand from waiting room to waiting room. She carried her toys with her, knowing that she would be there most of the day, and that there would be another "there" tomorrow.

Throughout her extended ordeal she remained good-natured and calm, a professional patient carefully examining patient professionals. Perhaps that was the problem. Perhaps we should have taken her to someone who would have shouted and screamed and railed at the injustice of it all, and actually done something. There is a belief that the true professional is the one with the reassuring manner, however, in my experience, it is the over-the-top raging lunatic who is the one you should back every time in a crisis. They really fight on your behalf, and absolutely refuse to let you go. Your death is their death, and they aren't about to give up on either of you. That is what my surgeon was like. I was lucky.

On the other hand, if you are a parent, your biggest anxiety is that your mortally sick child becomes either frightened or intimidated. You quiz your friends and acquaintances over the reputation of each consultant, waiting for someone to say that Mr. So-and-So really looks like he knows what he is doing. Unfortunately, the one who will actually do what is necessary is often the one everyone describes as "a bit out on a limb." We are talking about the consultancy business here. The most successful consultants, in terms of revenue and reputation, are those who look the part and offer a safe, if fatal, choice.

Inevitably, Louise's slow slide towards the grave raised the question of "Why her?" On the basis of any sort of merit where life is the prize, it was inconceivable that this plucky, beautiful, courageous, honourable and frail child should be singled out for this gruesome treatment. "Why her?" My mother discussed it many times with her priest, who confessed that he could not begin to phrase an answer. She questioned each successive medical professional how it could have happened. Each one had his own list of potential causes from electro-magnetic currents, to pollution, to diet, to genes, but none was conclusive. We asked each other the question many more times besides, knowing it was rhetorical, and that we were more giving expression to despair than expecting the other to attempt an answer. The only acceptable and appropriate response was for me to shake my head dolefully, and ask her if there was anything she needed, giving her the opportunity to suggest once again "a miracle". Please, please.

From what I know now, I can still not venture any explanation beyond that life is morally random. Lottery winners are seldom saints, and child victims are rarely sinners.

You can comfort yourself with the notion that we all have to experience life, and for the very best of us God says after only a few years "They are ready for the next life. They have nothing more to prove. They have graduated", before whisking them away. I think that this is rubbish, but it is some consolation.

Strangely, Louise never asked "Why me?", or at least not that I ever overheard. She accepted that it was her immediately, and followed the trail of her fate with great thoughtfulness, and minimal dissent. It was all happening to a child who had her body, and who wasn't really her. It is a remarkable phenomenon to watch, and a much better one to be spared.

The second to last time I saw Louise, she was lying on the grass in the garden, watching some ants. She liked ants. Our mother had bought an ant colony kit which was a plastic container into which she poured sugared sand. You could see the ants burrowing away. Louise admired their ceaseless energy.

The last time I saw her was when she had already slipped into a coma over the weekend. I had been away, sleeping over with friends, and my mother believed that it would be too distressing for me to be recalled to join her at Louise's bedside. I remember thinking that it was odd that the sleepover was lasting so many nights. My friend Rupert's parents came up with some plausible excuse or another.

The death bed of a child is especially grim. It affects the hospital staff as well as the family, as well as anyone who happens to be passing. It is so against our desired order of things. We want to believe that everything has its time and place, and that a child has no place dying. We want to believe in meritocracy, such that all smokers, and drinkers, and drug abusers, and child-batterers, and wife-beaters, and rapists, and traffic wardens should go first. It is not that way. The hospital beds of thousands of young children tell you otherwise.

"Oh God, why her?"

I prayed for special powers to save her.

Chapter 4

Have you thrown this book down yet, Inspector? You must be shouting "Get on with it, Julia. Get on with it." You must want to get to the heart of things, and you are only getting to the heart of me. Maybe that is some compensation. I am trying to get to the heart of me too.

I am taking my time, I am afraid.

I am giving you a privileged insight into how my mind works because we have sat so many times together, talking, that it is only fair that you glimpse everything, and that you realise that I know everything—your every thought.

Maybe you are getting hot under the collar. That flush that starts as a thumping in the chest, and rises to a heat buzzing through your ears. Then the cold feeling descends, and the terrible realisation dawns. She knows everything?

And when you have read this, and we meet again, you will be attempting that impossible task—not to think something that you are already thinking about. "Do not think about pink elephants", we used to challenge each other, and laughed as we realised that we could not subsequently banish pink elephants from our minds for the duration of the task. "Do not think about my naked body as we talk, Inspector." One of us will be deeply uneasy throughout our conversation. We will never be friends again, because you will be unavoidably aware that I will have a detailed map of what you are thinking as we talk, and that the playing field can never be level between us.

I get a map, and pictures too. It is a three-D neural map, the sort of map you see if you buy brainstorming software where you can link any concept to any other concept. On my map, labels shimmer as they are in a constant flux of re-evaluation. On one side of my brain I get the live pictures, either in scanning mode (where the most interesting mental pictures around me zap in and out of my consciousness), or in personal mode (where I can lock in on every visual and aural thought a specific individual has).

I can also scan groups, monitoring what each person is thinking of the other. You can imagine that what you get is not what you see. I must have spent most of those first few weeks with my mouth open, physically reeling, occasionally laughing out loud.

You may have the impression by now that I am the sort of person you definitely do not want to spend time with any more. I am too bizarre, too scary. I am not at all the person you thought I was.

That is the question everyone asks, don't they? "Will they still love me when they find out what I am really like? If the one I love had unlimited and total access to every thought I have day and night, what would they think of me? Would they forgive me?"

Our first reaction is that they would despise us. They would know about our greed, our peevishness, our anger, our pettiness, our spitefulness, our contempt, our desire for serial adultery, our hope that our parents will die so that we can inherit all the money from the sale of their four-bedroomed detached house, our wish that our children would up and leave us at the ages of 28 and 24, our almost irresistible urge to pick up a shotgun and shoot all those people who really annoy us.

Actually, maybe what they would mostly discover is how nice we are. They would find earnest, generous thoughts. There is a strong desire in us all to do our best for everyone. When the person next to us is in trouble, we want to help. Social rules often discourage us from doing so, but we really do want to drag the person out of their mire, at some considerable personal inconvenience.

Take mothers and their children. I am not a mother. I will never be a mother. I am not cut out for it. However, I have watched them. The amount of worry the average mother gets through in a day planning how her children can have a pleasant, invigorating, rewarding, educational 24 hours! And that is the tip of the iceberg. Mothers strategise every few minutes as to how their children can develop, and grow, and find fulfilment and happiness over a whole lifetime. Whenever anything goes wrong for their children, their first concern is whether the mishap hurts now and how it can be remedied, but the very next thought is how this incident might blight their children's entire lives. After this, will they ever be the same again? They are constantly searching for things that will change their children's fortunes for the better, and dreading those that will change them for the worse.

Men are not like that, even the house-husband types. They are generally baffled watching this stream of uncertainty flow through their partners. They are more physically aloof, but that is not it. Men simply worry less about people, themselves and others. They have more of a sense of the transitory nature of the world. Things will go wrong. Things will go right. You cannot have the ups without the downs. Women worry about people. Men worry about finances.

❋   ❋   ❋

You must, by now, be wondering if I will ever get to the point when I arrived in Hanburgh, and still more whether I will give my side of what happened there.

Allow a woman to tease you, Inspector, and to tease out the real truth for herself. We women are wilful creatures, especially in front of a willing audience.

The answer is yes, definitely, I will tell you all, and it is all just about to begin.

I came to Hanburgh for one reason only. I became very, very rich. Less than five years after I had been virtually annihilated as a person, I became a super-person, someone who no longer cares about the rules, or the consequences. I can afford them all.

I do not suppose you know what it is like to be exceptionally rich. You have no doubt met such people, and found us either exceptionally decent or exceptionally arrogant. I flatter myself that my wealth did not change me much. I was always both.

The secret of my wealth is no secret. I invested every penny I could get my hands on in a market as it swept up like a tsunami wave, and I bailed out before it crashed into all those high rise buildings lining the beach, killing everyone still aboard or in its way.

I remember just sitting back and watching the numbers whizzing round. And such large numbers, bigger and bigger every time I looked at them. I sat there laughing helplessly, the uncontrollable giggling of the supremely lucky. How can anyone have had this much luck? I was not even anywhere near the richest woman alive. What must she feel like, no doubt many years on from me? Was she still feeling lucky, or bored, or angry, or euphoric about the world? Where would I be by then?

Of course, I know the answer by now—bemused, and disassociated, out of the swim of humanity, sidelined, alienated, afraid to lose what I have, and to be lost in what I have. I am about ready to complain to some young person in a bar about the burdens of wealth. Oh my God!

I remember the day I leapt out of bed and said "Enough! Get out before everyone else starts flailing around." I offloaded the lot over two months without anyone noticing, I believe. Three months later, the Internet bubble starting blowing air through its anus, stinking out the financial world as it shrivelled away.

And I have all that money in the bank, and bonds, and precious metals, anything other than shares. It is all sitting there. I can do almost anything I want.

With the voices of the world in my ear, I am almost godlike. Is it time for hubris to lengthen its shadow over me?

So let me talk about Mary Knightly, the first person I ever heard of in Hanburgh. The woman my mother hated with a passion.

My mother warned me many times about people like Mary Knightly, with whom she spent some of her childhood in Hanburgh. "You must believe in people," my mother would counsel me. "Most people are good, even when they are behaving badly. They are willing to help, and to share, and to enjoy others' enjoyment alongside their own. It is foolish to be cynical about people because you are afraid." Then she would take hold of my hands and kneed them with gentle strokes. "On the other hand, there is another type of person. They are usually deeply unhappy people. They absolutely must be feared, and preferably avoided. They will introduce you to hell, and they will never stop. They will never get better, and there is no strategy for dealing with them. They are destructive, out and out."

"And how would I recognise them?" I would ask.

My mother leant forward and whispered. "You cannot hear them."

"Not at all?"

"When they are being silent. In the spaces between their words."

"You cannot hear anyone when they are silent."

"You can if you are listening carefully."

"You can hear them when they are saying nothing?"

"Yes."

"Mummy, you are losing it."

Now I know differently. I can both hear and see what people are saying, and I know that my mother was more right than she can even have been aware of. She was guessing. I know.

I misuse my powers, I am afraid. I have a little stratagem that I try out from time to time. It is a miraculous sleight of thought. I synch into your thoughts and travel alongside them. I can make comments that astonish you by how much we believe in the same things. I have heard you exclaim "Extraordinary! That is what I think too." I normally blushed modestly, and said something like "Well, yes, we do seem to be of like mind, Inspector." Then when we were running down the same track, I would insinuate a deviant suggestion, encouraging you into a direction that you would not normally have entertained. You cavilled for a second, and then you chose to re-align with me. That like-mindedness was just too cosy to abandon. I built on this disorientation of the psyche to push you further. Within minutes, you were flat out with me, whatever I said.

I am sorry to have treated you like a laboratory rat, but it was just so wonderful to watch, to have this power over you, over everyone.

However, it does not work on people like Mary Knightly. They have some sort of disruptive technology that resists empathy. If you lock in on what they say, you find that they have dodged elsewhere. Unlike everyone else, they are not interested in whether you agree with them or not. They are only interested in whether you do what they want you to do, which is inevitably unreasonable. They insist on being unreasonable. If they were being reasonable when you complied with their suggestion, then you may have obeyed them merely because what you thought they wanted was the right and proper course of action. That is no test of their power over you. However, if they are totally unreasonable, and you still follow their wishes, the only possible cause is because they have power over you. You are their creature. So, all the time they test whether you are still enslaved to them by being rigorously unreasonable. Are you with them, or are you against them? Do you dare to be against them?

I cannot read their thoughts. I hear silence. I approach a zone of white sound. Nothing can be heard. The air becomes eerily still, and a little cold. There is a blank expression to their mind. And then I know that I have to be watchful, on my guard.

The good news is that they do not seem to know who I am, or at least there is no indication that I have ever detected. There again, as their thoughts are silent, I would never know. Either way, they do not glance at me or in any way acknowledge my presence. They pass me by.

And how would you spot them? It is not as easy for you. That is why you do not recognise them, why you are taken in by them, why you victimise others before falling victim to them yourself.

Now let me tell you the story as it happens.

❄   ❄   ❄

Before I do that, I must tell you one more thing about myself.

After I had my accident, after I was reconstituted by the surgical team, after I learnt about my new powers, as I began to come to terms with them, I made a strategic decision.

There are two types of Mary Knightlys in the world. There are the minor league Mary Knightlys, like Mary Knightly herself, and there are the major league ones, like Joseph Stalin or Adolf Hitler. They are the same creatures underneath, living on different scales.

With my new-found powers, I could take on either. I could use sympathetic suggestion to get a personal audience with the appropriate dictator, I could enter the room, I could shake him by the hand, I could flatter him and make him laugh. Dictators have no discernible sense of humour, but they laugh when you flatter them. Then I would kill him.

How would I do that?

After the accident, I was visiting South Africa and I went on a three-day safari. It was magnificent. I saw all the big game in their natural habitat, and they were magisterial. On the third day, we were standing next to the jeep, and suddenly a lion leapt out on us. According to the guide later, this was most unexpected behaviour from a lion. The lion came at us very quickly. Involuntarily I stepped in front of it to shield the rest of the group. As it made ready to spring, I suddenly felt this energy welling up inside me, my eyes flared like fire, and my brain exploded. The lion was on its back legs, starting to leap, then it wobbled and it dropped at my feet, its jaws gently encircling my ankles.

The group was flabbergasted. They wanted to thank me out of sheer relief, but it was not obvious what I had done. Because the situation was otherwise inexplicable, the guide rapidly explained that this particular lion was in the process of being monitored because it had a heart problem. Obviously it had got over-excited at the prospect of making a kill and had suffered a heart attack. Having had the situation explained to them, the group came up to me one by one to congratulate me on my courage in stepping into the path of a rampaging lion.

What the guide said was untrue, because I heard him. He was panicking as to how to explain this apparently super-human feat, so he made up the story of the lion's weak heart. He did not want to acknowledge to himself what had happened as it defied nature, and he wanted to reassure the others too.

I knew what had happened. I had killed the lion with my thoughts.

So I could kill a major league dictator too, using the same powers, but only one of them. I would be arrested and the rest. I would be a bee that could only sting once, not a wasp that could attack and sting many a foe.

And would I improve the world with that one sting? I am not sure that I would. My favourite social scientific law is the law of unintended consequences. For anything that you do, there could be the one intended consequence (and that is not guaranteed) and the two or three unintended ones.

Kill a dictator, and who comes to the funeral? Maybe worse—does anyone come to the funeral? There is, apparently, according to political science, a significant difference in the way that conservatives and socialists think. Socialists think that any change is for the better. Conservatives know that change can go both ways. Your investment can go both up and down.

And say I were to kill Putin in the way I have just described. He almost certainly deserves it. What he has done in Chechnya, the way that the people have suffered for their desire to be independent, is utterly reprehensible. He has tortured, maimed and murdered on the cynical calculation that he is fabricating an enemy that will unite the Russians and keep him in office. In its way it's as disgusting as Bush's calculation that if he invaded Iraq the price of oil would shoot up, and he would make himself fabulously richer.

The question is, what happens when I have killed Putin? Is the world a better place? If I were to kill Bush, it would be simple. The Americans would get rather upset for a few days, the network TV companies would drown in cash, there would be an election, and in a few weeks nobody would remember who he was.

For Russia it is different. Russia is always in the process of falling down because it has never been given sturdy legs to stand on. It has always been led by dictators who lend it their own legs and do not see any benefit to allowing the country to survive independently of them. If they die, the country may well collapse. It is not worth the risk of subjecting over 200 million people to misery and maybe civil war in order to rid the world of one would-be tin-pot dictator.

And most of the ugliest dictators run countries like that, ones that will descend into chaos if they fall. That is why I dare not strike at that level (plus I am terrified of pain, and I know exactly what would happen to me if I were to bump off everyone's favourite dictator who keeps the privileged in power, even if they could not prove it was I who killed him).

So my decision was to focus on the micro-dictators—the Mary Knightlys. In their way they do an enormous amount of damage, and yet the fall-out of their demise is minimal. Everyone shrugs their shoulders and says "Good riddance. I am glad to see the back of that one."

To deal with a Mary Knightly is to commit a good deed acclaimed by all, except of course by Mary Knightly, at minimal risk to myself.

So, I admit it, Inspector. I came to Hanburgh as an act of revenge, with the intention of killing or otherwise destroying those people whose acts had driven my mother to suicide. I knew whom I was after. First of all Mary Knightly, the woman my mother regarded as being the most evil person in the world. Then Dr. Berringer, for a reason I shall explain later. Then the man who raped my mother, leaving her pregnant. Those were my targets as I drove up to Marshalls the estate agents in Church Street looking for somewhere to rent in this village.

And then I found myself in the middle of someone else's war of revenge, I assume. Someone decided to kill off quite a different set of people for their own reasons, or perhaps out of their own unreason. It is a shame that our lists have never coincided. We could have co-operated. Instead, the killer blocked my sights. Mary Knightly is still alive. Dr. Berringer is still alive. And I still do not know who my father is.

So what does it feel like to know that the person you sat opposite during all those lunchtimes had murder on her mind, was a criminal in thought if never in deed? Would that shock you, or surprise you, or leave you unimpressed? Do you assume, as I have now come to understand, that everyone is a murderer-in-waiting; everyone wishes to kill; that we would all be murderers if we were certain that we would get away with it? And, let's face it, someone is getting away with it. Even though two of the people they killed were very special to me, and I am extremely angry about that, I must admit that one part of me says "Good on you for your courage. Now I would like to revenge myself on you."

❈   ❈   ❈

Chapter 5

The first person I meet in Hanburgh is Tom Willows. He is walking along the beck with a spade in his hand.

I am watching the ducks and swans diving and scratching in the mill pond.

He walks slowly, as if surveying his estate, and as if anyone discovered there should be noted and accounted for.

"Good morning," he calls. "Prospecting for lunch?"

I smile. "After London, this is a peaceful change."

"Ah, you are from London are you? The Big City. The smoke."

"I am not sure that we ever call it that."

"Probably not. Probably not. So what brings you here? I am Tom Willows, by the way." He moves forward and offers his hand. He scrutinises me intently. He gets right inside my guard, as if he wants to climb into me to rummage around and understand what I am about. It is not overtly threatening, but I feel uncomfortable nonetheless. I recognise it as a technique.

"I am taking some time out. I am thinking of living here."

"Do you have any connection with the area? Any relations?"

"Not that I know of."

"So why Hanburgh?"

"It is in a part of England that is rather off the map. Different. I fancy living off the map for a while."

"Off the map, eh?" He laughs. "And there are some people who think that Hanburgh is the centre of the world." He laughs again.

"And you? Have you always lived here?"

"Always, always. My father, my grandfather, my great-grandfather, many generations. We have always lived off the land around here, with greater or lesser success. It is very fertile farming land . . . . and," he looks me directly in the eyes in an almost challenging way, "I had better get back to it. Good luck with your house-hunting . . . ."

"Julia. Julia Blackburn."

"Good luck with your house-hunting, Julia, and we will no doubt bump into each other again if you decide to live here." He walks on several yards, and waves his spade over his shoulder cheerfully but dismissively in a salute, without looking around. A minute later, he waves it again to someone he has spotted across the village, and he wanders over to talk to them.

❋   ❋   ❋

Mary is very relaxed after a day lounging on the beaches of Cap D'Agde, forty minutes from here. We have bought a Smart Roadster to get us around, or mostly to get Mary around—I spend most of my time typing this. We love the Smart car and, with the rainy season arriving anytime now, we may have to buy a covered Smart Car to keep us dry. A couple of Smart cars, that describes us well—deceptively sophisticated, chic, no room for past baggage, Mary laying herself wide-open, me more enclosed and egg-like.

Mary has heard of Cap d'Agde's reputation for sexual promiscuity, and has been indulging in a bit of voyeuristic tourism. She did not come across anything noteworthy, but the thrill added energy to the day.

So, in this late September sun, she lay out on the beach, watched and waited. The light breeze ruffled her skin. The sunlight was intense. The sea was still warm enough to swim in, while becoming increasingly restless. She read, she slept, she sipped her water. She awaited a proposition from a beautiful young man or woman. I have broadened her tastes. Would she accept it? I don't know. Maybe. After twenty years of playing it straight, the spell broken, Cinders might like a ball.

She slipped back into the house fifteen minutes ago. She is nervous about interrupting me. I am the one still at work, and paying for this adventure. I wish she were more at ease with me, that she viewed us as one, not as two parties to a contract which has to be balanced and equal. She starts to prepare dinner, pouring herself a glass of rosé. I stop my writing. She smiles at me, and brings me a glass of wine.

"Was it all you were hoping for?"

"No, there was nothing," she smiles innocently, "but it was wonderful, peaceful. I wish you could have come. Will you come next time? You do not have to write every day, do you? After all, he is not paying you to do this. You are a free agent."

"It must be my work ethic. I cannot bear taking a holiday until after I have finished my task. You must help me. Force me to take a break."

"In that case, come back with me tomorrow. We will have a picnic, drink some wine, and scandalise the strays on the beach with our passion for each other. If we can find the right beach, we can even make love out there in the open, in front of other people. I have never done that. The wildest time I have ever had is with you, me and Frank." She laughs. "Poor Frank, he really did not know where to put himself. And he so wanted to. A gentleman in the bedroom is a bit of a liability, don't you think?" She comes over and strokes my hair and my neck, then sits on my lap. I fear that she is getting heavier.

"I do not think that two women fondling each other on the beach will change their world perspective."

"No, but we will enjoy it, and we have not had much time together since we have been here. I miss you, Julia. What you are doing is immensely important, but so are you. Let us enjoy this little bit of heaven. It will not be for ever."

"Why do you say that?"

"We have complicated lives, you, me, Frank. This is a moment of simplicity. Let us savour it."

I do not like the intimation of finality, fatality.

"Are you thinking of leaving?"

"No, not yet, but I do need to have more of you, to be a part of you. At the moment, I am some useless adornment that gets to wander off and be frivolous while you are hard at work. It does not make me feel good about myself, and I am concerned that I will run out of things to do. I have worked all my life, Julia. This interlude is idyllic, but it will soon become tiresome if it drags on. We need to find a way of living with each other, you, me and Frank. Frank has been incredibly generous. He has allowed us this time to sort ourselves out between us, to forge our relationship. When we get back to Hanburgh, we must concentrate on building a special relationship with Frank too, so that we can all three be at peace. Do you think we can do that?"

"We have discussed it many times, Mary. I have said that I will do anything I can." The mention of Hanburgh has introduced an anxiety into my surroundings. England, cold, wet, intrigue, murder, complications. What I really want to do is to have Mary to myself out here forever. How do I persuade her? I don't think I shall. Mary is affectionately accommodating, but you cannot deflect her from her inclinations as to what is best for her. She is a typical Libran; "maybe" means "no".

We go for a walk in the garden and into the vineyards. The grapes have been harvested, leaving the occasional bunches that have been overlooked by the blind stilted machinery that crops them. We collect them up into a bag, and take them home. The locals dismiss these gamay grapes as being unfit to eat. However, from the experience of four bottles from two different vineyards, they are somewhat better to eat than to drink in this particular village, at least.

❋   ❋   ❋

The house I am interested in is Hanburgh House. It is up Hanburgh Hill, below Hanburgh Hall. I noticed the For Sale sign as I was touring the village.

The top gate is locked, solid and too high to see over. The bottom gate is open, so I wander in. They have a strange concept of security around here.

The house is looking run down. It may have been uninhabited for a while. The grass is long, the weeds have risen high in the flower beds, the roses have not been pruned, the apples have not been picked. Two windows are replaced with hardboard on the ground floor. I wonder if it is supposed to be haunted. Having a few ghosts of my own, I feel some affinity to a possessed house.

I ring the bell, and knock on the front door immediately afterwards. I never trust doorbells unless I can hear them. Silence. I listen for a footstep, a shout, I watch for a light. Nothing.

I walk around the house down a mossy concrete path in the shadow of the walls. There is a basket ball hoop deprived of its net on the back wall, a bank of ivy, a single stable, a greenhouse, then a double-garage. An open door leads into a tiny damp courtyard and to the back door. I knock there too. No response again. I try the door. It is locked. I stand back and look at the windows facing onto the courtyard. There are many windows, reflecting the sky. I search for faces. No faces, although I can imagine them.

By the time I return to the front of the house, I have decided that this is provisionally the house I want to buy. Maybe the interior will be a disappointment. I will ask for a viewing, and hope that no-one else is on its trail.

I return to the village, and march into Marshalls Estate Agents. Vincent (Vice) Marshall greets me. He is a fleshy man, with pockets to feed.

"Good afternoon."

"Good afternoon. Could you help me?"

"I will do my best." He gives a strained, practical smile.

"I was wondering about Hanburgh House. Is it still for sale?"

"There is a great deal of interest in it, but yes, it is still available."

He is lying about the level of interest. Years of brokering deals would have provided me with that intuition, even if I could not overhear his thoughts. He is thinking "Play it cool, Vince, play it cool. Nice looking girl. Clearly plenty of money (will check in a minute). Might be able to get a premium. Stick to the higher numbers."

His face betrays none of these thoughts. He is a hardened semi-professional. I would guess that the business has been handed down to him, or that a friend got him into it, or something. He does not seem to be a natural-born estate agent.

"Do you have any details?"

"Surely," he replies, "now where are they?" He lays his podgy hand on them quickly enough. £450,000. That is quite a price for this area.

"To whom does it belong?"

"The house is being sold by the family."

"Can I have a look at it?"

"Surely. We can go now if you like. I just need to lock up."

We are back at the house within ten minutes.

"It is a very spacious house. Eight bedrooms. Are you interested in it for yourself or for a family?"

The empty rooms echo.

"For myself."

"Oh."

"I like to have spare rooms."

"For when people visit you?"

"To lie empty. I like to be surrounded by empty rooms."

"Ah. Each to his own. Her own," he corrects himself.

"If I were to offer £425,000, do you foresee any difficulty?"

The rooms are all of a goodly size, with plenty of nooks and crannies and obscure rooms—butler's pantries, dark corridors, single toilets, cellars, back stairs. I love it.

"I would have to put it to the family."

"Please do so."

The next day, Vice phones me on my mobile to say that the family has agreed to my offer. They must be dancing in the streets, but I really cannot be bothered to negotiate such things. I want a big house in the village that conforms to my tastes, and I want it now.

While the sale for Hanburgh House went through at record speed, because the Markham family was desperate for the money and I was paying cash, I was staying at the Hanburgh Arms, a white-washed eighteenth century coaching inn (I know you know this, after all we spent enough time there together. I am just adding in some final details for the sake of the completeness).

The rooms are well kept, and rarely used. Hanburgh is not a tourist village, and no-one hires a room for the night at the pub except occasionally to save money on business travel. As a business hotel, it misses the necessary formula. There is no bathroom, shower or toilet en suite, the rooms are small and low—if you are taller than 5'9", you have to duck. They have TVs in the rooms, but no porn channels, not that I wanted them personally.

I spent four weeks there; four increasingly lonely weeks. I can be solitary in my own house away from anyone, so long as I am surrounded by my own things, by myself. Living in a room that is no more than 12' by 10' hurts. What do I do? I continually visit my new house, I walk in the village and greet passers-by, I introduce myself in the shops and explain that I am moving into the area ("Ah, you are the one buying Hanburgh House!"), I drive around the countryside, I visit the towns, but I cannot even buy anything. Where would I put it?

I therefore pass more of my time than I would like in the pub itself, talking to Brenda the barmaid, who is just as bored herself during the bar's many quiet hours. The smell of leftover smoke, yesterday's beer, and dim lighting haunts me.

Brenda tells me where Mary Knightly lives, which is not difficult because it is immediately opposite the pub in a small, manicured cottage close to the village green, near the church and its cemetery. I overlook it from my room, and while away some time trying to get a glimpse of the woman herself. The cottage is an innocuous setting for Mary Knightly, white sash windows, white door, brass knocker, window boxes. It is only a few yards away from where I met Tom Willows. I see the lights go off and on in the house, yet never see her even briefly. She must use the back door. There is a car park behind the house. Watching the house at night, I imagine that Mary Knightly looks out of her window and converses with the dead before going to sleep.

In stereotypical fashion, Brenda has accumulated all the village gossip. She does not like Mary Knightly, not at all. She describes her as insufferably bossy in her drive to climb onto the higher social slopes of the village. She disports herself as an aristocrat in waiting (not Brenda's words exactly). She is a stickler for manners, and officiously humiliates anyone she can for social ineptitude, whoever they are and for however little. She fights gloves-off, but insists that on the surface all must appear civilised. Civilisation is very important to Mary Knightly.

Brenda believes that the most pertinent fact about Mary Knightly is that she was adopted by the Berringers when she was four or five years old, having been brought up until then by her impoverished family living up in a council house on The Mount. Her parents were killed in a car crash, and the Berringers took on Mary, but not her sister, who was older and reputedly already wild and uncontrollable. Anyway, the sisters never got on. The adoption brought with it a sense of trauma and shame, and conversely a taste for social respectability, because Dr. Berringer was until recently the local GP. Someone walks over Brenda's grave. "I wouldn't have wanted to be adopted by him. She cannot have had an easy time of it."

"Why? Was he strict?"

"Very, and that is the start of it. Poor Mary. You have to be sorry for her sometimes, except she doesn't thank you for it. She really can be evil, and she is totally devoted to her father. She has no time for Phyllis at all, but she dotes on Jeff still, despite. She won't hear a word against him."

"Are there lots of words against him?"

"He is a very dangerous man," she declares, but refuses to be drawn further.

The object of Mary's greatest scorn, or perhaps envy, is Samantha James, who was born in Hanburgh Hall, next door to my new home.

There is a story around Samantha James too. Her mother, Julie Fothergill, fell pregnant at fourteen while living at Hanburgh Hall where her parents were house-keeper and odd job man. Freddy Fothergill, the owner of the Hall, immediately took responsibility for her condition, and married her as soon as she reached sixteen. However, he was never prosecuted, or even investigated, and no-one ever believed that he was responsible for her condition. "I would bet it was Jeff Berringer," Brenda says, with an expression and a grunt that suggest she may be spreading malicious gossip, "or it could have been Tom Willows," she adds. "Julie saw a lot of both of them, and too much of one of them, I suspect. Everyone loves Freddy It is typical of him to step in and cover things up. He is a real gentleman, if rather too fond of the booze. He is getting a bit grumpy nowadays, too."

Mary calls Samantha "a bastard daughter of a whore". Samantha calls Mary "a jumped up little poisonous turd".

"I wouldn't get on the wrong side of either of them," Brenda comments, "although sometimes we get no choice in the matter."

❋   ❋   ❋

I am excited beyond knowing how to settle. I rove round the whole house, from room to room, without any greater purpose than to assimilate the atmosphere and the interior structure.

This is the start of a grand project, and I love projects. I am not, however, any expert at interior décor. My skill has been to make money. I will have to hire someone.

When I am not in the house, I spill out into the garden. I like wild gardens, and I am half-tempted to leave it as it is, and even to let it grow yet more jungly. However, it has been designed as a formal garden, and it therefore does not adapt well to the wild. The structure of the lawns, of the beds, and of the hedges imprint themselves unduly on the wilderness, and render the garden merely unkempt. Brenda tells me that Tom Willows is my man.

Tom saunters up the driveway, sweeping his eyes this way and that, taking careful note of everything. Behind his studied casualness is a mastery of, and devotion to, detail.

"It needs a bit of work, doesn't it?" he greets me.

"I was hoping you could help."

"It'll take me a while I am afraid, unless you want to hire me an assistant, or two, or three. Then we could make quicker work of it." He scans the garden again, and makes a calculation. "I would estimate about 60 man days." He waits for my reaction. "Or 90-plus woman days." His eyes glint with challenge.

"So, 90 days or so to do it properly," I riposte.

He hesitates a second, caught in mid-air, and immediately recovers. "Yes, that would be about it. 90 days of careful gardening, or 60 days of shovelling any-old-how."

"Do you know anyone we could hire? I would appreciate a rapid transformation."

"I could arrange that."

"Thanks. I am also looking for an interior designer-type person. Any ideas?"

"Mary Maloney." He smiles. "Mary Maloney is excellent. It is not her mainstream work. She does the books for her husband, Frank's, transport company, but I have seen a few things she has done on the side. They are really interesting. You will like her. Do you want me to contact her for you?"

"Please. Perhaps you would both come round to lunch."

"You can cook?"

"Funnily enough, yes."

"Any particular day?"

"No, I'm free forever."

"OK, I'll arrange it."

❈   ❈   ❈

It is funny, and I am not sure in which sense, to recall that first lunch party with Mary and Tom, watching Mary as, I am now, in front of me contentedly reading a book on the sofa.

It is a cliché, but the minute I greeted Mary at the front door and saw her face, I was captured by her. So beautiful, a little overweight, perhaps ten years older than me. Not the most obvious thoughts to be provoked by instant infatuation, yet they were.

She had, and she has, both a vivacity and a sadness about her, continually flickering between the light and the dark sides of her nature. I used to calculate that she would switch mood each day, and count the days forward up to a specific event—good, bad, good, bad, good, bad, damn. Now it is much less predictable, with longer spells of both. You are never sure when she will turn from being bright and breezy to cold, even chilling.

In those first meetings, I never saw, or perhaps registered, the shadows behind her eyes. She was all smiles and reserved charm.

I noticed the way Tom looked at her. I guessed that he was as close to being fond of her as he was ever likely to get. He was much gentler and more attentive in front of her than was his general habit.

It was not during that first lunch party, but several months later, that Tom admitted, in front of Mary, that if he were ever to marry, it would be to her, not that she would see it that way.

"Really?" I responded. Mary remained silent, and knowing.

"It is not going to happen, by the way," he added. Mary nodded. "I am a confirmed bachelor living off the fat of the land. I fell in love once. That is enough."

"So, who broke your heart?" I asked. I assumed Mary knew, although I neglected to ask her for some time.

He considered me. "You wouldn't know her. She left Hanburgh many years ago. I am not sure even Mary ever met her . . . ."

"Yes, I did."

"She's dead now, sadly."

"Were you really in love with her?" I press. Why was I posing the question? I think it was because I wanted to use the word "love" in front of Mary.

His expression said "Why are you carrying on with this?" He actually said "It was one of those situations where we just missed each other. After a promising start, she decided not to have anything to do with me. It was a missed opportunity from my point of view, and pointless, I suppose, from hers."

"And then she died?"

"Much later on. Even when I knew her, there was a kind of death wish built into her, although I could never work out whether she was planning to kill herself or those who got close to her. Most people said I was mad to go anywhere near her. She would destroy me at a thousand paces. A moth to a flame. Well, I was badly burnt, and she is dead."

"I am sorry."

"You needn't be. It was over probably before you were born."

"A lady never discloses her age. And nothing since?"

"Anyone in the village will tell you about my love life." He glanced at Mary. "I am sure Mary would. Lots of life. No love."

"Whatever rows your boat."

"My boat is adrift, which is OK so long as everyone understands the rules."

He was telling me the rules.

"I understand what you mean."

"You do?"

"Yes, I do. I have led that sort of lifestyle myself, without your excuse. My heart was never broken. At least, not in that sense."

"By what then?" Mary interposed. I was flattered by her interest and I answered her in an uncharacteristically straight way. "By the death of my sister, then my mother, I suppose."

"That must have been hard for you." Mary commented quietly.

"My sister's death was really hard. She was only six. She died of leukaemia. My mother's death was more predictable. She was depressed most of her life, and she eventually committed suicide when I was sixteen."

"Then what happened?"

"I went frantic for a bit, and then completely off the rails by going into the City."

Neither laughed.

"Did you make a lot of money though?" asked Tom.

"Yes."

"So why are you here?"

"As I said by the stream . . . ."

"The beck . . . ." he corrected me.

"Beck?"

"Yes, that is what we call it around here."

"Well, as I said by the beck, I want to live off the map for a while. I want a break from my frenetic life. I want to come to terms with myself."

"Yes, but why Hanburgh?" His calm grey eyes transfixed me determinedly. "I don't buy it, Julia. There is a reason that you have chosen Hanburgh, whether personal or cosmic."

"Then it must be cosmic."

"We'll see."

Mary got up and went to the toilet. When she came back she declared that nothing had ever happened in her life.

"Time to start living," pronounced Tom.

"Not your way, Tom," Mary riposted, but she gave him a smile nonetheless.

"No, you would never do it my way," Tom assured her. "Frank and Mary were childhood sweethearts. I think that the first bed they shared was a cot."

"Near enough," Mary confirmed. "I met Frank in the playground when I started going to the village school at the age of four. Even then he looked out for me."

"A traitor to his sex," Tom observed.

"I think he has been amply rewarded for his treachery," Mary said. "Crime obviously pays."

"Well, you have to make ends meet in the transport industry somehow."

"Don't I know it, Tom. It is murderous, especially at the minute."

"Even more cut-throat than gardening?"

"Definitely. If I knew anything about gardening, I think I would really like it. It is like Frank's fishing. I could never bring myself to sit on a chilly river bank for hours, pestered continuously by gnats, but I can sort of understand why Frank loves it so. Country pleasures, quiet, slow, and something to show for it in the end."

"Your supper."

"And a lot of gnat bites. They don't half irritate him. He rummages round the house for hours scratching his scalp. I keep telling him that if he doesn't give up fishing, I will leave him. He doesn't pay a blind bit of notice."

I remember watching Mary all the way through those afternoons, trying to squeeze the essence out of her and into my mind. There were moments when she behaved typically middle-aged, in her thoughts and even in the way she shuffled in her chair. Then, she would be twenty, full of enthusiasm, teasing and astute. Playfulness. Softness. Toughness. Calculation.

I was less interested in Tom once I had set my sights on Mary. He began to irritate me with his sawn-off ways. I have met plenty of really hard men in my life, and several equally hard women. Some people would say that I am one. This provincial strutter was not hard. Mary is harder than he was. He just nursed his bruised heart behind a monumental lifetime sulk.

Curiously, though, women found his sulking irresistible, even Mary. She was doing everything to suppress any intimation of it, but I could hear her calming herself down, dampening her spontaneity. And the more I came to like her, the more upset I was by it, and the more resentful of Tom.

I admit it. Sometimes I wanted Tom out of my way because he was interfering with the relationship I wanted to build with Mary. So long as he was around, I thought that Mary would not even register me. The chances for me were slight anyway, but Tom threatened to erase them entirely. Tom was from her world. I was not. They had shared a childhood together. I hadn't. Tom was a man, and I am a woman. I have never been able to tell whether a woman is turned on by other women. I thought that Mary was as straight as they come.

I stopped our lunch parties because I became too jealous. I felt too left out.

I tackled them separately from then on.

❋　❋　❋

Madame Quelque Chose de Quelque Part, as we call her, has just been up to collect the rent.

It really is not that difficult for her. She arrives, we pay her the money in cash, and she goes.

However, she insists on turning the whole banal non-event into a suppurating drama. You can see it churning in her mind. Will the house be damaged? Will they pay? Will they make outrageous demands? Will they be engaged in lewd acts of indecency?

She stands there as if dealing with very naughty children who should be punished, but she will let us off with a severe warning this time. She clicks her teeth at anything she dislikes, real or imagined, as she surreptitiously checks as much of the house as she can find an excuse to inspect. I really do not think that the French have got the hang of service. In France, it is the seller who is in charge, not the buyer. "La direction" decides what goes and what doesn't.

I tried last month to explain to Madame that we were the clients, and as we were paying, she should settle for that. "Pay? Of course you pay," she replied. "It is normal."

"Yes, we are behaving normally, as you say," I declared emphatically.

She gave me a look to the effect that two women of our age sharing a house was far from normal, and that we were lucky that she was prepared to tolerate it.

I suggested that she might prefer us to rent another house.

"You must give one month's notice," she warned. "That is the contract."

Mary and I like the house, but it is nothing special. I am sure that we could find a hundred houses similar to this one around Béziers. We have stayed up several nights discussing whether to leave or not, but have yet to come to a decision.

Madame QC de QP's husband refuses to address us at all. He nods as he passes us, but cannot be lured into a conversation. My French is nearly fluent, but he feigns unintelligibility.

Their children are different. Thibault, who is in his mid-twenties has visited us a few times. He believes himself to be a fellow citizen of the world, although he has never in practice left the Pays d'Oc. He comes round to eat our food, drink our wine, and to learn about life and everything. I think that we are a fund of stories for his friends.

Alice, his younger sister, on the other hand, is genuinely interested in us. She is gay, and has not yet had an opportunity to explore her sexuality in this highly conservative region. "It is not Paris," she keeps repeating, although she has never been to Paris to judge it at first hand.

She asks a lot of questions about us, and especially about how we found each other.

I have noticed how much more relaxed Mary has become socially when she is with me. She drops her pretence at demure, mature conservatism and reveals the passionate side of her nature. She does this particularly in front of Alice whom I think she views as her younger self in need of careful guidance.

"So how did you get to know each other? Is it difficult in England?"

"I should think the same as in France."

"Had you ever dated another woman before?"

"Not me. Oh, no way. It never even occurred to me as an option. There are many strange sexual practices in our village, but women together is definitely not one of them. Julia had, though."

"Had you?"

"Oh yes, I have been with many women. I always knew I liked girls, from the start."

"Was that compliqué, complex, for you? Were you ashamed?"

"Until recently, not at all. It seemed entirely normal . . . ."

"Normal?"

"Yes, it was what my body wanted to do, so I wanted it too."

"So, how did you know which women, girls, would acquiesce? How could you differentiate them?"

"I couldn't. Well, some are obvious, but mostly I did not have a clue. I just tried it on."

"Were they angry?"

"Yes, sure, it happened. I even got hit once or twice. And sometimes their boyfriends would threaten me."

"You were menaced? What did they say?"

"Well, usually, they asked me what I was doing. Did I not know that she was with him? She had no interest in me, so they didn't want to see me again, that sort of thing."

"They are very tolerant in England. If this village knew about me, no-one, no-one would talk to me. They would close their lips, and look away. Call me a pervert. I would have to leave."

"Yes, that happens in England, too."

Mary laughed. "You should see some of the looks we got in Hanburgh. Luckily, my husband Frank has a nasty temper, so they did not say too much."

"You are married?"

"Yes, I have been married for 25 years."

"And it did not feel wrong?"

"No, it felt right. Frank and I are very good friends. We are still very good friends. It will work out in the end."

"That is strange. You English people arrange things very strangely."

"We don't welcome too much emotion in England."

"It is evident. So what happened? Do you mind if I ask?"

"Not at all," Mary and I said together. We glanced at each other.

Mary started.

"Julia invited Frank and me round for lunch. We all got on very well. Frank likes Julia. Then Frank wanted to go fishing. My husband is very keen on fishing."

Alice made a face. "OK."

"Julia and I carried on our conversation. As we talked, I began to feel this incredible closeness to Julia, as if we were twins. We kept coming out with the same thoughts. We found ourselves laughing all the time. We had a ball . . . ."

"A what?"

"A ball—a good time."

"OK." Alice giggled.

"Then?"

"Then we were kissing each other. I don't know who started it. It just came together. We couldn't help it. We had probably drunk the best part of a bottle of Chardonnay between us, we were connecting so strongly, having a riot, and I had this irresistible urge to kiss her, and to hug her, and for Julia to kiss me?"

"Wow! That is really cool."

"It was nice."

"And then?"

"Surely you don't want all the details."

Alice hugged her knees. "Yes, I do."

"Why?"

"Because it is something I have never dared to do. It is a marvellous thing for me. I want to know it can be done."

"Oh, it can certainly be done," I said. "Much harder for it to be undone."

"Undone?"

"Stopped. To forget that it had ever happened."

"You wanted that?"

"Me, no. Mary did for a while."

"It took some time for me to come to terms with the situation. Those kisses overthrew a whole lifetime of beliefs."

"Did you do more than kiss?"

Mary chuckled indulgently. "This girl is very persistent."

"Everyone says I am very persistent."

"Well . . . ."

"Tell me!"

"Well, what is there to say? We took our clothes off and we made love."

Alice turned to Mary. "Did you know what to do?"

"No, not really. I followed Julia. She knew exactly what to do. It was a revelation." Mary faced me as if asking whether she should say more. She hesitated. Finally, her new found role as Godmother to this girl imposed its demands and she added "and when Julia went down between my legs and started licking me, I nearly fainted. I had never experienced anything like it. Frank never did anything like that to me. It was so intimate, and rather crude. It was so liberating."

Alice nodded "I would like to try that. Would you help me?"

Alice is cute. Very sexy. It was not at all difficult for either of us to decide that we would wish to help her, but we hesitated. We had both been in bed with Frank, but he is Mary's husband. I was not betraying Mary in any sense. I was sticking to our agreement. We had not discussed Alice. We had not taken any view on whether we would consider having sex with a third woman. However Mary might react now, how would she behave tomorrow, after deep thought? I was really unsure.

Mary stroked Alice's hair. "We will help you. If that is what you really want."

"I really want it."

"Then where would you like it to take place?"

Alice looked around nervously. "Not here. Someone might be watching. That would be terrible."

So we returned to the house.

Mary put her arm around Alice in the garden. Alice shrugged it off. "Not here. It isn't safe."

Alice resisted the salon too, so eventually we ended up in the bedroom. Mary and I worked together to remove her clothes. She began to tremble.

"Are you absolutely sure you want to continue?" Mary quizzed her.

"Absolutely sure. I am just a bit anxious."

We removed our own clothes. We were all three naked in a row. I concentrated on her top half, Mary on everything below the waist. We were quite a team. Alice remained rather tense until Mary slipped her tongue inside her, and that unlocked her as it had released Mary when I had done if for her that first time. Once Alice had come, which didn't take long, she turned on us. It was like being attacked by a puppy, all wetness and enthusiasm and lots of gauche moves. Neither Mary nor I reached a climax, but we had a great time.

"Will you two do it together while I watch?" Alice asked.

"No way," Mary replied immediately. "That would be too weird." So we all got under the duvet, and we fell asleep.

Chapter 6

You must admit, Inspector, that while this book may not solve your case, you are getting some titillation on the side. Does it turn you on, the thought of three bare-breasted, bare-bottomed and bare-minded women in a bed, and all of us beautiful? You know all about Mary and me. You have not seen Alice. She is dark, Latin, skinny, full of attitude and some resentment. You would like her physically. Her behaviour would almost certainly irritate you. It would depend whether your mind or your body was in control at the time.

I wish I could introduce you. To do that, I would have to know where she is. I assume that she is with Mary somewhere, if they are still together; if they were ever together. They probably are.

Who is paying for them now? They took all the spare cash I had in the drawer as they left, and they "borrowed" two of my credit cards, but I blocked both of them after a few days, and the money must have run out. At least, I have assumed that they took them. Mary and Alice went missing, the money went missing, and the cards went missing, all at the same time. I haven't heard a thing from them. I am beginning to be more worried than angry. Surely, if they could at least e-mail me. They could find a cyber-café anywhere, although Mary probably wouldn't.

I am still hoping that what happened is what I feared would happen. It is a strange thing to hope that your fears have come true. However, it is better than any likely alternative. If they have been abducted, that would be really horrific. I do not wish to imagine it. They could be held in a cellar in Feyrargues somewhere by outraged, puritanical villagers, or whatever the Roman Catholic version of puritans are—possibly Cathars—this is Cathar Country, the motorway signs proudly proclaim. If so, why am I not there too? It doesn't make sense, so I doubt it. I think they have simply slid off, forever, for a month, maybe for a few weeks. Maybe they will be back when the money, or the lust, or the fascination runs out. Maybe I will never see them again. There will be a huge gap in my story which is the future-history of Mary and Alice which I will never learn.

Three is never a good number. It has inherent instability. It induces neuroticism, and I am a neurotic character. I am not afraid of people. I am not afraid of direct danger. I am afraid of situations and how they can develop to destroy my life. At base, I have no faith in the universe, no faith in a generous and protective God, no faith in people. We are all on our own, watching out for ourselves, making choices that we believe further our best interests, even when we describe them in altruistic ways. Human beings are animals. We may not be the most successful living beings on the planet (I cannot talk to beetles, mice, dragonflies, birds and crocodiles), but we are certainly the most aggressive and domineering. You see something, you take it, and you try to get away with it. Or, if you are more cunning and calculating, you try to work out the last bit first.

At this moment I hate Mary and Alice, I am not sure which more. Alice is a thief, an amoral twenty year old thief. Mary has betrayed me. I think that the betrayal is worse. When a thief steals something from you, she has made no commitments to you. She has just found something of yours which has sneaked itself loose, and she has seized it. She is a predator. Mary, on the other hand, committed herself to me and I to her. She took all my secrets, all my fears, all my hopes, all my future away with her, leaving only their dark shadows—guilt, anxiety, and helplessness.

The car is still there. Everyone has been searching high and low, and no-one has tracked down a taxi picking them up from here. The nature of my car is my best alibi. Nobody believes that I could or would transport two trussed or dead bodies in an open-top Smart Roadster, and there is no evidence that the police can find that I have hired a car in the area (I haven't, since before we bought the Smart).

I have not written anything here for weeks. I was first wrapped up in our relationship with Alice, then with their relationship with me, and, finally with their departure and the hole they left behind. There were no rows, nor even obvious disagreements, only increasing tension as Mary and I vied for Alice's affections. I didn't realise it was serious, that we were strategising to grab Alice and run off with her. I would never have left Mary for Alice. She is a young girl, fickle, dangerous, as yet loose in the world. She would never have been a long term solution to any problem I can think of. Mary clearly saw things differently, although it may be that she was not seeing things clearly at all. She is surprisingly naïve sometimes. She goes with the flow, without due consideration of the consequences. I find (found) that exceedingly frustrating, even if we would never have got together at all if she had thought about it.

I wonder whether I should phone Frank. "Frank, if you think you have lost your wife, I have too! She's with you? Oh, thank God for that!" or "We have been looking everywhere for her. I am sure she will turn up . . . . yes, she has been missing two weeks now. I know I should have called you earlier. I didn't want to panic you. I know. It was a bad decision. I am sorry. We are doing everything we can."

The longer I do not contact Frank, the more difficult it is to do so. I have built up a hope that Mary is back with him, another of those hopes based on a fear. If I phone Frank, I will know one way or the other, and I don't want to know about either. I don't want to have lost Mary to Frank, and I don't want to have lost her altogether from sight. I prefer the anxiety and reassurance of evading the truth.

Madame Quelque Chose de Quelque Part (and I no longer find that nickname funny—it was a shared joke between Mary and me) has gone to the police. They came round to ask where Alice and Mary are. They are, of course, minimally concerned with Mary's welfare. It is Alice they want to get back. Madame QC de QP is ringing everyone she knows, or has heard of, in the police hierarchy to get some action. They all keep coming to me demanding to know where Mary and Alice are, have they contacted me, have I traced their use of my credit cards, what did they say before they went?

Only Thibault is staying well away. I suspect that it is now all too much of a story for his friends, and he no longer wishes to be compromised by our acquaintance.

A large part of the speculation is whether I have done them in. Why does death trail me? I moved to London to get away from the deaths of my sister and my mother. I fled to France to recover from the death of a girl, Marianne, I had been living with for two years, and who died from a drug overdose. You did not know about that? The overdose wasn't deliberate. She used a medicine-chest of drugs, many of them obtained on prescription, which made her impossible to manage or cope with. People on drugs are a hell to those who live with them, always broke, always moody, either plangently unreasonable or ridiculously happy. I have met many partners of drug addicts. We talk, even as we remain isolated in our separate hells, never daring to find common cause lest we become unwilling to help those who continuously crucify us. We are loyal dogs. We have made a terrible mistake, and we foolishly stick with it. Our drugged-out former loved ones are so vulnerable. We adopt their survival instinct. We look out for them as they bounce off the walls seeking the next hit.

I came to Hanburgh in order to come to terms with death, only to find more of it. I came here for the same reason, and now Mary and Alice are missing, progressively assumed dead.

I say that it has nothing to do with me. Alice was a frequent visitor to the house, she fell in love with Mary, and they eloped. Don't blame me. I spend my time writing a book about my life in England. I am not their keeper. Except that I have blatantly not been writing anything over the last few weeks, and I was intimately involved in the events leading up to their disappearance.

Well, Madame Quelque Chose de Quelque Part, you really have something to click your teeth over now.

❋   ❋   ❋

My stuff has arrived. The removal van did not fit into the driveway, so they had to park it in the street at the bottom of the garden, and carry everything fifty yards up a narrow, slippery path to the house.

The removal people were furious, and moaned and sulked. I was the inconsiderate enemy. I had bought a house that had no easy access, a sin compounded by the weight of some of the furniture I had bought over the years. I am sure that the older, stocky guy is still muttering.

They took the furniture and the boxes directly to the allotted rooms, and snorted whenever I was unsure as to where they should go. Oh to be a man at times like this.

Two days later I received a customer satisfaction survey. I filled it out with some venom. I haven't heard back from the company.

It will take weeks, months, even years to get everything sorted out. It is not that I have so much, more that I am physically lazy and cannot be bothered to work at it for any length of time.

I was inspecting the photo albums earlier, and decided to sit down and leaf through them. I suddenly realised that these photos of my mother's childhood took place in this village. I know that I deliberately came to live in Hanburgh because my mother was brought up here, but I had not emotionally connected this village with her until then.

I desperately wanted her to walk into the room, to stand there, and to talk to me, without her habitual sorrow and pain. I would like to hug her, to welcome her back, to hear the stories of her childhood recounted with awe not hatred and anger. At least I would like to find something of hers in this house. Why would I? Her family was poor. There is no relationship between the Hanburgh she knew and the house I have bought.

She must have walked past this house, though, climbing up the hill, reflecting on the luck of the upper echelons of the village. Did she know anyone from this house? Were there children? Maybe she played here. I want to feel something of her here, and I can feel nothing except her absence.

The time in this house speeds by. There is everything to do. The carpets arrived yesterday. I panicked when I suddenly realised that the carpet people might have to haul several enormous, heavy, struggling carpets up the garden. However they were able to drive straight up to the front door.

The previous owners covered all the floors with cheap plastic laminate. I should tear it all up, but I cannot face the inevitable necessity of having to replace all the floors. I shall not be in Hanburgh for long. I cannot spend my entire stay leaping from joist to joist.

The garden is my domain. I stand there and I look around, and I tell myself that all this is mine, all this is me. It is surrounded by walls, trees and hedges.

They are my natural curtains from behind which I peer into the village. In fact, I see very few people pass by on foot. There is always some activity around the beck, but they are usually strangers.

When I march down the path the removal men struggled up, and let myself through the gate into the street, time changes down to a careful pace. No-one hurries around the village, not even the children. People enter and leave the shops one at a time. You would think that there is nothing going on here at all, that nothing has ever happened, that everyone is dormant here year-in year-out.

And you would mostly be right. Even the rivalries and the squabbling are small things, marginally significant to anyone other than the central players. And yet babies are born here to spend most of their lives in this village, at least they were. Mobility has reached even this part of the world.

❋   ❋   ❋

I keep looking at the floors. I need to get rid of that stuff. It isn't even modern laminate—it is parquet, old, bobbly and, if anyone trips over it, they could sue me.

No-one has really been here yet, except Tom and Mary, and they have not been for a while. I am embedded in my isolation, in my superfluity of rooms, and my bars of chocolate, and acres of time. I feel luxuriant, sleepy, honest. There is nothing to lie about when I am lying about these rooms.

The fireplace in this room is tiled. Fifties, I would think. A rather mean fireplace. An ugly surround. Convenient to clean.

There is a ring at the door, then a knock. Maybe it is Mary. I jump up and bound down the stairs to the front door, frightened to miss her.

It is somebody I don't know. She smiles at me. "Sam James," she says. "From next door. Up the hill." The "up" appears to have social significance.

I point towards the little hallway behind me. "You live there, do you?" It is a ridiculous statement. No-one lives in my little hallway, among the coats, in front of the basin, and next to the toilet. Nonetheless, Sam responds to what I mean.

"Well, not any more," she corrects me and herself. "I used to live up there at the Hall. I was born there. Now I live up in the dale. Top of the hill, turn left, one mile on your right."

"I see."

"Have you been there yet?"

"Yes. There is a nice view of the river."

"That is the other way. Straight on."

"I know."

Sam appears strangely disconcerted, given that she is the local and I am the intruder. Even more surprisingly, I actually want to unsettle her. I don't want to speak. There is a power in silence that I often use, even when I have no purpose for using it.

"Come in."

"Thank you," Sam smiles, "but I must be going. I jut dropped round to say hello, and to invite you to one of our coffee mornings, well get-togethers." My expression must have dipped at the mention of a coffee morning. "A few of my girlfriends."

Being rather fond of girlfriends, I accept. Then I remember that Sam could be very useful to me. I hope that Mary will be there. "When?"

"Tomorrow?"

"OK. That would be nice. Thank you."

"It would be really good to get to know each other."

Why is she saying this? I search her face, without gaining an answer. It is friendly but the expression is blank. What makes me someone that she would want to get to know?

"After all, we are sort of neighbours," she adds.

For the present, the fact that she hates Mary Knightly is enough for me. Perhaps we can be allies and, failing that, I will almost certainly learn something. I am about to fight a war. I need to recce for intelligence.

"See you tomorrow then. 11:00."

"Thank you."

We are not fooling each other. We will not be friends.

❋   ❋   ❋

The girls are flopped where they are. I like that in girls. It is aggressive in boys.

Melody and Julie were on the town last night, trying out a new restaurant belonging to a friend of theirs. Mich (short for Michelle) stayed in and watched a horror movie in which everyone ended up down a well, menaced by a fiend with a contorted face and an enormous knife he was not afraid to use.

There is only sporadic conversation.

Everyone is expecting me to speak, and even keen for me to do so. I don't. I smile and say nothing. It is the sphinx in me that controls Sam, but visibly irritates Melody, who is not naturally harmonious, I would suspect.

"I have just seen everyone traipsing into Mary Knightly's house," says Julie. "I bet that is a wild party."

"She is organising the festival again," says Sam.

"Are you going?"

"I would not miss it for the world. Let Mary have her day of glory. She can be relied on to spoil it by insisting on taking all the credit." Her eyes open and glow maliciously.

"Is Brian singing again this year?"

"I would think so. If they invite him."

"I thought he got rather annoyed last year."

"He did. More than. He was absolutely livid."

"Poor Brian."

"It was his own fault."

"Yes, it was rather."

"He won't do that again."

They all laugh.

Apparently Brian threw a chocolate gateau at Tom and hit Brenda straight in the face. Sportingly, Brenda who was startled at first, recovered her composure and burst out laughing, thus conserving the reputation of fun-loving barmaids everywhere.

"No he won't do that again. The cleaning bill cost him £35."

I am lost in the conversation. I haven't a clue who Brian is and it is not obvious to me why Brian should be throwing a cake at Tom, although I do empathise. It would be a true moment of achievement to mess up that edgy smug expression of his. I really do dislike Tom, while being drawn to him against my will, my taste, my reason. There is something in that wiry body of his that sucks you in. Something absolutely physical. I am usually entirely averse to the charms of men, I don't like him, but my body seems to crave him.

"Who is Brian?" I ask.

"A friend of Sam's."

"More than a friend of Sam's", laughs Mich.

"Just a friend," Sam replies.

"Oh, come on!"

"We can do things together, and still just be friends," Sam retorts.

"Doesn't Tony ever say anything?"

"Who is Tony?"

"Sam's long-suffering husband."

"Rubbish. I am Tony's long-suffering wife." Sam giggles girlishly.

Julie leans forward towards me. "Sam and Brian have had a thing going for years. Brian is married to Katie, who is really lovely and is a good friend of mine. Sam married Tony because he is rich and handsome, and she can do anything she likes with him. Brian hates Tony—he thinks he is a complete wimp. Brian hates Tom . . . ."

". . . . I know Tom."

"Yes, we all know that."

"Why would you know that?"

"Everyone knows what Tom is up to. He always latches onto the new face in the village, especially if it a pleasing face. It is a territorial thing."

"I am not having an affair with Tom, thank you." I put the speculation firmly in its place.

"Apparently not," Julie continues. "We are all waiting to see what will happen next. Are you married?"

"No."

"Divorced?"

"No."

"Looking?"

"No."

"Oh come on, everyone is looking," Melody declares aggressively.

"I am not looking," I reply flatly. "Only for peace and quiet."

"Well, you will certainly get that."

"Will you take a bet, Julia?" Mich asks me.

"Why?"

"For fun."

"What is it?"

"Will you take it?"

"I know all about betting. What am I betting on?"

"I am betting you."

"About what?"

"That you will end up with Tom at least once."

"Oh no I won't." Sam is watching me nervously. I do nothing to lessen the threat in my composure.

"It's a bet then?" Mich pushes me.

"I wouldn't take your money."

"But it is I who will be taking yours."

"Why would I have anything to do with Tom?" I am genuinely puzzled.

"You are his type."

"A real ball-breaker," Melody adds, unnecessarily.

"No, a challenge. Tom is a hunter. He loves a challenge."

"He doesn't stand a chance. Why am I discussing this?" I sweep the room.

"Well we were discussing Sam's love life, and it is a way of breaking the ice."

"Sam's love life is an open book," observes Julie. "Brian, Tom and Tony if she has to."

"In that case she will hardly want me to end up with Tom."

"Everyone ends up with Tom, unless they are a les-y." The question hangs in the air.

"Mary Knightly is a les-y," smirks Melody. "And even she had a fling with him."

"Now, now, Mel," pronounces Sam. "Mary may have many, many faults, but she is not a les-y. It's a shame. It would make her more interesting, and give her an excuse for being a revolting little creep."

They are all watching me to see how I am reacting. What am I supposed to be reacting to?

❋   ❋   ❋

I have explained how Mary and I got together. I invited her and Frank over for lunch. Frank went fishing. We got drunk.

Mary looks at me from the floor. She is shame-faced, and embarrassed in the lull, yet visibly excited. "I don't know what to say," she says. "What do we do now? We shouldn't have done this. It was incredible." Her eyes beseech me under her lashes. She wants to reassure herself that she will not be going straight to hell. Hell cannot be like this.

"I'm glad you enjoyed it."

Mary laughs. "I did. But now what?"

"Why is there a what? We can do it again."

"I don't think we should. I don't normally do this kind of thing."

"You seemed natural enough to me. I didn't have to rape you, however much I have wanted to over the last few weeks."

Mary is shaken. "You planned this?"

"Yes, no. I hoped that it would happen. I thought that it would."

"Why? I am not a lesbian. I have never been a lesbian before."

"There is something very open inside you. There is no need for you to be a lesbian to do this with me. I am not a lesbian either."

Mary chuckles derisively. "Who are you kidding, Julia? You are in denial. You are definitely a lesbian."

"Technically, I am not."

"Technically, how?"

"That is a long story."

"I am listening."

"I am not telling."

Mary waits. She stares me out. Nobody can out-stare me. She breaks, and she kisses me to ease the suspense. We start again. Her body is so soft, her lower lips are so eager. She even thrusts them onto my hand.

"I am getting so fat," Mary observes as she dresses to go. "It hasn't mattered to me for a long time. You make it matter to me now."

"It suits you."

"It doesn't suit my clothes. They were designed for a thinner me."

"Don't wear your clothes then, at least not here."

"I will have to sometimes, and then I look fat."

She kisses me good-bye. "I don't know how we make this work, Julia, but I really want it to work."

"So do I."

For this moment our eyes twinkle. We are two bodies as one.

❅   ❅   ❅

Chapter 7

At last, it is time to enter the Mary Knightly's den. I have plotted to meet Mary here for so long now. I am a predator and a victim.

In truth, I am unsure as to exactly what she did to my mother, what harm she caused her. My mother described her as "pure evil". I would argue with her. The definition of evil precludes purity. Purity precludes evil. Perhaps she might try "totally evil" or "entirely evil" or "undiluted evil". My mother would always give me a glare to suggest that I was picking a fight on sacred ground, that I was desecrating her fragile being. Eventually she tossed at me angrily "Go look up 'oxymoron' in the dictionary, will you? Then try 'smart-arse ignoramus'." I did, and her point struck home to the extent of strafing my pride with shrapnel.

No-one seems to like Mary Knightly, yet she carries on doing whatever she does. She has not run away. She has brazened out her short-comings and the negativity they provoke. That, at least, is admirable.

So, I am as prepared to appreciate her as to hate her. I doubt that I shall ever like her.

I already realise the sort of person she is. I have picked up the vibe. Nervous, spiteful, scared, aggressive, poisonous.

You could say that I have used my Mary to get to her. She is on the festival committee, and she has suggested that I join it too, given my undoubted organisational abilities. Why do people assume that because you are rich you can organise anything?

What do I do with Mary Knightly once I am in contact with her? All I have is an inherited hatred and a sense of enraged injustice emanating from a vague evil.

After all, my mother was a flake, cooky, a cross between Goldie Hawn and Joan Crawford. Dizzy and depressed. Sexy and viperous.

And why Mary Knightly? Who was she to my mother? Who is she really to anyone? For these answers, I must wait.

I will have to imagine what Mary Knightly was doing before I turned up at her house for that first meeting.

She is laying out the white china coffee set with gold rings. The sugar cubes are mini-boulders. She agonises a little over the cream. Is double cream perhaps old-fashioned? Should it be at least single, or maybe even skimmed milk? The biscuits are easier—Hobnobs, empirically tested.

The tray with its seven cups, saucers and silver tea-spoons is centred carefully on the Georgian coffee table, with a gold inlay. It is exactly equidistant from the seven chairs, and precisely in the middle of the room.

The doorbell goes. She saunters across the shagpile carpet to answer it. "Claudia! So nice to see you! You are the first!" They kiss one cheek each.

"Such a morning!" declares Claudia. "Such traffic!"

"I know, dear! It is getting impossible!"

"Beyond impossible, if you ask me! Will they never get the roads mended?"

"Well, come in and have a cup of coffee. The others will be here in a minute. George is just doing the washing up."

"Good for George!"

"Ah, that's the bell. Hilary!"

"Hello, Mary. Terrible weather we are having! Even the roses are looking bedraggled! Ah, thank God! I could murder a cup of coffee!"

Mary (Maloney) and I arrive together. "Mary, this is the Julia I told you about."

"Welcome, Julia, to our little circle" she says in greeting. She barely looks at me, but her senses are all out

"I love your annuals, Mary, "says Mary M. "They are so beautiful set into the lawn like that!"

"George complains all the time about those. They make it difficult to cut the lawn, but somehow he manages."

"It's worth it!"

George enters the room. "George, make yourself useful. Get Mary, and Julia, a cup of coffee, will you my dear?"

"Of course, dear."

"OK," announces Mary. "To business. The musical festival."

For a second everyone is disorientated, then we settle into the free chairs, and the sofa where Mary and I sit.

"Georgina, have we got the field yet?"

"Most certainly. And we don't have to pay for it."

"Well done, Georgina."

The meeting goes well. Much progress has been made. Several semi-professional nephew-tenors have been tracked down, as has a cousin-soprano. The local band will play some jazz. There is even a comic who is willing to compere, although Mary is not so sure about that. "He is very good," Hilary reassures her. "He did our Kate's wedding ten years ago. He had us in stitches. Nothing out of place."

"Well, we can approach him," confirms Mary. "We can decide later."

The event is to be run for the fifth year as a benefit for multiple sclerosis.

Mary does voluntary work for many good causes—breast cancer, the lifeboats, the RSPB. She prefers charities patronised by members of the royal family. Greenpeace, Friends of the Earth and Amnesty International unsettle her. "They are so aggressive. Quite unnecessary."

Most of the women are of an age. Only my Mary and Georgina work full-time. Hilary is a receptionist two days a week at the local GP practice. Claudia helps out at the village school with reading tuition and singing.

Without appearing to do so, Mary Knightly is watching us. Is it us, or is it me? Has she heard that I have been invited round to Sam James'? Does she pick up on those vigilant social antennae of hers that Mary and I are more intimate than anyone in the room, and the village, would find acceptable? She personally finds lesbianism abhorrent (what do they do in private?), and she certainly does not want her good name tainted by it. She can imagine what Samantha James would say. "Mary Knightly and her lesbos . . . ." It would be hard to recover from that.

How does Mary Knightly perceive me? Long dark hair, a still expression, and a neat, slim body, to contrast with my Mary's more voluptuous and up-front frame and disposition? Am I a threat? Or am I simply a nobody, a stranger to her and the village she need not trouble herself with, yet?

"Have you seen Tom, Mary?" Hilary asks La Knightly.

"Yes, Hilary, I did see him the other day, wrestling with an apple tree that he was going to plant in the garden."

"Did you ask him for his p.a. equipment?"

"Oh damn, no, I forgot."

George glances quickly at his wife. It is unusual to hear Mary Knightly swearing on official occasions, although in private there are certain words she considers acceptable, and even cultivated—damn(ed), darn(ed), bugger and shit." The rest are beyond the pale.

I cannot wait to go. I am eager to return to bed with the body sitting warmly beside me. My Mary may be relatively new to lesbian gymnastics, but she is catching on fast (and for Mary Knightly's information, there are many adventurous things to do if you have the imagination and a few pieces of equipment).

I am expecting the festival to be naff—amateur singers, a ramshackle band and an unforecast downpour of rain. I will be surprised. Mary is an excellent organiser.

❋　　❋　　❋

"There is something I think you should know, Mary."

"Come in Hilary."

They both enter the drawing room. George is asleep in his chair, snoring softly with a newspaper across his knee and his glasses askew on his face.

"George, dear. George, dear. GEORGE!"

George stirs. "Yes, dear?"

"Hilary would like a private word with me. Do you think you could make us some tea?"

"Of course, dear."

George gets up from his chair, carefully folds his newspaper into the brass journal rack, and shuffles off towards the kitchen.

Mary and Hilary sit down in adjacent chairs, knees pointed towards each other. "What is it, Hilary?" asks Mary.

"Well, I was just walking back from the practice for lunch, as I always do, and I was passing Mary Maloney's house, and I saw that new Julia's car in the driveway."

Mary waits expectantly, a pussy-cat look on her face.

"Did you notice the way Julia and Mary were sitting together on the sofa when they were around here earlier?"

"No," Mary lies.

"I thought that they were looking overly-familiar with each other. Anyway, I walked into the driveway, thinking I would drop in and say hello . . . ."

("Snooping," Mary thinks to herself.)

". . . . and I had rounded the corner to approach the front door, when I noticed there was a window open. And you will never guess what . . . ."

("Sex," thinks Mary. "Got them!") "No, what?" she says.

"There was a moaning coming from the window. For a second I thought that Mary had hurt herself, so I was rushing to the front door, ready to knock it down if necessary . . . ."

("Well, you are built for it," Mary thinks to herself.)

"Then I realised that it wasn't a distressed moaning, but a passionate one. When you have been in the medical profession as long as I have, you can tell the difference." She smiles proudly.

("What a boring way to find out," thinks Mary, scornfully. The medical profession? She is a receptionist.)

"I know what distress sounds like. So I hesitated for a second, and retreated back to the street. I was totally shocked."

"I cannot think what Mary is thinking of," responds Mary. "I cannot imagine that she is usually like that, not in all the years I have known her. Frank is perhaps not the best company for her with his fishing and his hours spent down the Hanburgh Arms, but he is very dependable and he gives her a good living."

"I have, of course, come across lesbians before . . . ."

George enters the drawing room with a tea set carefully laid out on the tray, and hears the word "lesbians" which sounds a much more promising topic than interminable finer detail discussion of the arrangements for the music festival.

"Thank you, George," says Mary. "You are a dear. How you look after me. You can go now and enjoy yourself in the garden."

"Yes, dear."

"I have come across lesbians before, but I never expected any of my friends and acquaintances to join them."

"No, it is most unfortunate."

"It is not seemly for our organising committee to have those two billing and cooing over each other all the time."

"No, it is definitely not."

"So what do we do, Mary?"

"They will have to leave the committee, frankly, before Samantha hears about it and generates a major hoo-hah. But how?"

"I'll ask Henry," suggests Hilary. "He is very good at this sort of thing." Henry, Hilary's husband, is an undertaker. He is about to become a busy man.

Mary and Hilary discuss the game plan, and Hilary leaves the house to consult with her husband, Henry. He in turn mentions our relationship to young Becker, his assistant, who tells his girlfriend Charlene (normally known as Charlie). Charlie tells everyone in the village.

My Mary is, naturally, the second to last to know. Frank is the last. Nobody wants to disturb his tranquil hours spent lazing on a river bank, nor create an ugly scene in the pub. For all his studied calm, Frank has a violent temper.

When she finally finds out, warned by her good friend Kate, she tells me that perhaps we had better cool it. She loves me, she adores my body, but the gossip is flying around and it is not fair on Frank. Besides, she does not know how Frank will react, what he will do to me and what he would do to her. She lies awake at night panicking about this, as Frank grunts gently beside her.

I tell her I understand. It is a pity, but I understand.

I am mad at her cowardly betrayal. Is her commitment to me literally only skin deep, a hand across my body, a kiss on my lips, her finger inside me, declarations of undying devotion, then starting like a rabbit at the first hint of scandal? "I love you but I don't want to see you. You are a freak. Leave me alone."

At this moment, I could kill her.

❄   ❄   ❄

I go immediately around to see Tom Willows.

He is in, and apparently caught off-guard to find me on his doorstep.

I am in no mood to mess around. He has a reputation for womanising, so he can womanise with me. I want revenge, this instant.

It does not take me long to get his clothes off. After all, I am very attractive.

Tom is very skilled in bed. I appreciate that. He smells sweetly of the outdoor fragrances of summer leaves and freshly-cut grass, he caresses me lightly with his hands, and licks firmly but subtly with his tongue over every crevice in my body. He hops on me lightly, without ever squashing or pinching me, rhythmically riding me until he is led to believe that I have climaxed, whereupon he follows suit.

To be fucked by Tom is to be fucked by a master.

I get dressed slowly, chatting away to him. Tom lies back on the bed. He almost enjoys watching me getting dressed as much as undressed. Smoothed back into shape, I kiss him, lie back down beside him for a minute, kiss him again on the forehead, and let myself out of the house.

That is the first and last time I sleep with Tom. Shortly after I leave, Tom goes downstairs to get a bowl of cereal, and sits at his desk eating it while reading the newspaper.

A shadow appears behind him, and there is a faint whoosh, and an almighty crack. Tom's head is cleaved almost in two by his own double-handed long-shafted axe. The murderer is protected from the spray of blood by one of Tom's large bath towels which is immediately lowered over his head. The murderer has left no footprints, finger prints, or sightings.

I, on the other hand, have been seen by several people in the village leaving Tom's house around the time of the murder.

Which is why you came to see me, Inspector, the first time we met.

I am sitting across from you in that hell-hole of a police station. I cannot bear the smell. I cannot bear the paint in its chronic despair. I cannot bear the flattened echoing sound that the corridor makes, the position of the door handles, the x-ray neon lighting.

And I cannot bear the sight of you.

I have resolved to hate you from the moment I woke up on the sofa this afternoon.

I imagine that there are rumours flying around the village that I have murdered Tom Willows. They will be standing grouped in the shops, they will be gossiping by the beck, they will be commanding a shock-enraptured audience at the Hanburgh Arms. "You don't say! She was only staying right here a few weeks ago! We could all have been murdered in our beds!" I arrived, I bought, I killed. What will they fabricate as my motive? Jealousy, rage, refusal, rejection, the humourlessness of lesbian wimmin?

What I could not have guessed at this moment is that those same rumours are accompanied by another set implying that I may also have AIDS, caught off Tom. Vilified as the village lesbian, I am the unwitting victim of salacious irony.

I watch you with my careful eyes, and an iced-down heart.

"Did you know that Tom Willows was probably suffering from AIDS, Miss Blackburn?"

I smile at your impertinence.

"Oh dear. Did you ever sleep with him, Inspector?" I ask.

"What?" you reply, cocksure aggressive.

"If you haven't, then you have nothing to fear."

"No! I do not sleep around."

"You are missing out, Inspector, although in your case buggery can make your anus drop out."

You shift tack.

"Tell me," you begin. "What is it like for a woman to make love to a woman?"

I raise one eyebrow. "You get paid by the police force, not to mention the tax payer, to ask these sorts of questions?"

"I am free to ask any question that can lead me to the truth."

"In that case, for the benefit of the greater knowledge of the police force, I will tell you that making love to a woman, when you are a woman, is a whole lot better than making love to most men. Tom was an exception."

"And you claim that you had left Tom Willows before he was killed."

"Yes."

"Was he dressed or undressed?"

"Naked."

"Had you just had carnal relations?"

"Yes."

"Did you have a fight, or angry words?"

"No, we were too busy fucking."

"Do you have any idea who killed him?"

"Yes."

You pause, surprised. "Will you tell me who you think it was?"

"No."

"Do you understand the situation you are in here? You could go to prison for life, or you could be released and yourself be killed by the murderer if he suspects that you know who he is."

"He doesn't."

"If I can arrest someone else with reasonable grounds to believe in their guilt, I can let you go."

"You will let me go anyway."

You sit back in your chair. "And what on earth makes you think that, Miss Blackburn?"

"Because you know that I am innocent, and while you may have your faults, you will not knowingly lock up an innocent person for twenty years. Besides . . . ."

"Besides?"

"Besides."

Of course, I do not know who killed Tom. How could I know? I barely know Tom, or the village, or anything about the current situation. It seems to me, though, that you will be more respectful of me if you think I know who did it.

I watch your grey eyes. I watch your lips working. I hear your mind. Much as I hate you, I feel strangely at ease with you. It is almost familial. Our rhythms are the same. We can insult each other in the same breath and we will literally be conspirators. I have never had this experience before, of utter safety with another human being. I am totally sure of you.

I know the story between us as it unfolds. You are as fixated with me as I am, in an unexpected way, with you. It completely escapes me why I would bother with you for an instant. You are not especially attractive in any way I can think of, but there is still that relational chemistry between us. It is not sexual on my side. I would not necessarily be revolted by the idea, but it is at least lower than 500 on my list of desirable things to do, somewhere below doing the washing up or taxing the car.

For you, I realise it is different. The fixation is physical as well as mental, and it started in this interview. I behave in a way that is atypical, challenging to your authority, playful, wounding, brutal even.

Like many of your kind, determined bullies committed to a crusade of self-righteousness, you are vulnerable to the coolly efficient counter-attack. At first you bite harder, then you admire and, in my case, ultimately you are ensnared. You want to be with me. You accord me powers that are almost supernatural. I do have a few of those, I admit, yet I do not believe that those are the ones you are thinking of.

I smile affectionately at you. "You seem to be having some difficulty keeping your tie straight."

You give me a "what on earth are you on about?" look.

"You are a bit of a messy eater, too. You need a good woman to take some care of you."

"Did you have anyone in mind, seeing that we are wandering off the subject of a murder investigation in which you are currently the chief suspect?"

"I do not know the village very well, Inspector. Nor you. Nor Tom, come to think of it."

"But you still believe you know who the murderer is?"

"Yes."

"How could you possibly know that?"

"Women's intuition."

You cough over the coffee you are not drinking.

"You are having me on. No wonder I have problems solving my cases."

"Men are much less observant than women. You talk more and you listen less."

"And do you know what I am thinking at this moment?"

"Of course I do, Inspector. And I am flattered, without being inclined to share your fantasy."

You are uncertain as to whether to shout at me, or soften your approach.

"You flatter yourself."

"May be I flatter you. I can help you, and maybe I flatter you with the sense to realise that it is better to work with me rather than against me."

"I think that I get to choose that."

"My point precisely."

"Well, you are certainly arrogant."

"Why would I deny it? I have a lot to be arrogant about. And you need a lot of help. Be an obstinate man, if you wish, or solve this case. You will do it a lot faster if we share ideas. I am not going to straighten your tie, but I can tidy up your mind."

You get up abruptly. "Enough of this. I will come back later." That is bravado. You are considering carefully what I am saying.

❋   ❋   ❋

Mary is there. I march down the stairs mid-morning, having had rather too much to drink the night before, and there she is, her shoulders to me, sitting at the kitchen table, ruminating over her coffee.

She turns round sharply. "I thought you were a man for a second."

She appears angry, not repentant, or sheepish or even ingratiating. Is this how she handles shame? It seems ungracious to me.

I join her at the table.

She meets my eyes. "How have you been?"

"OK."

"Just OK?"

"Just OK."

"It has been hell for me."

"Why?"

"Do I need to explain?"

"Mary, you do not need to explain anything to me."

"Then I won't say anything."

"Fine."

Mary is daggers drawn. "You are totally devoid of emotion, Julia, aren't you? You do not feel anything at all. You are dead."

"And it is nice to see you too."

"But there is nothing there. You are not angry. You are not hurt. You are not relieved. You are not welcoming. You haven't stood up and walked out. Nothing."

"Which of those would you like me to do?" I smile ironically. "Then I will know that it is really irritating you when I do not do it."

"That is how you get your revenge, is it? How small-minded of you!"

"Up until now, I was thinking how broad-minded I was being."

"Hooray for heroines then," she snarls. "A heroine and a martyr."

"I am not dead."

"No-one is dead, dear. Just hurt. I am just hurt."

"Is that why you are trying to hurt me?"

She glances down at her coffee, and up again. "Yes."

"OK. That's OK, Mary. It is quite useful my not having any feelings sometimes."

"But not the rest of the time."

"No, maybe not."

Her hands are working around her cup. The coffee is becoming tidal. Her eyes widen. "Will you have me back?"

"Of course I will."

"Really?"

"Yes."

"Why?"

"Because I love you."

"Love is not enough."

("Oh, for God's sake!"). "And because you still owe me some money."

"That all went weeks ago."

"And Alice?"

"Don't ask me about Alice."

"OK."

"Don't ever ask me about Alice!" she repeats vehemently.

"I may not, but everyone else will, unless she has returned home."

"I don't know. I doubt it. She kept saying she wanted to. Who knows?"

"What do I tell people?"

"Nothing."

"What will you tell people?"

"Absolutely nothing. I have nothing to hide, and nothing to be ashamed of. If Alice were a man, people would respect my silence."

"She is a young girl. If she is not back at home by now, I assure you that they are not going to be respectful, not Thibault, not Madame, not the police, not anyone. They are going to want answers, Mary."

"They are going to have to want, then. I don't have any." Her Manchester accent has slipped back in. I had forgotten her Manchester accent.

"It's up to you, Mary, but I do not think that silence will satisfy them. They are going to cut up rough."

"What can they do? We spent a few days together, then she moved on. It is hardly a sin is it?"

"They will certainly consider it a sin."

"In that case they can just fuck themselves!"

"Oh well. I am going upstairs to have a bath. Are you coming?" I take her hand to lead her.

She pulls it away again. "I am going to finish my coffee. I may see you later."

✻   ✻   ✻

I slip the key into the lock and the door slams open. I didn't mean to be that clumsy. There is a scent to the house that I do not remember. It feels still. The plates are on the table where I left them. I go over to the cabinet and extract a packet of cigarettes.

I have not smoked for a while.

It feels good, the smoke edging down into my lungs and lightening up the whole of my body. I feel myself again.

I sit back on the sofa. Now what? So little can happen in weeks, and your life can be destroyed in 24 hours.

Where is Gargoyle? "Gargoyle, where are you?" They must have taken you to the kennels. After a quick search I find a note by the front door. "Your dog is with me. Ugly, isn't he? Goes with the name I suppose. Love (I am sorry), Mary."

There is a knock at the door. It is Sam. I let her straight in. She is taken aback by the speed with which I open the door.

"I am sorry to disturb you. I know that you have been through a terrible time. I just felt the need to say hi."

"Come in."

I gesture Sam through the lobby towards the sitting room.

"I am really sorry about Tom."

"I am sure you are. You knew him well, too."

"He was the best."

"Yes, he was."

"I will miss him."

"I will keep him."

Sam looks surprised.

"In my heart," I explain.

"I didn't know you smoke."

"I don't."

"Will you come out for a meal with me? We can get drunk. Any excuse to get drunk"

"With my reputation? Can you afford it?"

"I can afford it. Come on. Let's phone a taxi. Can I use your phone?"

"What, for you to phone a taxi for us to go out?"

She looks alarmed. "Yes," she says hesitantly.

"Then do it, girl."

She laughs in relief. "Where is it?"

"Just there. Don't forget to pay."

"Are you going to be like this all evening?"

"No, I have finished now. Sorry. It is the shock. I suppose that Mich wants her money."

"She is meeting us there. She says that you can pay for the meal. Do you want to invite Mary?"

"No, not tonight."

❋   ❋   ❋

Mme. Quelque Chose de Quelque Part is extremely agitated. She is visibly shaking, and her face holds a continuous "moue". The policeman, the local one from Feyrargues, is alternating between trying to ignore her and attempting to appease her.

"Where is my daughter, Alice?" she demands in French.

"I don't know," I reply.

"Cannot Mme. Malanny help us here? She must know something," the policeman intercedes.

"She refuses to tell me anything at all. She says that Alice left her, and she has no idea of where she went—perhaps Paris."

"Perhaps Paris . . . ." The policeman himself makes a "moue" at that.

"Perhaps Paris!" snorts Mme QC de QP. "What would my daughter be doing in Paris? She has never been to Paris; she does not know anyone in Paris . . . ."

"It may be exactly for that reason."

"For what reason?"

"She may be ashamed. She may be embarrassed. She may simply have wanted to explore new possibilities."

"Shamed! Embarrassed! She had nothing to be ashamed of until she met you two. You have done this to her!"

"In a sense, yes we have. In another sense, we have freed her from her prison."

"Prison, yes, prison! That is where you should be!"

"Did you ever have any experiences with Mlle. Picard?" the policeman asks me.

The pricking in my ears warns me that this could be a trap, or that at least in answering the question I could ensnare myself. What is the legal age of consent in France? How do I warn Mary when they ask her the same question?

"No, of course not," I declare resolutely. "She is young enough to be my daughter."

The policeman is silent.

Having fed his képi twice through his fingers, he adds "If Mme. Malanny does not wish to speak to us here, it could be better that she accompanies us to the station where we can record the events in a proper manner. What do you think?"

"I have nothing to say. Mary has to make her own decisions."

"It would help us if you accompanied us too."

Not another police station! I cannot bear sitting in another police station.

"Please inform Mme. Malanny that she must accompany us now."

I turn to go upstairs.

"My vase! You have broken my valuable Sèvre vase!" Even the policeman starts.

"What are you talking about, Madame?" I retort. "That vase was cracked before you were born."

"No it was not. You have broken it. It will cost you a lot of money! A lot of money!"

"Madame, I assure you that the vase was damaged when we arrived. Look at it. That crack is ancient."

"Well, we will examine the inventory together. If it is declared on the inventory that the vase is cracked, then you will be right. Otherwise, you must pay me. The inventory is the document of record."

The policeman is clearly distressed that his resolute course of action is being sidetracked. "This discussion is for another time. Now we must all return to the police station to continue the process of finding Mlle. Picard."

"You will pay for my vase nevertheless," Mme QC de QP hisses. "I will not forget. It is a family heirloom. You are not taking the proper care of my things, of any of my things."

There is impure hatred not only in her face but in the hypertension of her whole body.

Now I am outraged. Yes, I understand that she is afraid and upset, but this is complete dishonesty and, worse, I really do not know how to deal with it. We have no evidence of its being damaged when we arrived. Mme. QC de QP mentioned the crack herself, and perhaps for that reason we never thought to record it on the inventory, because she had already acknowledged it. She really is a spiteful woman. Well, one way or another, I am going to set her straight. She is stepping into more dangerous territory than she knows. I am not the type to tolerate that sort of nonsense.

In the meantime, Mary has arrived in the hallway, momentarily disorientated. "Mme. Mallany, are you willing to come with us to the police station?" inquires the policeman.

"Of course," replies Mary. She looks at me. "Should I have a lawyer?"

"I don't know how to play it. Maybe we should. He or she can deal with Madame's little games at the same time."

Mme. QC de QP is listening carefully. She obviously understands more English than she lets on.

"Dirty slut," I add.

Madame steps back as if she has been slapped. The policeman is bemused. "What did she say?" he asks.

Madame shrugs her shoulder. "I do not know, Thierry," she says. "I do not speak a word of English."

"We need a lawyer," Mary declares decisively. "Madame calling Mr. Plod by his Christian name is not a good sign."

Chapter 8

"Hi!"

"Hello."

"Hello. I am Mandy Hawke from the Manchester Evening News."

"Hello."

"And you are Miss Julia Blackburn."

"I am she."

"Excellent. I was wondering if you would not mind us having a quick chat about recent events in the village."

"No, I do not mind."

"Excellent. Excellent. Do you think I might come in. It is rather hard talking, and writing, and standing up all at the same time."

"Why don't we go and sit in the hammock over there?"

"That's a good idea. It is a beautiful day."

"Isn't it?"

We settle ourselves down, which means that we have to synchronise our rhythms otherwise the hammock becomes a very stormy sea. Mandy smiles a lot.

"So how long have you been in Hanburgh, Julia? You are a relative newcomer to the area, aren't you?"

"About two months."

"Do you like it here?"

"I used to."

"Yes, events have turned rather traumatic. Why did you choose to come here? You are not from around here, I gather."

"No, I used to live in London. I came here for the peace and quiet." I smile ironically, as I am supposed to do.

"Well, mostly it is, I should think."

"Mostly, yes."

"And had you known Mr. Willows long?"

"Funnily enough, he was the first person I met here, and he asked me almost exactly the same questions as you have. He cleaned up this garden for me, too. You are looking at his work."

"Wow! It is a beautiful garden."

"Well, he did not lay it out, but he did restore it to its former glory, with the help of some hard labourers."

"What did you think of Mr. Willows? What sort of man did you judge him to be?"

"I am sure that you know his reputation better than I."

"Frankly, I am having a little difficulty getting past that. I would like to be able to write something more insightful about him than that he was the village lothario. Could you help me?"

"I can try. His being the village womaniser, and a very gifted gardener, are the two most obvious things about him."

"What did women see in him? Was he funny, was he comfortable? He must have been sexy . . . ."

"No, I would say that he was none of those things. More determined, I would say."

"Determined?"

"Yes, determined to fill his day, and his life."

"By sleeping with people?"

"Well, specifically with women."

"So sleeping around filled his day, you think?"

"Yes. It certainly passed the time."

"What did he want from these women—their love, their affirmation, their warmth?"

"I never got close enough to him to find out."

"But you were the last person to see him alive and, in this context, the last woman."

"Yes, I was probably the last woman to sleep with him, as far as I know. I suppose he could have snuck in another quickie."

"How does that make you feel?"

"Afraid."

"Why afraid? Do you think that the murderer might come after you, or that he might have killed you at the same time if you had still been there?"

"Yes, I feel vulnerable, both to the murderer, and to life. Something like this reminds you that anything can happen at any time. And being interviewed by the police is not that funny either."

"How was that experience?"

"Daunting. Police stations are not pleasant places, and policemen are not that pleasant either."

"Did Inspector Frampton question you for a long time?"

"Quite a long time."

"And then he let you go."

"Yes."

"So he doesn't think it was you. That must be a relief, anyway."

"The crime was pretty obviously done by a man."

"Well, women can do most jobs nowadays."

"I would think that handling a double-handed axe precisely would take a lot of practice. I have not known many women lumberjacks, or even many of us who go out and split the logs for the fire. There again, I have lived nearly all my life in London in a smoke-free zone."

"What did you do in London?"

"I was a City trader."

"So you made your money and got out before you burnt out."

"I don't think I was in any danger of burning out but, after the crash, it was not going to be much fun or, more importantly, very lucrative to work in stocks and shares for a while."

"Good for you. You must be quite upset that your new-found peace has been invaded."

"Yes, I am. I am a very private person."

"And now you have to lock all the doors at night."

"I always did that."

"Does it make you feel afraid, being alone at night, if you are alone at night?"

"Yes, it does. I think we have covered that."

"To be honest, I think we have covered everything. Thank you so much, Julia. It has been very nice talking to you."

"It has been my pleasure. This must be quite a good assignment for you."

"Well, I have been the crime correspondent for the Manchester Evening News a couple of years now."

"The Manchester Evening News has a full-time crime correspondent?"

"Sure. There is lots of crime around here. Quite a few murders, actually, most drug-related. We don't get many old-fashioned village murder mysteries, like this one."

"Perhaps Tom grew cannabis on the side in a sunny corner of his garden."

"I don't think anyone gets murdered for grow-your-own. You are hardly likely to corner the market, are you?"

❋   ❋   ❋

In a way, I have lived alone all my life. If you were being trite, you might try to classify me as a loner, but that is not really it. It is not that I have ever chosen to be alone, and I am rarely physically alone at all. OK, yes, in this precise interlude of my life, I am more alone than ever. I have a large house, and I rattle around in it. Isn't that what you are meant to say in these circles? "Julia rattles around in that large house up there." Mary visits often, but she is not here most of the time, or anything approaching that. People call, but they are mostly strangers. I have met up a few times with Sam. Contrary to my initial expectations, I like Sam. She is more original than I would have imagined, more weird. Her thoughts flutter around like a bird's wings against a wire cage, not overly distressed, yet not still—absent-minded energy.

It is more that I cannot avoid being alone. I am alone amongst the wildest company. I am alone even with myself. What does Durkheim call it? Anomie? I am not quite sure how you spell that. Anomie is where you are adrift from the natural concerns of society, almost sociopathic, although even more desperate than that, and too lacking in spirit to kill anyone, never mind everyone. I am not that either. I scrutinise with great care what happens in society, and I am frequently moved by what I see, often to anger. Human beings feel so little respect. They are reckless and stupid about themselves, and careless for others. They are slobs, half-baked, pointless wander-abouts. Dazed and confused and pettily nasty. They have brains like tins of baked beans (is that where the "half-baked" comes from?). The most exciting moment of their lives is when they are picked up and shaken so that all the beans are spread evenly through the sauce. Then someone brings out a tin opener, and they die.

I cannot live in this world. I hover over the surface of life, occasionally dipping my toe in, but refusing to go in deeper, even up to my knees. I cannot imagine immersing myself in it. I would never get out. I would slip into a relentless, unpitying, unsatisfying, interminable life. I would become a zombie bumbling around the everyday of shopping and gossiping and television. My God, what a terrifying fate! I couldn't even be sure of being allowed to die, or of when.

My mother was always half out of this life, from as early as I can remember, forever knocking back pills like peanuts, and being carted off to hospital to be pumped out. "Isn't it nice to have your mummy back again, dear?" Oh yes, and for how long exactly this time? "She is rather weak, though. You will have to look after your mummy, won't you?" Excuse me, flittery thing, I am five, my mother is a grown-up, isn't someone meant to be looking after me, indeed us? Louise here is this squirming, howling baby lying on the sofa. What is anyone doing with her? I try to help. I have even attempted to change her nappy. That was really messy. "Oh dear. Baby's nappy has come loose. Poo everywhere." No, it didn't come loose. I tried to change her. Give me some credit you blind old bat. Oh well, by the time mummy is dead, I will probably know how to do it.

Just imagine that, at the age of five I was counting the days to when my mother would die. How can a child know all about death at the age of five? Well, I didn't know all about death exactly, but I did know it existed, and that my mother was heading straight for it like a kangarooing old banger, stop-start, stop-start, stall, re-start, splutter. I did not think about what would happen to me, us if she died. I only knew that she would not be there, and that left a hole in my stomach. What I did not know or expect was that Louise would be dead before her. I am glad that I did not even consider this, although when she was a baby I would probably not even have cared. Babies are not really human to a small child. They are an articulated disposal bag waiting to be something.

My crazy mother! It is small wonder that I never really entered this earth, given that she was so desperate to leave it, and that we barely passed on the stairs.

Sometimes when I hear a low-pitched radio squeaking slightly a long way away, I think that is what life is like—a distant voice played over the airwaves almost out of earshot.

Alone in this house, my telepathy is like that too. Thankfully, there appears to be a geographic limitation to it. Really strong emotions, like when Sam and Brian are together, sometimes march in and bang me over the head, but usually it is a low-level wisp of sound.

Is this what it is for God? Quiet babbling whispers across the universes? Is that how He bears it? In that case, lucky for Him because when I am with people, it is like a crowded pub on New Year's Eve, everyone shouting and passing thoughts around over other people's heads for friends to reach over and collect, with much incidental spillage of emotions.

I sometimes wonder whether my telepathy isn't a madness, whether a wire wasn't left buzzing loose during the operation, short-circuiting my mind. I discount the thought because what people say and what I hear them thinking appear to be closely related, except when they intend them not to be (which is 50:50) but that could all be a delusion too, a déjà-vu, a false belief that I am making two elements connect when there was only ever one.

Anyway, it is a constant social tinnitus I suffer from, illusory or real.

Hell, I am bored of all this soul-searching. I am going to kick off my shoes, hug Gargoyle close ("Hello, boy! Hello, boy! Hello, boy! Did you miss me? Ah! The tongue! Gargoyle, that is disgusting. Do it again."—Frank returned him this morning), open a bottle of fridge-cold chenin blanc, strip a bar of chocolate and vegetate in front of a film. I need to drown out the noises from my own head, generated by me.

Perhaps my whole crusade is wrong. Perhaps I should go and kill a real dictator after all, and not trawl these village green fiends. I am beginning to feel sorry even for Mary Knightly. How much trouble can she be?

❀　　❀　　❀

"Father! What a pleasant surprise!"

I am not thinking of Mary Knightly, which is unusual when I visit this part of the village. As I leave the jangling bell of the post office and turn left towards the Hanburgh Arms, my first flash of thought is invariably that I will be passing Mary Knightly's house from the back, where she parks their car. Will I see her?

Today, I have someone else on my mind, because my ex-Mary (and indeed Frank) live in a mid-size Victorian house set back from the road, almost opposite Mary Knightly's. It is a beautiful brown-bricked Victorian house, copying the Georgian town house tradition, with windows like sashed eyes and a front door like a dainty nose, and ivy like Rabelaisian hair—the sort of house Prince Charles would like about 25 million of the UK population to live in.

I miss Mary, and I am wondering whether I should stay here in Hanburgh. I might just return to London, or go abroad, almost certainly to France. I fancy some reliable sun, promenade beaches, shell fish, and a house filled with red wine and chocolates. It will have to be the South-West, then.

I am wondering what has happened to Inspector Frampton. I haven't seen him around, and he hasn't called in to tighten the noose on his enquiries. Funny, I thought you would have returned to me as a suspect by now. I had that sense as I was released from the police station, as I stopped helping the police with their enquiries, that I represented unfinished business. The quick flick of your eyes told me so.

"Hello, Mary. Hello, George."

My head shoots round. There like kangaroos assembled at the side of a dirt track, are Mary Knightly and George with a tall perma-tanned, silver-haired, distinguished man, somewhere into his seventies, I would guess. So, this must be Dr. Berringer.

He is the handsome man who ruins my theory of deceptive appearances. He would stand out from any crowd, and he actually looks cruel, which is quite a feat for an old man. He doesn't leer, and he bears no outward scars, but he has steel-grey eyes and an imposing, arrogant manner. I have no problem tagging him as a doctor, nor as someone who would terrify a small child. He is not looking my way. He is not really looking at anybody at all. His gaze is into the air, as though man addressing God.

I want to hear this conversation. Where to hide? I could stand the other side of the wall, but that would be arrestingly obvious to any a passer-by, and I have my social pride. Ducks! I'll feed the ducks at the mill pond. It is easily in earshot of this little group, as if I needed to hear them in that sense, and I have just bought some bread.

I scuttle round, pinned to their conversation.

"Such a glorious day," Dr. Berringer opines.

"Come inside and have some tea, father."

"I think I would rather stay out here, Mary. It is beautiful out here."

"Do I hear you are off to Spain again, Jeff?"

"Yes, that's right, George. Tuesday morning."

"And how long are you away for this time?"

"23 days."

"That will be nice."

"It is always nice to catch up with our friends out there, and to catch some sunshine."

"We will miss you, father. Is there anything you would like doing?"

"I was hoping that you might look after the plants while we are away."

"Only too pleased," George volunteers. "Do you want a lift to the station?"

"No, we are driving down this time. We may spend a few days in London when we get back."

"So, we won't see you for a bit then."

"Well, perhaps I will have a cup of tea after all."

They move inside and shut the door. They are still talking, but I doubt that they will ever have anything interesting to say.

❉   ❉   ❉

I continue onto the Hanburgh Arms. The place is empty, with the exception of Brenda wiping some tables. I am always intrigued by the materials people use for cleaning. Brenda is using an old shirt sleeve, checked and ragged. The buttons are still attached, and clack against the wood. Brenda picks up the ashtrays, turns them over, and wipes their bottoms. The smell of disinfectant penetrates the smoky atmosphere to double its repugnance.

"Hi."

"Hi, Brenda."

"What have you been doing?"

"Oh, murdering people, that sort of thing."

"Not even as a joke, Julia."

"Sorry."

"That's all right."

"I forgot you took a cake in the face for him."

"I have done many things for Tom," Brenda laughed, "including the cake. Poor Tom. Who told you that story?"

"Sam and her friends."

"It was all Sam's fault. She was trying to make Brian jealous, and she succeeded. I don't think he forgave Tom until the other night, then he came in here and broke down. He had the whole pub trying to calm him, even Sam's husband Tony, which is ridiculous, when you come to think of it."

"Do Brian and Tony get on?"

"Not in the least. Tony knows full well what Brian is up to with Sam. He doesn't do anything about it, but I don't suppose he is particularly grateful. If I was him, I'd flatten him, like your Frank did with Jeff Berringer last year. That was great . . . ."

"My Frank?"

"Well, Your Mary's Frank, then."

"She is not my Mary, not any more."

"Oh, I wouldn't bet on that, Julia. Hang around a bit and see."

"So why did Frank hit Dr. Berringer?"

"Nobody is quite sure, but he was absolutely livid. In fact, he was so angry we could not really make out what he was shouting about. Anyway, Jeff sidled into the pub in his usual way, hoping that someone would stand him a pint, and Frank marched straight over to him, started roaring threats about if he ever saw Jeff doing that again, he would bloody kill him, then he thumped him really hard in the mouth. There was blood everywhere, and Jeff lost a couple of teeth for a short while. Funnily enough though, Jeff never did anything about it. He never pressed charges. Everyone was absolutely stunned. We had never seen Frank like that before, even though people have always said that he has a nasty temper on him if he gets really riled up. He was certainly that."

"And you don't know why?"

"It was almost certainly because Jeff was up to his old tricks, and Frank caught him at it. Jeff cannot keep his hands to himself when there are young girls around."

"Young girls?"

"Yes, I mean very young girls. Teenagers, and younger. He is always turning on his distinguished GP charm and pawing them. Somebody usually tells him to stop, but I don't think he can help himself. Frank must have seen something rather serious. Anyway, George dragged him off Jeff in the end. You wouldn't think that George would have the guts, or the strength, but he is a surprisingly strong man, George, when he wants to be. He is as protective of Jeff as Mary is. There's nowt as queer as folk."

"Is that what you meant when you said that Mary must have suffered a lot with her father?"

"Yes. Mary was an attractive young girl once, and a really lovely one too, from all accounts, before she was adopted by Jeff and Phyllis. Then she turned really mean, and she hasn't turned back since, I can tell you. She is Jeff outed, except that I don't think she has all his particular demons."

"What about George?"

"George? Oh no, he is a real softy, although terribly boring with it. He is a born accountant. He plays everything safe to the point of stupidity. He won't hear a word against Mary, or against Jeff. He protects them in every way he can, and he scowls if anyone mentions any gossip about them in front of him. He is rather on his own is poor George. If he just relaxed a bit, I think he would have quite a few friends around here, but as it is . . . ."

"Is he still working?"

"No, he retired a couple of years ago. He has a good pension, I think, so that makes Mary happier than she has been for most of her life. And, for the rest, I think he just does what Mary tells him to do, without a hint of rebellion, at least in public. He must get irritated sometimes."

"It sounds like that old quote 'It was kind of God to have Mr. Knightly fall in love with Mrs. Knightly, thus making two people unhappy rather than four'."

Brenda considers this for a second. "Except that I am not sure that Mary and George are that unhappy together, and Mary still takes great pleasure in upsetting everyone else. And nothing is going to change that now. She will be like that until she dies and, being as she is, she will probably last forever, heaven help us."

"Do you think I should bump her off, too?" I hold out my hand as Brenda reacts. "Only joking, Brenda!"

We are both forlorn as we get out of the car, having driven back from the police station. We are not talking to each other. I wonder if this will ever end. Mary simply refuses to explain to anyone what happened between Alice and her. The police, got more and more menacing, but she stonewalled it. Not a murmur, except if you were standing in the corridor as I was, and overheard the shouting of the interrogator punctuated by Mary's short, flat responses. Twice the policeman (l'Inspecteur Herbert) hurled himself out of the interrogation room and slammed the door behind him so hard that the partition walls visibly vibrated with the shock waves. He came down the corridor and stared at me. "What is it with this woman? Why won't she talk to us? What is she hiding? Does she not see the pain she is causing Mme. Picard and her family? Do you two think you can come in here and hurt families who have lived here for centuries, without repercussions? Watch out, I say. Watch out!" He then stormed back into the interrogation room, and roared at Mary all over again.

I have to say that I was not feeling the empathy for Mary I should have. I should have been sitting in her body, scared and alone in the face of this onslaught, hiding maybe some terrible secret, wishing it would all end. I should have been beside myself, crying in the corridor, begging them to stop hurting her, begging Mary to relent and give them what they wanted, however compromising, however terrible. I should perhaps have screamed the house down until they stopped, roasting every gendarme, or whatever they officially are (I don't understand the French police compartmentalisation and hierarchy either) as they stood apologetically in front of me, I should have demanded a lawyer and got one.

But I did none of these things. I let Mary sort these things out for herself. What they were asking of her was perfectly reasonable. There is a young girl of the village missing, she went missing, it is to be assumed, while she was in Mary's 'care', so why is Mary refusing to talk? Nonetheless, if I were a better, more committed person, I would have protected her. I think she would have done that for me. Perhaps a few months ago, I would have done that for her. We have become estranged from each other's needs, and especially I from hers. There is a coldness about me that always saddens me. It is part of my refusal to become embroiled with the world. To get in there and fight would be to become human. I don't want to be human. I don't want to be that foolish, and I don't want to be that hurt, and I don't want to be that ground down and crushed by the emotionality of being human. I prefer to live a separate life, in life but not of it.

So, as we get out of the car, I am sure Mary feels sad and betrayed. She won't look at me, and that usually means that she is controllably angry with me, an ice dagger that cuts deep and melts into invisibility. I have not protected her, and she will lacerate me.

"Mary, let's talk," I suggest.

"Don't you dare say a word to me!" Her eyes flash at me. "Leave me alone. You are good at that. I don't know what I am doing here, I really don't."

"Then go somewhere else. Go back to Hanburgh, to Frank."

"You know I can't do that. How dishonest can you get? I despise you. You are disgusting!"

"I accept that. What shall we do about it?"

"What will you do about it? You! What are you going to do about it?"

"I am not sure that there is anything I can do. I am me. Take me or leave me."

"I certainly don't want you anywhere near me. I cannot bear you anywhere near me. I want you to go!"

"No, I am sorry, Mary. I am not going anywhere. I am renting this house. You walked out on me. You lost Alice along the way and are refusing to say where she is, provoking the police to drag us off to their station and shout at us. You could easily say where she is . . . ."

"I do not know where she is!" Her eyes are red and tired and watering. There is a despair temporarily eclipsing the anger. "Why will no-one believe me that I do not know where she is? She left without a note. I woke up and she was no longer there, her clothes were no longer there, there was no trace that she had ever been there. She never said that she was planning to leave. She never gave the slightest hint of it. We had a good time the night before she left, then I woke up and the room was empty of her, and I have never heard anything of her since."

"Why didn't you tell the police that?"

"It is none of their business. I have done nothing wrong. Alice is her own responsibility, they must talk to her."

"They don't know where she is."

"I don't know where she is! Can't you fucking get that into your thick skull? I don't know where she is!"

"Explain that to them, not to me. I am not the one looking for her. She can be where the fuck she likes as far as I am concerned."

"Lucky for you then!" I am not at all sure what I am being accused of this time—not caring about a young, complicated girl, who walked out on me, without saying goodbye or thank you, with my partner, without saying goodbye or thank you for her either?

I cannot help comparing your interrogation technique, Inspector John, with that of the French inspector, l'Inspecteur Herbert. I have to say you are much quieter, although I suspect that you are both highly subtle and highly professional in your different ways. Under whatever techniques you use, you both glint through as being caring human beings. It is a glimpse of you that makes us want to talk. L'Inspecteur Herbert is younger than you, much more handsome, much more still, more giving, but he can also rave and shout. You are older, mousier, more biting and visibly less in control. I feel that I know you and that I unnerve you, that I want full-out to unnerve you. I do not feel that with l'Inspecteur Herbert. There is no need, and I would be frightened of doing it, either because it would hurt him, or because he would hurt me, or, more probably, the one and then the other. He did not manage to persuade Mary to talk, although she claims that she had nothing much to say. He did not even unearth the nothing much. It was the same between us. I knew virtually nothing, but I failed to tell you the one fact that I could have told you, that I saw Sally Willows disappear into the alleyway down the road from the house as I slammed the front door shut and, as you know, she claims not to have been in the village until the next day, when she heard the news about Tom. There is something for you, at last. Have a play with that. I cannot believe that she would have hurt Tom, but you have to ask yourself "Why was she there, and why did she not admit to being there?" Clue number one.

Actually, there is the same situation here. I noticed Mary shoving a bloodied piece of clothing into the washing machine shortly after she came home. It could have been menstrual, who knows, but it sets the mind computing. It makes me anxious. Is Mary really here to accompany me, or is she here to keep an eye on my progress? Is she reading this while I am out? If she was keeping watch on me, why did she leave with Alice? If she was here out of a companionship or love she no longer felt when she decided to leave, why did she come back? What part did Alice play in this? Did Alice find out something she could not be allowed to divulge? Is she lying in some scrubland somewhere, dead? Am

I in danger even as I write this, exactly because I am writing this? Was Mary so jealous that she killed Tom? No, I don't think so. Killing Tom was a man's work, and neither Sally nor Mary are men, I am pretty sure of that, although you never can tell, can you?

Chapter 9

"Hi, I am from The Sun newspaper. My name is Dave Chevey. Here is my badge. May I come in? Quite a place you have got here."

"I doubt it, Dave."

"To be honest, it is virtually impossible to write, talk and stand up all at the same time."

"And especially if you are a Sun reporter." I smile sweetly.

"So you are not looking to chummy up to me, then?"

"No, I shan't be doing that."

"You are not nervous of bad publicity, then?"

"I have good lawyers."

"OK, so that is well understood. Where shall we talk, then?"

"Who said we were going to talk?"

"I don't know if you know anything about the press, Julia, but it is much easier to get it over with. We hang around until we have got want we want. So let's go inside, I'll ask a few questions, you will answer them as honestly as you can (honesty is the best policy with us—we always find out everything in the end . . . .)"

"But you are not always allowed to print it."

"That is true, Julia. Anyway, I think that co-operating with us would be very much to your advantage."

"To be honest, Dave, I don't care a flying fuck what you think."

"Well, can we sit in the garden then, if you won't let me into your house? Why is that, then, by the way?"

"I doubt I would ever be able to get rid of you."

"Well, you are definitely gorgeous, darling, but not that gorgeous. I have had better."

I consider for a moment telling him to piss off, or slapping him, or just slamming the door in his face. I consider doing all three. There again, I am sure he can be a complete pain in the arse if he wants to be, so it may indeed be better to give him what we wants, and be done with him.

"I'll get out some chairs. The hammock will still be damp from the dew this morning."

"Anywhere you like."

I drag out a couple of folding plastic seats from the hammock. "I think that the grass should hold up, but you might find yourself sinking in a bit."

"That's OK. So, Julia, you are a newcomer to the 'hood."

"Yes, I arrived here a few months ago."

"And you have no connections with the village."

"None whatsoever."

"So why did you come here?"

"For peace and quiet."

He laughs.

"So you were the last person to see Tom Willows alive."

"No."

"No? How is that?"

"The murderer saw him last."

"OK, I'll re-phrase my question. You are the last *known* person to have seen Tom Willows alive?"

"Yes, so far."

"And you had just had sex with him?"

"Delicately put."

"We don't mess around."

"Ordinarily, neither do I."

"So you weren't planning on having a long-term affair with him? You weren't his new girlfriend?"

"I don't think Tom had girlfriends in that sense."

"Children. Did he have any children?"

"I don't have the first idea."

"He must have a few little bastards tucked away around here somewhere, with his reputation."

"Perhaps the women always came well prepared, with his reputation."

"And you?"

"I can't have children."

"So what was it like having it away with someone, and the next minute they have been gruesomely murdered?"

"Are you trying to delve into my deepest emotions?"

"Nah. I don't write that sort of stuff. I just want words like 'shocked'. 'horrified', 'it tore my world apart', that sort of thing. Something quotable, and quick. We don't have that much space. 200 words. That's nothing."

"You can use 'shocked' then, and 'frightened'."

"Yeah, those are good words. Had you known him long?"

"Not intimately, no. I knew him as a friend. He did this garden up for me."

"So, it is not the end of the world for you, then?"

"Only for him."

"OK, that's it then." He tugs his ear. "Oh, look, here comes Steve. He is my photographer for the day. You don't mind us taking pictures, do you? The house, the garden, you?"

I turn to Steve. "Hi, Steve."

"Hi."

"Dave here tells me you want to rape me."

Steve mutters uncomfortably "I wasn't planning on doing that."

"It certainly feels that way."

"I am sorry. We won't be long."

"Rapists seldom linger, Steve."

"Yeah. Well. I'm sorry."

"Just a shot of the house full frontal from here, Steve. I don't think we will bother with the garden after all . . . . However, on second thoughts, as Tom was the guy who did it, perhaps that would be a neat bridge. Then a few of Julia, looking lovely, eh, Julia, and maybe just a touch forlorn."

"You don't want me to be sticking my fingers up at you, then."

"You're joking. I can't think of anything better. We might even be able to get you on the front page if you did that. The editor would love it. However, if I were you, I would stick to 'demure' and page 7, unless old Frampton can pin the murder on you, that is. Yeah, take a few shots, Steve, just in case."

❈   ❈   ❈

Mary and I are back together again. It is wonderful. She came round this morning, there was a slight hesitation while we stalked around each other, then we were straight into each others arms, naked and satisfied on the sitting-room floor.

It is so calm holding Mary. I know it is love. I know she is in love too. I can hear her, twittering and trilling away, so happily. It is worth listening to all that multitude of unsolicited moaning and whining voices in my head to be able to hear Mary's private conversation about her love for me. I am so sorry that I cannot reciprocate. It would be a total revelation for her to hear my thoughts, although we would probably get stuck in some infernal loop, both sharing the one thought round and round and round.

It is so unlike making out with those girls when I was sixteen, just after my mother died. I was distraught because she was a fantastic, if tragic and exasperating, mother, and to lose her suddenly like that to suicide was a blow I shall never fully recover from.

Why was I not enough? I used to ask myself that before she died, when she was deep in her depressions and threatening to kill herself, and of course afterwards. I adored her. She loved me. We were extremely close. And it wasn't anything like enough.

I asked her once if she had always been depressed. She said it had no doubt started when her parents were killed in a car crash when she was seven, and she was adopted by a couple where the woman did not want anything to do with her after a while because she was so hard to handle. Her younger sister had been adopted by another, very respectable family, where she was also severely mistreated. At fifteen she was raped by my father, and had me. She followed this with a series of failed relationships, after one of which she gave birth to Louise. Then Louise died. Life was too much for my mother. It did not give her a chance.

After she died I went totally out of control. All these young girls came round to console me, and would do anything for me. I was of the age and the mentality to take total advantage, so I made love to many of them in my bedroom as I now had the house otherwise to myself. In a way I was getting my own back on my mother. Look, mother, at what you have done to me. Look what you are making me become. As if my mother deserved any more punishment. The girls and I got very sticky together, sometimes more than one at a time. It was a huge release for me, a necessary one. I think that they must have felt pretty guilty about some of the things we got up to, especially after I started introducing the drugs to enhance the experience. Yet, if they got nervous, they still came back for more, and I have never heard that anything untoward ever resulted from our activities.

That lifestyle naturally continued when I became a City trader, the pressure of which encouraged cathartic release into alcohol, drugs and women, paid and unpaid. It stopped with the car crash that mutilated me, and psychologically and physically took years to recover from.

So being here with Mary is totally different from that. We are together, we are in love, and we are talking and thinking incessantly. Occasionally I get caught out responding to a thought that she has not yet said out loud. She stops and looks at me, and asks "Did I really say that?" and I say "Yes." And she says "I certainly thought it but I cannot recall saying it. Weird." And I say "How else could I have known?" and she says "Weird. Weird."

I am afraid I am deceiving her already. I am not telling her the truth about myself and what I can do. I will. I promise I will. It is not time yet. We have also started discussing whether and when we should tell Frank about us. Mary is extremely scared of doing this, for obvious reasons, but she thinks we have to. It is only fair to Frank. She does not want to humiliate him by leaving him as the only person in the village who does not know what is going on. He does not deserve that in return for all his loyalty to her throughout their lives. The village does not know about us getting back again, how could it? It was only about an hour ago (so give them another hour). We have a little time.

Mary asks me if I would be prepared to accommodate Frank, sexually speaking. He only likes it occasionally, although, with a young girl as pretty as me, he might work himself up into a frenzy for a week or two, until his fishing and the pressures of business drag him down to earth again.

I say that I would. He is a nice man, and a considerate one. I am sure that it cannot be too unpleasant.

Mary replies that Frank is not Tom, not by a long chalk. She laughs. It suddenly occurs to me that Mary actually knows that Tom had a long chalk. "You did it with Tom?" I exclaim incredulously.

"No."

"It sounds like you did."

"No, I have never been unfaithful to Frank before you, and I am not 100% certain that it even counts as adultery with you, being a woman. Can a woman commit adultery with another woman, technically and legally speaking?"

"I don't know. So how do you know about the length of Tom's chalk?"

"I have never slept with Tom, but I know many others who have. Tom's chalk has slipped out into the conversation, so to speak, on more than one occasion. I have never consulted Tom about gardening, and I have never even sat on a sofa with him, so I am untouched. Sadly, forever."

"Yes."

"I am sorry to bring Tom up."

"Well, I did more really. He was in my thoughts first, before you mentioned him."

"So I can read your thoughts too, now, can I? It must have been terrible, terrible, terrible for you."

"It was."

"And I got you into it all by breaking off with you because I was so scared of what Frank would do, and what the village was thinking. I was such a coward, such a fool. I am honestly, honestly sorry."

I am wondering why Mary is apologising to me. If she were anyone else on earth, she would be demanding abject apologies from me, and then still not forgive me, maybe forever. To bury my own confusion, I hug Mary close and give her a deep kiss.

To celebrate our getting back together again, we are starting a new game. We are sitting on each others' knees, our thighs and our buttocks splayed. We are totally open to each other. I slip my finger inside Mary, withdraw it, and suck it.

"Ugh, disgusting," says Mary.

"No, it's not." I do it again. "Strawberry flavour."

"I bet it jolly well isn't." She dips her finger inside me and tastes it. "That's not strawberry, that's melon."

We try it a few more times. We come to the honest conclusion that it does not taste of anything much at all except the perfume we are wearing.

Mary then offers her finger for me to suck. "Try yourself," she suggests. I do. It is strange tasting yourself as a coating on someone else's skin. I like her finger in my mouth. That is really sexy. I return the flavour.

So, there we are, being extremely intimate, more intimate than I have ever been with anyone, as perfect a moment as one could conceivably have.

The thought has just popped into Mary's head of what would happen if she slipped her finger up my bottom instead. Would I still lick it? She wouldn't, she decided. Bliss has its limits.

The jury is out on this side of the twin-backed beast. I think I probably would. After all, it would only be me.

"I don't know why you admire him so much. Let's face it, Tom was nothing better than a common rapist."

The whole room draws breath at the same moment, and they begin to stutter their protestations. They are probably also wondering whether I killed him after all.

Melody is the most composed. "He certainly slept with anyone he could," she admits, "including you, Julia, but I have never heard anyone even suggest that he raped them. You all fell for his charms, or for his technique, willingly enough, as I understand it. That isn't rape."

Under some pressure to respond and to justify my provocation, I take a moment to collect my thoughts. "My mother would have called him a rapist," I assert.

"What has your mother got to do with it? Does she know him?"

"No."

"So?"

"My mother was always very precise about the exact boundary between right and wrong, and she would have called him a rapist." I am fully aware that my statement has a private meaning that I have no intention of communicating. This is a conversation with myself, a monologue, in the presence of strangers.

"Bully for her, Julia." Melody turns to Sam. "Do you think Tom raped you?"

"Of course not." Sam flushes slightly, despite her usual brazenness on such matters. "He most certainly didn't rape me. Not all those times."

Everyone laughs, even me.

"Sam was a bit of a favourite," Julie explains. "She has no sense of guilt, only of fun."

"Right on," Sam declares, throwing her arm into the air.

"He lied to you," I challenge her," didn't he? Didn't he make you feel special . . . .?"

"Very," Sam giggles, and they all giggle along with her.

". . . .and didn't you think that you were more than a quickie?"

"Yes. Still, I should have known better. Not that we were all that quick."

More laughter.

"Perhaps he should have known better. Definitely he should. He lied to you, without question, and you cannot consent to a lie, so that constitutes rape. He had sex with you by means of deceit."

I can see that around the room they are starting to realise what I am alluding to. As my argument becomes clearer, they are beginning to relax with it.

"I still think that you are being very harsh," says Julie. "And he has just been murdered. Spare him some generosity of spirit, Julia."

"Well, my mother would have called him a rapist, and so would I. As it happens, I was about the only woman he did not rape, so I feel that I am capable of being entirely objective here. I came much closer to raping him."

Melody again: "I still don't see why your mother keeps turning up in this conversation. I think you should leave her out of it. You are a little too old, if I may say so, Julia, to keep invoking your mother. With respect, what she might or might not think is irrelevant here."

"Not to me."

"Is she still alive?" Julie asks carefully.

"No. She died a few years ago."

"Then she is past caring," Melody cuts in.

"She cared very much."

The room lapses into silence.

"Have you seen Brian, Sam?" inquires Julie.

"Not really. He has gone strangely quiet since Tom's death. I think he has gone to ground."

"Kate will be pleased," remarks Mich. "She can have him to herself for a change. Here comes number five!"

I do not really take any further part in the conversation. As an outsider, here at Sam's invitation, I have the privilege of being able to appear and disappear as I wish, and I am not sure that her friends will ever resent my silence as much as my presence. Perhaps that is to be overly neurotic. Melody is the most aggressive towards me, and she is like that even with Sam, so I am probably simply no-one special to her in any sense. Julie is friendly enough, if somewhat perplexed by me, as is Mich, who has a tendency to say very little, especially if the conversation is tendentious.

And Sam? I still cannot make Sam out. We do not gel, so we cannot really be friends, yet she appears to have a need to connect with me, which is strange. She has an established position in the village, and she is entirely self-assured to the point of being rampant, so why would she bother with me unless we hit a chord, which we don't, at least as far as I can tell. Perhaps she experiences it differently. Maybe for one reason or another, she either needs my approval or my endorsement, but it is not at all obvious that she either needs them or seeks them from anyone else.

Here is a bit more background on Sam, Inspector.

From what I have heard or can deduce (given that she is the most talked-about personality in the village), everyone is agreed that she married her husband, Tony, wholly for his money. She rarely spends time at their home, preferring to hang around the Hall.

Tony is very rich and surprisingly nice, but he lacks the spice that Sam needs. He is not dangerous. He looks good, he does good deeds, he wants children, he is kind to his fellow man, he is a bit boring. However, according to rumour, there is a lot more to him than Sam recognises, or would know how to recognise.

Tony spends much of his time sitting at his desk working. He works constantly. That is how he became rich, knowing how to buy and sell, and what to buy and sell, at the right price, at the right time, in the right location. He moves goods around the world from his desk in Hanburgh, all at the touch of buttons. Few people have worked out the financial benefits of the Internet better than Tony has. Few people know as many of the relevant laws, and customs. He has a knack for understanding markets, and how they ebb and flow.

He is good with people too. They like him, they trust him, they buy from him. He knows what motivates them, partly because, as with everything else, he does an enormous amount of research.

The one human being not to be touched by him, it appears, is Sam. He does not understand her at all, and she does little to help him find out about her. Her calculation was cynical. She wanted the power, she wanted his looks, she wanted his money. He is disposable, and she treats him as if the sooner he disappears the better. It may take some time. He is only fifty. He is fit. He works out and he runs, and he swims. He is lean. He rarely drinks, barely eats. His biggest risk is that his eyesight will go with the amount of time he spends staring at a screen.

He knows about Sam's flings. He lets them pass, although no-one knows what recriminations there may be in private.

Sam, it is said, has always been in a hurry throughout her life. When she was three, she wanted to be ten. She wanted to get there ahead of everyone else. At eleven she wanted to learn to drive, which she did in the park of the Hall. At sixteen she wanted to marry a rich man, and so she married Tony. At sixteen-and-a-half she wanted a divorce, so long as it did not jeopardise her alimony. Her lawyer advised her that she would get a great deal more if she waited a few years and had some children.

"What if I say that it was all a mistake, and that I didn't understand the nature of the commitment I was entering into?"

"Well, your husband is an older man and, it appears, exceedingly rich. These two facts will predispose a court to be generous to you, especially if you remember to cry," replied her lawyer.

"Oh yeah," said Sam. "I can do that."

"You will get more if you wait a few years, though" repeated the lawyer.

The reasons Tony married Sam were not admirable either. He had come from nowhere to make a lot of money importing/exporting. He was admired, rich and lonely. He wanted a wife to keep him company, and a trophy fitting to his status. A buxom young blonde from a wealthy family living in a semi-stately home would do it.

For once, he did not get what he bargained for. He got the wife to place on his elbow at events, but he hardly saw her the rest of the time. She turned out to be something of a home bird, but nowhere near his home.

One day he was sitting at the bar of the Hanburgh Arms sipping on a half pint of Fosters. He was the only person in the place. He got chatting to Brenda.

"How is Sam?" asked Brenda.

Tony would usually have said "Fine, oh fine, thank you," out of loyalty, a desire to keep his private life private, and to hide his mistakes from the world. However, this time, realising that Brenda was well-apprised of the truth, he said "You are more likely to know that than I am."

"Really?"

"Yes, really."

"That's a shame."

"Yes. It would be nice to see my wife occasionally."

"She will be burnt out by twenty-five, that one."

"No age nowadays," nodded Tony.

"You being funny?"

"It is the only weapon you have left when you are fifty, and your wife is running around with other men."

"You know about that, do you?"

"Yes, I know about that. She tells me all about it. The ups and downs of Brian. How he is so mean to her. What should I do in her position? She treats me more like a father than a husband. I think it might shock her to realise that she is married to me and that Brian is married to Kate with four children, and very unlikely to leave her."

"No, he would never leave her. He knows a good thing when he sees one. He is just in it for the ride."

"I wouldn't know."

"You always wonder why people are as they are. That girl has so much going for her. An indulgent father, and loving and generous husband, from all accounts . . . ."

"That would be me then . . . ."

"No money worries, and she insists on rebelling against it all, knocking about with Brian and Tom—I assume you know about him too . . . ."

"Oh yes, I know all about him . . . ."

". . . .and simply refusing to settle down, have children, get a job, all the normal things that everyone else does. It does make you wonder if anything happened to her along the way somewhere. There is obviously the fact that Freddy isn't really her father, then there is the possibility that Jeff Berringer is—is any of this new to you, Tony?"

"No, I have heard it all before . . . ."

". . . . and nobody would want Jeff as a father. I have heard rumours that he may have made himself rather more than her father, if you know what I mean."

"Not entirely."

"You will know that Jeff is partial to young girls."

"Yes, I have heard that."

"Well, I have heard it said that Sam is one of them."

"Even though he may be her father?"

"So it is said."

"That is disgusting."

"Yes, it would be."

"Can't something be done about him?"

"No, he seems to have immunity."

"We'll see."

According to Charlie, who picks up on all the gossip that Brenda misses, Tony subsequently confronted Sam with a demand to know what had happened between her and Dr. Berringer. Sam blustered, astonished that someone had briefed Tony on the subject (it must have been Brenda. What the hell was she doing?), and off-balance that he cared.

"Is he your real father?"

"How would I know?"

"Did he take advantage of you?"

"How would I know?"

"That is ridiculous!"

"So are your questions. It is none of your business. My past is my own, as is my present. If you are not satisfied with what you are getting, buzz off somewhere else. I am not stopping you."

Rumour has it that Tony plotted his revenge, and many business people will tell you that Tony James' vengeance is usually sure.

❀   ❀   ❀

M. Picard is at the door. It is a shock to see him. He has never attempted to speak to us before. This time it is clear that he has every intention of addressing us until he has an answer.

He marches straight into the house, as I hold the door, and turns to confront me.

"Where is she?"

"Mary is upstairs."

"I am not talking about your girlfriend. I am asking about my daughter."

"I know nothing about your daughter."

His hand whips me across the face. I have never been hit before. As I stagger back he announces that he is not here to waste his time. I stamp hard on his foot, and he strikes me again.

"I am going to phone the police".

"Do that."

I pick up the phone. He knocks it out of my hand, and hits me for a third time. I could kill him, and seek the means to do so. I run to the kitchen, and shake a knife at him. He corners me and I flash the blade at his eye. It streaks blood down his cheek. For the first time he stops. I am opposite him. He is calculating whether to lunge at me. That will be the end of me, I can sense it. I can hear it—a cumulus of expletives and misogyny. He darts forward. I carve a second gash into his right cheek. He stands back, then turns and leaves.

"A father has the right to know," he declares over his shoulder. "And I will find out. We will find out."

"And a woman has a right to defend herself."

He is gone.

Except that he returns as soon as it is dark, accompanied by many friends. Mary and I watch them as they snake with flashlights up the driveway. We are really scared, and for once this reunites us.

"What do we do?" she asks.

"There is little we can do," I reply. "But I'll shoot the first person through that door."

"Shoot?"

I show her my revolver.

"Where on earth did that come from?"

"Courtesy of Sally Willows," I reply.

"You can't use it. We will be arrested."

"We may have no choice, otherwise we may be dead. These people think we murdered their daughter, the daughter of their village."

"How can they possibly believe that? I keep telling you, Alice simply walked out on me."

"They do not believe you, and you have not been doing much to convince them."

"So this is my fault is it?" So much for our new-found solidarity, it lasted two minutes.

"Is it mine?"

"In a way."

"In what way?"

"If I had not gone off with her, you would have done. I was not going to be left alone here, penniless and humiliated."

"I had not intention of running off with her."

"She said that you begged her many times."

"The bitch! That is absolutely ridiculous. No way, did I. She is far too young, and far too volatile. I thought you were mad."

"I thought you were scheming."

"That at least explains something."

"Why would she lie to me?"

"She needed to get away from people like those knocking on our door." I consider for a second. Shall we try hot oil?

"Good idea!"

We scamper to the kitchen, and put the Extra Vierge on full heat in a medium-sized saucepan, adding a second and a third helping.

A window smashes. I take a knife and slash at the hand trying to lift the catch. It is removed with a curse. A second pane shatters. Mary does the same, this time with a heavy steel hatchet. It does not sever any fingers as they are withdrawn at lightening speed, but it makes its point at is thuds into the wooden frame. There is a frenetic discussion outside. They are going to burst in, from the back and from the front simultaneously. We wedge substantial chairs under both door handles and patrol the windows with blades poised until the oil starts to spit.

The timing is perfect. Just as they break both doors down, and emerge staggering into the house, we hit them with the oil at waste height. There are unmanly shrieks, and a total confusion as the leaders try to force their way back against the flow. One of them briefly catches fire. The burns must be savage, but we have kept any marks away from their faces, except possibly for a rogue splash. That way their fledgling lynch mob behaviour can remain their shameful secret. One, then two of them see the gun in my hand, warn the others, and they all run. Mary and I are abandoned to our little pigs celebration. They won't be coming down the chimney.

You are coming under a great deal of pressure to re-arrest me. Mary Knightly's set have made it a campaign. Georgina has phoned the local MP, Gerald McNaughton, to ask why I was released, and Hilary has written to you to the same effect. Everyone entering the doctor's surgery is invited to sign a petition for more effective policing in the area, which you take to mean that they want a result and, if not a result, a head.

You are, I am sure, familiar with the politics of policing. The public is invariably more comfortable with the thought of the wrong person being behind bars than that of having nobody there at all. It is nonsensical, but it is human nature.

The finger print crew have been round the house and found twenty-seven recent female finger prints. They thought their must have been a party.

A secret passage has been discovered, evidently frequently used. Tom's house dates back to the sixteenth century, so it has both a secret passage and a priest hole. This might be how the murderer got in and out of the house without being detected. Who would have known about it?

It is still puzzling the police as to why the passage is so well maintained. That must have been Tom. What was he doing using it when so much of his malfeasance was out in the open?

The police have also discovered a gun. It was hidden in classic fashion behind a loose brick in the darkest corner of the passage. What would Tom have been wanting with a gun? Stranger still, it is a woman's gun, a Ruger. This baffles you even further, and makes you very crotchety.

For the hell of it, you decide to go and interview Mary Knightly. You cannot imagine what she could have to do with Tom's murder, but having exhausted the most likely leads, you have decided to attend to the least likely.

George meets you at the door, and looks rather startled. "Good afternoon, Inspector."

"Good afternoon, Sir. Is Mrs Knightly at home?"

"Well, yes, she is. Would you like to see her?"

"That would be most kind."

George turns. "Dear, there is the Inspector here to see you."

Mary Knightly appears at the door. "What a pleasant surprise, Inspector. Do come in. We were just wandering what little tasks we should be doing this afternoon and you have saved us the bother. George, dear, please get the Inspector a cup of coffee."

"Thank you, Madam."

"George's pleasure, Inspector. He makes a very good cup of coffee with that cartridge gadget he has. Give a man a gadget, and you have a slave for life. Sit down, sit down."

"I assume that you must have known Tom Willows a long time, Madam."

"Oh years, Inspector, absolutely years. We have both been in this village all of our lives. We were at school together. We sang in the choir together. Tom has been most helpful in supplying equipment for my musical festival, and he is an excellent gardener. Will you be attending my music festival, Inspector? You don't sing by any chance?"

"I used to, Madam, but I am more into brass bands."

"Do you play in a brass band, Inspector?"

"I do, Madam. Twice a week."

"I am very partial to a brass band myself. Your band wouldn't be available for the festival, would it? That would be something really quite different."

"Well, I can ask the lads, Madam."

"Please do so, Inspector."

"Now, Madam, I have a favour to ask you. You have lived in this village all of your life, as you say. Who do you think might have killed Tom Willows?"

"Well, he was a bit of a ladies' man, Inspector. There is plenty of room for jealousy there, I would say."

"Any candidates?"

"Well, the obvious one is Julia Blackburn. She is rather unstable, I would say. Visiting Mary Maloney one minute, and Tom the next. I assume that you are aware of that. Yes. It is what I call fishing with a wide trawl. Anything and anyone."

"Why do you think she would want to kill him?"

"As I say, jealousy. She is new to the area. She does not know our country ways, and she probably did not know Tom's reputation when she got involved with him. She is a strange girl. There is something most definitely odd about her. Everyone notices her looks first. I noticed her eyes. I would say that she is extremely vengeful. Not one to cross. I never mean to hurt a fly, but I would be very much more comfortable if she were behind bars. If she has not committed a murder yet, I would be very surprised if she does not do so in the not so distant future. Frank will come back from the pub or fishing or something unexpectedly, and catch them in flagrante, there will be a fight, and Julia will shoot him. Something like that, or do you think I am being too melodramatic?"

"It may be too early to say."

"That is the problem with crime. You only know that you were right after the fact."

"Tell me about it."

Chapter 10

"Miss Blackburn."

"Hello. Good morning."

"Good morning, Miss Blackburn. My name is Simon Stanley. I am the local vicar here . . . ."

"Oh, hello. I am pleased to meet you, come in."

"Please call me Simon."

"I am Julia."

"Hello, Julia."

There is an embarrassed silence while we shuffle momentarily on our respective sofas.

"You have been through a terrible ordeal."

"Yes, it has been an awful shock."

"Do you mind talking about it?"

"Do I mind? I don't know. I mind talking about it to the press, especially to the Sun. To you? No, I assume that you will give me a fairer hearing, and be less intrusive about the more personal side of things, or at least the physical personal side of things. I am not a church-goer, I am afraid."

"Very few people are, Julia. If I had to survive on the contents of my collection plate, I would be half the size I am."

This is a self-deprecatory joke. Simon Stanley is about five foot ten and seventeen stone.

"I cannot remember the last time I went to church, beyond going to weddings, that is."

"Then it cannot have been too bad."

"Or maybe I was asleep."

He smiles passively. "You know, Julia, that I am here to listen any time you would like to talk to me. I cannot claim to have had much experience of life, but I am a friend, and we in the church are not at all judgmental about whatever we hear. And we hardly even mention God nowadays, so we do not put any pressure on you to believe, or to pretend to believe."

"I do not pretend to believe, yet maybe I do."

"What do you believe in, if you do not mind me asking?"

"I believe that there may be a God."

"Good. I believe that too. There are a few of us left."

"In life, or in the church?"

"Both. The press suggests that the ratio is about the same, but that has not been my experience. The people I know in the church are very honest, questioning believers. Seekers after the truth, so to speak. I think that is a vast improvement on the past. As you accept the possible existence of God, do you think He is a loving God or a judgmental one?"

"An accidental one."

"An accidental one? How intriguing. In what way accidental?"

"I consider it at least a possibility that He made the world by mistake, and then did not know what to do next."

"The blind watchmaker."

"Yes, something like that, although I do not know that theory in any detail."

"Nor do I, although I believe that it does not necessarily postulate the existence of God."

"Yes, well that sort of thing."

"Would you say that you are a religious person, Julia?"

"Now that is a difficult question. Religious enough to ask questions, I suppose. Much like everyone else. More religious than church-going, anyway."

"I think that is the right way round. Good."

"Other than that, I have nothing specific to say. No burning need to discuss my life with anyone at the moment."

"Well, I am here anytime you wish to discuss anything whatsoever. Life can be very perplexing and confusing sometimes, and we all need to talk. And frankly, it is something of a relief for me to be able to talk to somebody and to be free to mention God. Most people treat me like a double-glazing salesman the minute I bring up the G-word. Which is different from the G-spot, by the way."

"Simon, vicars should not make jokes."

"No, I am sorry, Julia. I should definitely not have said that."

"Don't worry, Simon. I am not offended. I am just trying to give you some guidance. Mentioning G-spots does not make you trendy. And being trendy does not make you relevant."

"Thank you, Julia. I will see you around. I look forward to our next conversation together."

"Indeed, Simon. Thank you for calling in, and for being concerned about me."

"I get the impression that you are fully capable of taking care of yourself."

"Most days of the week, yes."

"Goodbye. And thank you for the tea."

I frown. "There wasn't any tea."

"Oh, whoops, sorry. So there wasn't. Everyone also offers me tea. I just assumed I must have had some. Sorry. By the way, this house used to be a vicarage, but you probably know that already."

"Actually, I didn't."

"Old Parson Markham built it. It was the first house in the village to have central heating. This is the first time it has left the family. Very nice people, too. It was as sad to see them go as it has been a pleasure to meet you. Good day."

"And next time you can stay for tea."

"Oh don't worry. I am not really a tea-drinker, to be honest. I am heartily sick of the stuff, and it is always embarrassing asking people to use their toilets. When you are doing your rounds all day, you always have to bear that in mind. I cannot keep popping back to the vicarage, and I am not as young and absorptive as I used to be."

✸ ✸ ✸

I went to see the remand hearing of Harold Shipman, the GP and possibly the world's most prolific serial killer, if you ignore the famed executioner of the Lubyanka who bumped off more decent souls in an afternoon, a bottle of vodka in one hand and a revolver in the other, than the 400 or so old women that Shipman killed in three decades of well-honed practice. If Harold Shipman had looked evil, if he had chilled the air as he entered the room, if he had sworn and threatened and openly abused, he would never have got past the first ten before being stopped. It was because he had a quiet, even gentle, air about him that he was allowed to carry on, and on, and on. He was in the dock a few yards away from me. He was small and humble looking. He had a bemused look on his face. He did not say a word, and he did not react other than the way any human being would react.

I am imagining Dr. Berringer at Stansted Airport with his wife, Phyllis, on his way to Spain. They have taken the courtesy bus from the long term car park, and are entering the terminal building pushing a trolley stacked with four cases. Jeff is looking for the screens to tell them where to book in. It is 4:00 p.m., so a reasonably long queue will already have formed—perhaps twenty minutes' worth—and they have two hours to go to take-off.

Phyllis is easily described as a rather silly woman with finicky ways and blue-washed grey hair. According to the Hanburgh gossip (Brenda again), when she first met Jeff, she was a nurse at the local hospital, and he was a junior doctor. She was shy and beautiful, he was handsome and a doctor. She lacked his class, but made up for it in sex appeal and compliance.

She is waiting for Jeff to tell her where to go next, and she often gives the impression to a casual observer of meek, foolish subservience. As ever, appearances deceive. In most aspects of life she has Jeff wrapped around her little finger. Her demeanour hides the steely vision of a determined social climber. She only had her beauty to commend her, so she was going to exploit it to hitch a ride in the lift up the social ladder. Do not think that she is ever far from the buttons. She also knows everything about Jeff's "other life", and takes it in her stride as a necessary evil. Luckily his conquests are all young girls, so he will not be bringing any diseases home with him, which is what she is most concerned about. She is a heavy user of Domestos. The house smells like a hospital used to smell when they still bothered to clean them properly.

If you try to unravel her world, she will fight you like a lynx. If you are about to succeed, she will kill you. When it is all over, she will protest her innocence and her ignorance.

As I saw him in the village, Dr. Berringer is a fit-looking man, with distinguished features and an underlying tanned sleekness. I imagine that his female patients used to look forward to consulting him, and would have thrilled slightly when he asked them to take their clothes off. In the surgery he was probably a model of propriety. His male patients would have viewed him as "old Jeff", the wise head and homely companion to be trusted and greeted with affection.

In his demeanour, he is courteous, considerate and gentle. He has a good bedside manner. He was an old-fashioned doctor who listened, speculated, explored and pronounced the solution, with a subscription to salvation. If you were terminally ill, and there was no saving you, he would visit you regularly, ask after your comfort, show concern for the other members of the family and how they were coping, and suggest that they phone him day or night if you deteriorated suddenly.

In his profession, he has made a lot of people very much happier than they would otherwise have been. He has been an effective doctor, and cured his patients of niggling complaints. Most people have left his company feeling better about the world. It is just that, like many of us, he has one central vice, and that vice happens to be a rot that destroys young lives forever.

He got to know most of his fifteen or so young victims because he was their doctor. For some, he was present at their birth. For most of the rest, he attended their mothers while they were pregnant with them. He has examined them as babies, judged them to be healthy, pretty young girls, helped them through coughs and sniffles, and won their confidence directly through his behaviour towards them and his reputation in the village.

Dr. Berringer mostly likes girls sexually when they are pre-pubescent, when their smiles are still straight and pure, their skin is fresh, their bodies athletic, when they are testing out their flirting skills, and of course when they are physically too weak to defeat him. For him, he is tasting their innocence, sharing it, and even initiating them into a greater stage of self-knowledge. Then, in the darker hours of his self-examination, he grudgingly, shamefully admits to abusing them. He is mortifiedly contrite. He shakes, he shivers, he becomes feverish with guilt. However, this contrition never abates his need for the tasting, and the sharing, and for the triumph of that initial penetration of a small, tight, rigid body.

Over recent years, it has been very much harder for him to gain unchaperoned access to young girls, even for professional purposes, because society has become much alerted in general to the risks young girls incur simply by being girls, and by being young. Then, of course, several mothers have been his victims and, beyond them, his reputation by now mostly precedes him. He is getting old, he tells himself. The experiences and adventures of youth must pass.

Twenty, thirty, forty years ago, his technique adapted itself to the circumstances. In some cases it was quite simply, and brutally rape. He found the girl unprotected, he coaxed her off to a quiet corner, he removed her clothes as she cumulatively flailed, and struggled, and screamed and cried. Eventually she would attempt to fold herself into a protective hibernation, from where he would resolutely prise her straight, and thrust himself inside her. Afterwards, he would threaten her that if she ever breathed a word to anyone about their secret, he would send someone to talk to her. Wherever she was, if she let slip the tiniest hint or detail, his friend would learn about it and find her. His friend would watch her all the time. This would be what she would later remember most of all, the booming, heathen godlike voice, threatening recrimination for the minutest betrayal. The rest she would try to suppress, or had already blanked out. And from then on, an unidentified, unrecognisable dread would track her throughout her life, striking every few days in unguarded moments. She must remain forever on watch.

With others, it took place in the surgery, when he would be giving them a routine examination on top of whatever minor ailment he was correcting. Their mothers would be waiting outside. He would look down their throats, using a spatula to press their tongues into place, he would listen to their lungs through a stethoscope, then he would work his way ever more inappropriately down their bodies until he was giving them a vaginal examination, without the impediment of gloves. Children are very astute in recognising the bounds of acceptability, but he was in a position and place of authority and, indeed, domination.

In a strict minority of cases, it was more like a seduction. He would initiate proceedings by sitting down quietly with them and creating an intimate atmosphere but, once in that situation for a few minutes, it would be the girls who would start flirting with him. They would sit on his knee. They would explore him to see how he would react. They would surreptitiously expose themselves to him. They would finger his groin through his trousers, wondering when he would stop them. He didn't. Eventually he would ease them onto him. At this point they would start to panic but find that they could not get away. He was far stronger than they were, and had a determined wiry grip. These girls would feel guilty for what he had done to them. After all, they were the ones coming on to him, teasing him, touching him, wanting to know what would happen next in this illicit game. They absolutely knew that what they were doing would be considered wrong by their parents and their teachers, but it was the fun of playing a daring game with a respected adult.

Then, when he ended the game by entering them, they believed that it was largely their machinations that got them there. They took on the responsibility. They were not yet wise enough to realise that they were too young to be responsible for that outcome, that they had been playing innocently against a stacked deck. And many years later they may still not have realised it. Guilt consumed them. They had been utterly bad, and all their parents' later lectures about how boys can behave, what is inherent in boys' natures, confirmed this. Any man will want to take advantage of them, it is how the world renews itself. It was for them to resist.

Some put the incident firmly behind them, suppressing the fall-out, and staying well clear of Dr. Jeff Berringer. Most kept their daughters at a watchful distance, and signed up to the practice in the next village, which in other ways was unfortunate as Dr. Jarvis there is an appalling, negligent doctor, devoted to prescribing antibiotics for any and every misfortune, however useless, and indeed damaging, they will be.

Two girls become his disciples. He was their first sexual experience, for good or for evil. He was extremely kind and generous towards them. He even loved them. He certainly cared for them. They were daughters to him. They felt rejected if they sensed that he had favoured other girls. They became needy and, in a way, the tables turned. They became predators on his time and his affection. Mary and Samantha vied competitively for his attention, and they became viciously jealous of each other.

Life plays tricks.

❋　　❋　　❋

At last, Inspector John, you arrive, twirling expectantly away from the front door, avoiding the gaps in the flagstones, I notice.

"Miss Blackburn."

"Inspector Frampton. We have played this scene before, and I ended up unconscious."

My quip unnerves you, as I intend. You are immediately agitated. You are not a patient man. "Come in."

"Thank you."

"How are you getting on?"

"Making progress."

"So why are you here?"

Your feet get caught up in a shuffle as you bob your head around to look at me, saying nothing.

Settled, if that is the word, in a chair, you start "I am having some difficulty locating anyone at Mr. Willows' house on the afternoon of his death, other than you."

I chuckle. "So things are not progressing then."

"Yes, they are."

"How can they be?"

You do not reply. "Can I call you Julia?" you declare, turning suddenly intimate. Is this a psychological trick, a professional question?

"Yes, of course."

You do not volunteer your own first name.

"Julia," you lean forward intently, confidentially, "the whole village thinks it was you."

"Fine. It shows what they know."

"No-one can supply a motive," you add.

"That would be difficult."

"Why?"

"There isn't one."

"There is always a motive, however obscure or twisted."

"Maybe, but not mine."

"What do you suggest?"

"I have no view at all. It is not my job."

"Wouldn't you rest easier if we found whoever did it?"

"Yes."

"So who did it, Julia?"

"I haven't the first idea. I do not know the village. I don't really know who has grudges against whom. I do not know whom Tom has humiliated and provoked to violence, except that it must at least have been a whole stack of people. My guess is that it must have been a man who killed him. Women cannot usually chop people in half." I shudder involuntarily.

"Defensive or offensive?"

"Me?"

"No, the killing. Was Tom Willows killed to protect someone, or out of anger or hatred, or for material gain?"

"I still do not know."

"Whom could he have had an angle on?"

"Everyone would say Dr. Berringer. He appears to be single-handedly responsible for all the true evil in the village, and he has been getting away with it rather successfully, for want of evidence, I assume."

"Yes, they would, but an axe does not strike me as being a doctor's weapon. A doctor would use something more precise—a knife or a gun."

"It might depend on what was around at the time. Maybe it wasn't planned."

Your eyes widen. "No, maybe not."

"And why use a weapon that points directly at you? A doctor can use an axe, a lumberjack can use a syringe."

"True."

"What would you use?" I ask.

"It has never occurred to me."

"What would you use to kill yourself?"

"Pills. I would probably take lots of pills. An overdose."

"So suicide has occurred to you?"

"We all like some control over our lives, don't we? And you?"

"Oh, I would commit suicide with a long-shafted axe." I laugh.

"Ah. I am disappointed, Julia. I thought we were being honest, making a connection."

"Where will a connection take us?"

"Maybe towards friendship."

"Can there truly be friendship between a man and a woman?" I ask teasingly. "Is there a Mrs. Frampton?"

"Only my mother. Ninety this year."

"Are you fond of her?"

"Very."

"Have you ever found anyone else to be fond of?"

"In my time. I am not just a policeman. And you?"

"Would you like to stay for lunch?"

"Why not?" You search my face to explore whether there is more on offer, then my body.

Over lunch I tell you a complete cock and bull story about my early life. I enjoy making it up, lying to a professional. You appear to believe me, or perhaps that is not what your mind is focused on. Several times I suspect you want to hug me. I let you get enticingly close, and will you to become excited, which you duly do if your squirming is a giveaway sign. Our power over men!

❅   ❅   ❅

The party is over, and Mary and I are feeling increasingly nervous and isolated. What will the villagers come back with next? Mary and I spend the whole day plotting. There is no lying on the beach, no writing, no relaxing. We are consumed by preparations for our self-defence.

I decide to phone the police and tell them what happened last night, minus the boiling oil. L'Inspecteur Herbert is not around. The policeman I manage to talk to cannot help us. We must wait for l'Inpecteur Herbert to return. He will be back in town this evening.

Why did we ever get involved with Alice? We ask ourselves this question time and time again. We were having a good time. I was overly wrapped up in my writing, but we were about to have lots of fun together, weren't we? Then Alice turned up, introducing jealousy and tension, provoking the misery for me of their elopement, the stress of Mary's return, now the fear of reprisals for no greater a crime than liberating Alice to be herself, an uncommunicative self as it turns out. She definitely wasn't worth it. Couldn't she just phone her family once to get us off the hook? The villagers may still ostracise us, but we can always shop elsewhere, and at least they will no longer be trying to harm us.

In the end, we cannot sit here nervously forever. We make love repeatedly, earnestly, sincerely, timelessly. It is the old days returned. We tremble on each others' fingers, we quiver on each others' lips. It has not been this good for a long, long time.

Then we pack and leave. L'Inspecteur Herbert will no doubt feel obliged to track us down. That is fine. So long as he finds us before the mob does.

I leave a note on the kitchen table. "Inspecteur, we have gone to Spain for a few days to avoid any more trouble. We will return shortly." Maybe he will not even bother.

We do indeed go to Spain. In the quiet of the early evening, we race through the streets of Feyrargues, lest anyone attempts to stop us, and we head for the motorway. Within three hours we are crossing the unpatrolled border. Within four-and-a-half hours, We are luxuriating in the NH Calderón hotel in Barcelona. The streets are still lively outside. We wander down to the Rambla. It is certainly very different from the atmosphere in Béziers. At the bottom of the Rambla, we are attracted into a small square, and have a late meal seated outside at Les Quinze Nits. It is very romantic, and a world away from a few hours earlier. We are safe, physically and as a couple. Mary is enchanted. She has never been to Barcelona before.

Meandering up the Rambla again, towards the hotel, a stealth thief tries to grab Mary's handbag. I confront him. He protests. I stick my revolver in his ribs. He disappears down a side street.

"I hate it," Mary says. "I hate the violence of the world. It is everywhere."

We decide to move on again in the morning. I am annoyed. I desperately need to do Gaudi again. Mary would love him, but she has lost patience with the city already.

❄   ❄   ❄

Chapter 11

I encounter Henry Spence in his funeral parlour, next to the post office. Letters departing for the next town; souls departed for the next world.

I have never been inside a funeral parlour. People have died around me (my sister, my mother, my girlfriend), I have attended several funerals, and yet this is my first encroachment inside this incongruous amalgam of a high street store and oblivion.

I am here to ask after Tom.

The atmosphere is kept purposefully reassuring and ordinary. Henry Spence is not planning to do anything unpleasant to you until you die. Having said that, working in a small village, where he has lived all his life, and where he has the only mortuary in the area, Henry is used to laying out the people he knows. In fact, if they come from Hanburgh, it is more than likely that he will recognise them. Some he has only heard of, and may have glimpsed once or twice in the street, others have been close friends or family.

Absolutely the saddest laying out, he confides to me in a deliberate sort of way, is that of a child. They look so complete, so miniature, so alive, and they have been abandoned by life so early. Luckily, he has only ever had one of those, little Jimmy Cuthbert who drowned in the beck by the church in no more than three feet of water.

Like all professionals, he revels in his expertise. Occasionally people question him about it, deferentially, carefully, late into the night of a dinner party, and Henry has a repertoire of gruesome stories to supply, such as the day one client suddenly sat up and burped at him, propelled by the gases of decay.

"Who was that?" they immediately ask.

"I really cannot disclose that," he replies with a pleased twitch of pomposity. "I cannot reveal my clients' secrets," although he can be persuaded to list a few of them anonymously—the scars, the tattoos revealing unlikely attachments, the operations, the deformities, the diseases (cancers like footballs, teeth rotted to the nerves, syphilis). For him, the dead are always his "clients", and the family is the "bereaved". No-one has ever heard him being disrespectful of either, except to observe that it would have been sometimes easier to have extracted the fee from the corpse than from the relatives, and he offers some excellent "don't trouble your relatives at a time of great grief" forward planning schemes accordingly.

Henry tells me about the suicides. There have been five over recent years. According to statistics, he would have expected to have experienced one suicide in a village of this size in his lifetime, and for it to have been a man. In Hanburgh, there has been one male suicide, Geoff Gibson, who got into overwhelming financial problems, and four women, two of whom were young girls.

Henry knew one of the girl suicides well. She was extremely pretty and lively, and the almost inseparable friend of Kate, his daughter. If you had looked at her sitting in the garden chatting away to Kate about boys and fashions and whatever, you would never have guessed that this girl would go to bed one night and swallow all the barbiturates she could find in the house, which was apparently better stocked than most chemists. While she must have been hiding a great sadness, it was not at all evident to anyone.

Carla Summers was different. She always was a strange one, and got stranger. She was into grunge before the rest of the world. You could almost say she invented it, except that Hanburgh has never been a leader in world fashion. She dressed like an apple-pie bed, had no friends, spent a disproportionate amount of her time daubing the wall of the Berringers' garden with painted insults, physically attacked Mary Knightly with a knife, and a few weeks later turned the same knife on herself to slit her wrists. "Poor lost creature!" they all sighed, repetitively.

She and Jenny Blair, the pretty one, died within a few weeks of each other during a hot summer about twenty years ago. It was a difficult month for Henry because his mother died then too, after fifteen years of heart trouble.

Henry tells me that as an undertaker, you never dwell on death. That would make your job virtually impossible to carry out. However, while "some of my persuasion" cut out all thoughts of mortality and fatality except to view them as a source of income (pray God for a long hard winter with lots of 'flu and pneumonia, we need the money), others do become philosophical about it. Henry is one of the latter. He does not obsess, by any means, over matters of life and death, but he does consider them. Why do children die? Why do the old take so long? Why do the nastiest people in the village never seem to die, apart from Frank Welbourne whom Henry is convinced was deliberately run down by that truck?

Seeing Tom dead before him really froze his thoughts. He liked Tom enormously, he says, he had spent all his life alongside him in the village, gone out with him in his youth trying to pick up the girls (Tom's invariable success usually left Henry to dawdle home alone having gained a peremptory goodbye kiss from the last girl he happened to be dancing with at the end of the evening—a pass-the-parcel moment). Tom had it all going for him, yet he had built so little. He had wasted his life "chasing skirt". Why? He was good looking, intelligent, sociable. He could have married a thousand girls, had children, built a business, and left something of substance behind him on this earth. However, that side of things had never interested Tom. He was quite content being an ageing roué and a gifted gardener who could turn a common-or-garden weed into a charming flower (he specialised in wild gardens long before that became fashionable).

In his thirty-six years as a mortician, no bodily sight had ever turned Henry's stomach. Tom's did. In fact, Henry told young Becker, his assistant, to stay away when Tom was brought in (Inspector Frampton had warned him in advance of what to expect). Even Henry did not have the experience to handle what he had to deal with, and he was sure young Becker would not cope, however callow a youth he might choose to be.

Henry looked at his good friend, his head cut in two accurately down the middle, his body lacerated in the search for clues. They had looked for drugs, no drugs. They had looked for food, just freshly consumed cereal, milk and coffee, no sugar. They had noted the traces of sperm and vaginal fluids on his penis and around his pubic area. They had ascertained the likely time of death. They had handed him over to Henry to dispose of.

"Poor Tom, what is left of you as a human being?" Henry asked himself.

Henry tells me that Tom's sister, Sally, is arriving today, and wants to see the body tomorrow afternoon. He offers to show me Tom. He is surprisingly considerate towards me. He suggests that however difficult it will be for me, especially as Tom is "not quite finished yet", I should steal myself to do it. It will represent a closure for me. The images may well haunt my dreams, and indeed my days, for a few weeks, but it will also close that chapter for me. Many people have told him that after seeing their loved ones laid out before them. "She looks so peaceful," they say invariably, "as if she is sleeping."

I wonder, snidely, whether it is not harder to deal with the clichés of bereaved relatives than with the bodies of old and diseased people who are ultimately lucky to have died.

Despite myself, despite his apparent generosity, despite his ability to analyse intelligently his role in the panoply of death, I find myself increasingly loathing the man. I look at him and I feel queasy. I examine his bespectacled face, and I am disgusted by his cheeks and by the razored stubble-tips lying below the skin. I cannot explain why. Maybe it is his way of delicately, sensitively, obsequiously handling sorrow that I detest. Maybe it is his loser friendship with Tom. Maybe it is because I do not believe a word he is telling me, or the authenticity of the emotions he alludes to. He strikes me as a complete phoney, a sour man under a soothing mantle. You get intuitions sometimes, and I pick up on his inner thoughts which are barren and cynical, not to mention personally intrusive. He is stiff, grey-cheeked.

"How on earth do I disguise this?" It is a declaration of despair, and I do not believe any of it. He relishes the challenge, the congratulations ("You have done an extraordinary job, Henry!"), and he continually resented the many humiliations Tom incidentally presented him with during his lifetime. The thought regularly flashes into his mind that Tom is another one he has survived, unexpectedly. That is his real response to Tom's death, a suppressed exhilaration of gloating.

The other thing I am picking up is his excitement that Tom's death necessitates that Sally return to the village. He cannot wait to see Sally tomorrow afternoon. Will she have changed? Will she have aged such that Henry will ask himself what he ever saw in her? Will she treat him as a funeral director, or as a friend?

After Sally left for London, Henry and his wife Hilary found each other, and it appears to have been a mostly happy marriage. With Hilary's surgery job and Henry's funeral parlour, they joke that they have both the living and the dead covered—a balanced portfolio, as those City types would say, not that there have been many City types around Hanburgh. Wasn't Lucy's son in the City somewhere? They have not seen or heard of him for years. Lucy committed suicide too, come to think of it. This must be the suicide capital of Britain!

So Sally is here tomorrow, and Tom must look at least presentable, as he always did when alive.

Henry withdraws the veil from Tom's body. It is a terrifying site. I search blindly for the toilet. Henry steers me bony-fingered towards it. I note that he is rather pleased with my reaction. I am copiously sick. You can try to anticipate the shock for days, make your preparations, rationalise away your fears. You will never be ready. It is the mind that captures the sight first and bellows it out in visual and verbal translation, before the reason can rush hurriedly around shutting the doors. Tom is quite simply revolting. I last saw him as an erotic, sinuous, soft body, alive, smiling, and pleasing. Somebody, within minutes of my imprint of that fading image, hacked his soul and body apart, and left his remains for the vultures of forensics to rip the flesh off. I cannot reconcile myself to his head, parted in two, peeled, congealed, at a crazy fairground angle. If Henry thinks that the sight of Tom will still anyone's troubled spirit, he is totally insane. Is he testing my reaction to unmask a murderess? Is he doing some private sleuthing? Is he showing off what he can stomach and I cannot? Is he simply a sadist?

And then I wonder: did he kill Tom? I rather hope he did. I would enjoy taking my revenge.

I spend some minutes thinking this over as I apparently worship at Tom's altar. Henry has not left me alone. He is hovering, observing, intruding. I am tempted to ask to be left alone.

Could Henry have wielded that axe? Certainly. He is tall, fit, and I would guess strong from manoeuvring so much dead weight. Would he know where to strike? Yes, anyway it is obvious if you are going to punch someone's head in two. Could he get intimate, unsuspecting access to Tom? Of course. Did he really hate Tom? I would not be at all surprised.

I will watch Henry from now on. Maybe I can use this Sally, plant some seeds, see what grows.

I stand back. "Thank you," I say. "Best of luck."

"My pleasure," he responds automatically, and I can believe it is.

I don't know what you think of the Tarot, Inspector, but I am fascinated by it. There is rarely a day that goes by without my consulting it to help me challenge and reflect upon my assumptions.

Some people find the Tarot sinister and evil, a direct conversation with the devil. Funnily enough, Old Nick has been coming up a lot for me recently.

Even if you can get over your revulsion for pagan, non-Christian rituals, you probably consider it less than a science. I do too, although I am beginning to wonder.

For something to be pure science, according to Karl Popper, the theory and the practice must be capable of reliably predicting defined outcomes. These outcomes must be stated in the negative—the null hypothesis. Which raises the question for me that, if when playing the Tarot, its predictions regularly refute the null hypothesis, should it be considered a science at least some of the time?

Certain cards turn up repeatedly over a period of days, and then I hardly ever see them again for months. I had a run of Death cards back in Hanburgh. Death does not necessarily mean death, most experts are agreed. It is more likely to be metaphorical, the death of the old self and the re-birth of the new. However, if you have any friends, relatives or enemies who are decidedly creaky, who knows?

For me, the question is not whether the Tarot cards accurately predict events, because only in hindsight does their meaning become clear (that would be a tough call for Karl Popper's theory—the cards uncannily predicting an outcome that you only know has been predicted once the outcome is known), more whether the same card appearing ten times out of thirteen defies the laws of chance and probability. I would have thought so.

Not only has Death turned up in an improbably high number of spreads at a time when there were several murders taking place, but I have drawn the Lovers unreasonably often too.

The Lovers card does not necessarily mean love any more than Death means physical death. It is more about choices that are available to you and that you must address. You will face dilemmas and you must choose between life-altering courses of action.

Nevertheless it is notable that it started appearing the moment I fell in love with Mary. Could it be that the Tarot has recognised me for the clueless interpreter of its sophisticated and nuanced pronouncements that I undoubtedly am? Is it speaking to me in words of one syllable, images where I need only to focus on the most literal of meanings? If I had got the Tower, the scary one, which is always depicted as crumbling, I would have fled Hanburgh, I can tell you.

The bit that spooks me out a little is that when I first started reading the Tarot (because my mother did) I just saw it as a harmless and informative deck of cards. Nowadays it comes with voices, similar to your (or your neighbour's) thinking voice, except more fuzzy and echoed. I pick up the cards and people are whispering to me. Am I going mad, or am I entering another spiritual realm?

Anyway, the Tarot has given me the all-clear now for the next few days, so I am hoping that Mary and I will indeed be happy at last in Granada, where we are headed. We need a break, a chance to rekindle what we had on a sustainable basis.

As I drive this Toyota Celica rather too fast down the motorway in a yearning to be settled, I am inevitably drawn back to the memory of my accident in the Alps, and then to Mary exploring the fading scars on my body. She was fascinated by them. She worried at first that I would be affronted to be asked about them, that we would even split up irrevocably if she even alluded to them. Her anxiety troubled me. Then she started to run her fore-finger along them, hovering a micron above them, teasing my nerves without touching the raised skin. Her gesture introduced the first line of questioning she was reluctant to voice.

"What happened?"

I am not at ease in my skin. I like sitting in a lotus position against Mary so that our pubic hairs prick each other, I enjoy the sensations of nakedness, but I am continuously apprehensive. I once felt overly delicate, I now feel bloated, as if bursting out of my frame, not just my skin. I am lumpen, a seat where the stuffing is beginning to protrude through the seams, where the structure is in danger of collapse. I sometimes visualise standing up quickly, and my entire body splits, then collapses. I am a miracle of surgery, and I am not at all convinced that the technology will hold out until tomorrow. You hear stories about people having cosmetic surgery that comes unstitched, and the left side of their face droops to their chin, and their breasts to the floor. I am every inch tacked together. What could happen to me?

It is impossible to relax with these physical anxieties. I agreed to my remorseless campaign of surgery because Dr. Eckardt persuaded me that my shattered body was no longer suitable to the sustaining of my everyday lifestyle, that I would be in a wheelchair until I died, fit for sympathy and pity, maybe antipathy, but never an equal human being again. After he had finished with me, I would have a new body, a refreshingly new existence. I could be what I had always wanted to be. I did not have to revert to the person I was. I could select my alternative. I could even adopt a Marilyn Monroe voice if I wished. I might become a prototypical Eckardt monster, but I could be sculpted into an object of great beauty, of adoration, of yearning. The expression the good doctor constantly used was that I would transform "from a chrysalis into a butterfly." It was a motivational phrase. He showed me in the mirror my chrysalis, my mummified body bandaged prostate head to foot, then he projected onto the wall pictures of beautiful women, women he had created, and whose ranks I could join. Women were his passion, his compulsion. He could make every woman stunning and alluring. Men, for him, were big, smelly, hairy things with deformed appendages and under-wiped bottoms. I would be magnificent. Would I choose my new life, my new power, my re-birth?

As you might guess, I delayed for quite a while. I had all the time left to me in this life to consider my options. I could not move. I could not breathe unaided. I could stare at a ceiling, and at the tops of the walls, and at the upper rim of the window frame. I could cough to clear my lungs, on each occasion flooded with a drowning desperation that I would never again become unblocked enough to breathe my way to survival. I could not feel any part of my body, except when I tried to move, and pain sawed through me like a jagged bolt of lightning. I wanted to ease my position all the time and, despite the agony, I often did, but there was no body attached to the pain, only vengeful electricity directly sheeting through my brain.

It was not what I would ever have devised for myself. It was not what I had ever dreamed of. You are lying there shattered to pieces, a garbage bag of leftovers from the Sunday chicken roast, and a crazed visionary appears, imbued with the compulsion to render you into his perfection, and you think "It has to be better than this. I believe this madman's obsession. I believe he can do it. I believe I will be able to walk and talk and function as a pneumatic human being again. I shall be alluring and seductive. That cannot be bad—a bit askew, yet not bad. If I submit myself to his godlikeness, I will be his artefact, his sculpture. I have no say in what he will create holistically of me, beyond an input into the selection of my spare parts. I will be an innovation, his moulded creation, reflective of his skills and his passions of the time. I will be Michelangelo's David with human flesh or, more exactly, Athene, goddess of war and love. I will have to adapt to that, however I have to admit that it will be a fitting me."

Once I had Athene as an image in my mind, I could not exorcise it. It was like viewing a house I could absolutely see myself living in. Dr. Eckardt could make me Athene. I had convinced myself beyond his evangelism.

So this is what I became. I look at myself in the mirror and, if I am distracted by other thoughts, I sometimes jump, even scream. Who is that? She is so beautiful, but who is she? Then my mind eases itself back into that body, and I recognise it as being me.

I am beautiful. I know that I am stunningly beautiful. And that is not all good. People try to exploit me ceaselessly, to flirt with me, to crucify me. I always get a reaction. I walk into a room and I am a provocation to enslavement or hatred. It is that instant, that programmed. Dr. Eckardt never explained this to me. I doubt he even cared. He is an artist of the human frame who creates his masterpiece, and leaves it to live its own life. I am a photograph in his slideshow, an exhibit of his collection. I have a right to no other feelings than to be determined to profit from his indulgent wizardry.

What Dr. Eckardt would never understand except perhaps in his dotage is that I am a human being with a mind. We all are. And however extraordinary our outward appearance, we are encased in alien bodies. We cannot explain them as our own bodies distorted by helpful prostheses. All his work is completed using only real flesh and blood. There is nothing mechanical, nothing inhuman. And yet the whole assemblage is inhuman. I am me, and this body is not. I am inhabiting a carcass, and will do so until I cease to be.

This is what I think in my lonely moments surrounded by Mary—that she is not loving a real person, only a revenant; that at any moment the threads that drew me together could split, and that I could fall as a random pile of head, torso, organs and limbs onto the floor, like a scene from a human rights atrocity dug up from its grave. I realise that this is ridiculous, and that the stitches are long gone, and that my body has long been inextricably fused together. It is nevertheless how I feel. I cannot suppress my unsolicited thoughts, nor can I assimilate them.

"I love your body," Mary preens. "It is perfect." She touches me intimately. "And it is all mine, to do with what I please."

"Your body is *really* perfect," I reply, emphasising the "really".

"Only if I had liposuction. I am past any ability or discipline to lose weight of my own accord. And I cannot entertain the idea of my surplus fat being turned into bars of soap." She winces, then laughs.

❋ ❋ ❋

I am climbing a garden wall. Dr. Berringer locked their garden gate before going on holiday.

Despite the reassurances, I am not convinced that this is a clever thing to be doing when Inspector Frampton could leap out on me at any time and try legally and enforceably to chat me up in the creepy confines of police station again. Any figure scaling their wall is visible for miles around thanks to the streetlights that abut the Berringer's house, like fully paid-for security.

Anyway, I am over and into the shadows of the garden, an exquisitely kept garden I have to say as best I can see it in the moonlight (if I want to visit it during the day, it is enrolled into the National Gardens Scheme, and so opened to the public twice a year). In this case, I doubt that the garden is holding any secrets I would benefit from knowing, although if the trees could talk as loquaciously as the Tarot cards . . . .

I have asked myself for days how I can get into the house, and it wasn't until somebody (well Claudia actually) mentioned that George comes here every night at 10:00 to water the plants and check that everything is OK (no burglars like me) that I recognised a solution. If George does not lock the door behind him, I am in with a chance, I thought. George is due now. It is chiming ten from the church tower, and here indeed he is, bumbling along with his thick-set glasses and shuffling gait like a Peter Sellers character. He rattles the key in the back door for a full thirty seconds, and he is in the house. Fortunately, he turns the lights on for every room he visits so I have a visible trace of where he is. He is on his way upstairs. There must be a cupboard I can hide in somewhere in the kitchen (lock the door as you go out, George).

There is. A nice big broom cupboard. Surely a male of George's age and professional persuasion would never look in there.

George is coming back downstairs again, humming. "I can't get no, da-da-da-da . . . .", not what I would have expected. I await his rendition of the Sex Pistols' "God save the Queen."

He has gone. I leave it a couple of minutes anyway. Silence. I creep out of the broom cupboard, and manage not to knock over the mop. They always make an unnatural din as they hit a floor. I have no idea of the topography of the house, so I will need to follow my nose.

I creep around the corner into what I assume could be the sitting room and, **Bam!**, I walk straight into somebody.

We both draw breath. One of us screams momentarily, and stops.

"Who on earth are you?" demands the screamer.

I consider running out of the house, except that all the doors are locked again.

"Julia. And you?"

"Sam."

"Sam?"

"What on earth are you doing here, Julia?"

"And you?"

"Probably the same as you."

"What's that?"

"Snooping around. Trying to work out what old Jeff has been up to."

"Yes that is why I am here."

"Good, we can work together then. I'll drink to that, and I have just stubbed my toe on the drinks cabinet, so I know exactly where to find it."

Sam chooses whisky for both of us. "Chin-chin," she says, chiming my glass. "Did you know that Jeff used to rape me regularly as a ten year old?" It comes out brazenly, challengingly, a truth that must be declared in a hurry, braced for rejection and regret.

"I had heard rumours. I'm sorry."

"Did you know that he is supposedly my father."

"Yes, I had heard that rumour too. That must be really hard."

"Yes, no, don't know." Sam shrugs her mind.

"What exactly are you looking for?"

"Nothing exactly. Just something. I'll recognise it when I see it. And you?"

"The same. Maybe I simply want to be in his house and get a feel for him."

"I've had that. Now I want the proof."

We search the house for two hours as best we can without turning the lights on. We find nothing. I suddenly realise that I cannot hear Sam's thoughts, which is disconcerting. Is she evil too, or have I lost my powers suddenly?

I am apprehensive. What if she stops pretending to rummage around the house, and takes that carving knife to me (for some reason I am not privy to she insists on carrying a carving knife around with her)? What if she pushes me down the stairs?

There is something about Sam I cannot make out. Are we acquaintances, or friends, or do I serve a purpose yet to be revealed? She appears to be behaving normally enough, for someone ransacking a house in the dark. She does not even consider tidying up after herself. There is mess everywhere. Is this how she is at home?

"Why are you not searching properly?" she challenges me.

"I was contemplating all the mess."

"Oh, don't worry about that. Nobody will say anything. They cannot afford to. Old George will clear everything up for us. He is a right old woman, that George, with baggy pants." She laughs.

"You are leaving fingerprints everywhere."

"And when they come round to question me, and I simply explain that I was looking for evidence that he raped me and countless other girls? I don't think so!"

"And if they did?"

Sam sits down on the bed. "If they did, it would be a relief, wouldn't it? No more sordid secrets. Out in the open. If I had told someone when I was ten, they would not have believed me, or at least would have chosen to pretend not to believe me. Even my father, the lovable Freddy, would not have taken on Jeff Berringer. He had already let it pass with his raping my mother. Forget it. I would have been fantasising about him, or trying to get him into trouble for some obscure girly reason, or something. This way, they are coming after me. I will coolly explain what he did to me (with a few tears in all the appropriate places, of course), then everything is immediately on the record on that interview recorder, and everyone has a lot of explaining to do—Jeff obviously, Phyllis, and even that flaming Inspector Frampton of yours, you are so pally with. He knows exactly what has been going on, and he has never done a single sodding thing to stop it. Berringer even raped his best friend, and he did nothing."

"Why should he know what Dr. Berringer gets up to?"

"Because he is from Hanburgh, you know. You didn't know? Oh yes, he is. He was born here. He was brought up here. He hung around with everyone you have met—Tom Willows, Henry Spence, my father Freddy, all that crowd. And then he betrayed them by becoming a copper. They never trusted him after that. They disowned him. That is why you would never realise that he is from here. Mind you, he was always a loner, so everyone says. The only person he really gelled with was Lucy Benson, the one nobody else dared go near. They were as thick as thieves, apparently, if you pardon the irony. Nothing happened between them in that way, as far as I am aware. She wouldn't touch anyone, so it was quite a revelation when she became pregnant and abandoned the village, and her precious John. He was absolutely heart-broken, apparently. So was Tom Willows. She was the one girl Tom couldn't break and couldn't charm. She tormented his ego, as he admitted to me once. That is how I learnt all about Lucy and John, from Tom. He was really angry that she befriended John, and despised him. I laughed at Tom when he told me this, and ordered him not to be so stupid, but it was no laughing matter. I thought Tom was going to strangle me. I am not surprised that whoever axed him attacked him from behind. If they had come at him from the front, he would have killed them. He was really dangerous, was Tom, but you already must know that."

"No, I didn't know Tom well. And, I must say that I did not like him much either by the end. He was a good fuck, that is all."

"That is what he thought of me, apparently. Mind you, he is not the only one to say that."

Her publicity hangs for a while, and I let it go. I am not sure what Sam is up to. She is certainly fucked-up, that is for sure.

"Do you think we will find anything?" I ask.

"No, I doubt it. What could there be? He could have kept a diary, I suppose, but it would have been written in code, you can bet on that."

"So why are you hunting around, tossing all his things around the room as you have been for the last hour or so?"

"To invade him. I want him to feel invaded. I want George to report to him that he has been invaded. I want him to worry about it. And maybe I want one of George's little visits. So there is no way that I am tidying up."

"What on earth are they?"

"Oh, if anyone threatens to spill the beans, they get a visit from George. He sits you down and tells you with great seriousness what will happen to you if you try to harm even a hair of Jeff Berringer's reputation. In fact, he frightens the living daylights out of you. You wouldn't believe that of old George, would you? Yet old women are the scariest, aren't they? And one day that will be us!"

"And what happens if you decide to go ahead anyway and denounce him?"

Sam lifts her eyebrows. "Who knows? No-one has ever done it. However, a couple of the girls did top themselves. Maybe they didn't. Maybe creepy George did it for them. Now there is a shadow we all have in the backs of our minds. Old George bumping us off to protect kith and kin. I believe it. Old George is capable of anything. Let's face it, he has lived with Mary for nearly forty years. He must have a constitution built from titanium. One thing everyone knows about George, he will protect Mary and her father, my father, at all costs. Good old George, God rot him."

❈　　❈　　❈

Mary is looking shaky. While she welcomes me warmly into her house, her mind is dense with pre-occupation.

As far as I can hear, both from what she says and what she is thinking (my inner-hearing is back again), her concerns are not specific. Frank is in there somewhere, and so are you, Inspector. You circle each other in her mind, like heads surfacing through water.

It is a deep fear, as yet not fully realised, throbbing beneath the surface of her consciousness.

She enters rooms she has no purpose in, she catches furniture with her foot, and glasses and plates with her hands. Nothing is either broken or damaged, yet she has a clumsiness one would not normally associate with her.

She is eating too much, snacking on chocolate, cakes and other sugar-drenched comestibles. She has shown me pictures of herself even two years ago, and she was slim. Now the body is rolling over the edges of her clothes, and her face is less sharp.

She has no solution to the problem she has yet to recognise or define. She is prodding it with a mental stick and hoping it will resolve itself rather than bite her. It is not going away.

In the way she approaches decision making, she could not be more different from Frank who worries at issues as he sits on the riverbank in all weathers, scrutinising the line as it trails towards the float in an oxbow, considering the ripples that appear and disappear, waiting for that slight tug on the float that will provoke him to jab with his rod to gain a hook-hold in the mouth of the panicking fish. All his decisions take weeks. He sees no virtue in sudden action. He does not believe in heroics other than of the quiet, relentless kind, driving home into the heart of the problem at a deliberate pace. He is slow to anger, even slower to act. He rarely forgives. Once his strategy has weathered all seasons, it is robustly built, founded on the interweaving of logic and morality. It would make no sense to abandon it.

Frank's drinking companion at the Hanburgh Arms nowadays is Tony James. When he is not working, Tony has an excess of time as Sam is rarely in the house, and has minimal need of him when she is. Frank knows that Mary awaits him at home, but has many years of precedent in allowing him space.

Seeing Tony and Frank together one evening when she came to collect her husband shocked Mary. Even if Tony is a relative newcomer to the village and not a natural gossip, he is clearly extremely observant and shares Frank's straightline morality. She can imagine Tony leaning forward in that affable way of his and intimating "Frank, if I were you, I would get home early tonight. Women should not be left alone as much as Mary is."

"That's kind of you to be so considerate of Mary," would come the mildly affronted response, "however Mary has no issues with my having the occasional pint in the Hanburgh Arms. She knows that I am up to no mischief here."

"That was not my concern, Frank. It is merely that you would be very wise not to leave Mary alone for too long. The devil finds work for idle hands."

"I certainly would not call Mary idle. She does my books, arranges all the financing of the business, keeps the men jollied along. A fine woman, is our Mary, and a very decent one."

"So why do you not spend much time with her?"

"Oh, we spend enough time together, I would say on behalf of both of us. You see, we got to know each other very young, and we have developed such an understanding between us that we are together even when we are apart. I never stop thinking about her, and she about me. We have no need to live in each other's pockets when we are quite so buried in here." Frank beats his chest. "You, on the other hand, are recently married to a young girl. The same considerations do not apply."

"Oh, I know what Sam gets up to. I know all about her escapades with Brian and numerous others. I would like to be able to console myself that when she has finished with them, she will always come back to me. Unfortunately, that would not be true in the least. She bounces from one to another, always on the rebound, and often back to Brian. She has a real thing for Brian. I am sure that all the others are there only to make Brian jealous, although she realises that she is doomed to coming second to Kate. That really infuriates her. Kate really infuriates her. What she would not do to that woman. We hate those we have hurt, as Tacitus once said."

"Not around here, he didn't. He did however say mine's a pint."

"Sorry, Frank. I didn't notice that your glass was empty."

"And some of those chilli-flavoured crisps, if you don't mind."

"Not at all."

Tony shuffles back his captain's chair, and approaches the bar. "Hello Tony," Brenda greets him. "Two more of the usual?"

"And a packet of chilli-flavoured crisps," they chorus together, and laugh. "It must be wonderful to be as predictable as that," Brenda observes, still grinning, "although not for poor Mary."

"I keep trying to persuade him to go home and keep her company, but he is not listening."

"Oh, he'll take it on board in time. He listens more than you think. I just hope that he does not take your advice suddenly, like. He can have a brutal temper that man. I don't have any special feelings for Julia, although she seems nice enough, particularly for someone who is so drop-dead gorgeous, but I am very fond of Mary. I would hate any harm to come to her. And I think it might if Frank surprised them."

"I think so too."

"So, if he does take your advice, give Mary a ring from your mobile to warn her, be a love."

"I'll do that."

"And I'll keep you up to date with what Sam is up to."

"I suppose I should be grateful for that, Brenda. Sometimes, though, I feel like a torture victim."

"You are, Tony, you are. And you keep asking for more. Go on, take Frank over his pint and his crisps, or he'll become all agitated. Take care of yourself, Tony."

"I will. You too, Brenda."

"I think you two have a bit of a thing going, if you ask me," says Frank when Tony returns to their table.

"Yes, it could be going that way," Tony confirms. "I wouldn't much mind if it did. She is rather a classic."

"Yes, there's not much wrong with old Brenda. Well, I'll knock this back, if you don't mind, and get back to Mary. I'll take your advice."

"You do that."

Mary lives in dread of Frank realising what is happening between us. Equally, she knows that as certainly as the arrival of the next electricity bill, he will find out about us one day. Then, like the Tower in Tarot, it will be a terrifying shock, followed by a cathartic feeling of liberation, if he doesn't kill her in the process. That would be a liberation none of us would want. I hope and pray that I will be on hand to protect us all.

❋   ❋   ❋

Chapter 12

Why are we running, down this s-bended Spanish motorway? The authorities must have built in so many corners to keep us motorists on the rims of our wheels.

I know what we are running from—fate, bad choices, evil, intolerance, communities, and blind injustice. So please tell me what we are running towards! I keep tormenting myself with this as I drive (I am the man in this relationship; I do all the driving, or at least most of it).

When you are behind the wheel, and the music is turned off (maybe even when it is on full-blast, competing with the wind), you have no choice but to think, eventually. You avoid it for a while as you scan the road ahead, you count the cars, you take in the scenery, you compute how many service stations you can pass before you have to fill up with petrol and dry packaged food. Ultimately, though, you are reduced to thinking, and that thinking concerns a problem. Maybe it doesn't for you, Inspector, but it does for me. I have had so many problems to solve in my life, I cannot waste my time reminiscing about happiness long gone past ("Exit 47", I call it. Salida 47, in this case). I have to build the next better moment and, to do that, I have to negotiate the everyday minefield, which used to start when the post arrived. Luckily, I don't receive much post nowadays.

My problem today is "us". Where do we go from here? And I am not referring to you, Inspector, although that would be another pertinent question.

Immediately, Mary and I are on our way towards a converted mill outside Granada which we found on the Owners Direct website. Cacin Mill. The Molino Santa Ana. It looks idyllic, contemporary international rustic décor, flagstones, round bath, rose-head shower, granite kitchen, swimming pool. However, nothing has yet been idyllic in our lives together. There have only ever been problems, with golden moments of reprieve. Do we love each other? I used to think so. When I met Mary, I was not looking for anybody, I did not need anybody. I was there on a mission, to take stock, to stop the cycle of violence with whatever means it took, then to go.

Insofar as I was planning a romance, I was planning it subsequently, and elsewhere. I did not know how to handle romance in my new form. I had only ever experienced it in my old one. I could not even envisage how it might happen. I considered bars, or a restaurant, or possibly a chance meeting in the street, and I could never escort my imagination past that pick-up moment, towards whatever would happen next. While I might have a new shape, which I was gradually wearing in, I was never destined to have a real life. I was going to spend my days in my wealthy isolation up in a farm amid the hills, with my animals and, maybe my servants, socialising with neighbours, playing with their children, attending quaint local cultural events, living a public life in private, and a private life in public, until I died.

I was not expecting to find a companion, much as I craved one. I did not think that anyone would accept me as I am, or that I could even forgive myself for being who I am. I expected to play the role of a just judge and necessary executioner, then of a recluse, maybe of a recluse on the run, although I doubted that. One thing I am certain of is that I am clever. If I were ever to commit a crime, I would get away with it. No-one would ever be able to pin anything on me and make it stick, not even you, Inspector.

And I know that for a while you considered "fitting me up", off and on. You stalked round Hanburgh, searching for an angle, without finding one. Maybe that alone was enough to persuade you that it was me. It almost persuaded me that it was me. I could not fault the taste of the murderer, whoever he or she was, until the final killing, and maybe that was an error on his part, mistaken identity or something. Tom, well, what good could you really say about him? He exploited people. Actually he exploited women. He fucked them and he threw them away. He treated us all as consumables. I even thought that he was my father for a time, fucking and abandoning my mother. I did not see him as a rapist until the day Sam told me that he could not seduce my mother in any other way, and God knows he had tried. And then there was good old George, the meek, compliant offender, who would visit young girls in the time of their most desperate need, and threaten them that if they were to even squeak a word against his beloved father-in-law, he would deal with them. Once Sam had told me about that, even I was ready to make him sign the audit of his life in his own blood.

And what I discovered that same day, Inspector, as you will have realised by now, is how kind you were to my mother. You were her only friend, the one who stood by her at all costs, while she was spurned and derided by all those who were singed by her originality. That gave me a huge respect for you when I heard that, almost a love for you. I began to see you as my mother might have seen you, as a committedly caring man, an outsider insider, unafraid to reframe yourself to face the realities of the world. It is a real shame that you are not my father. I would have been truly honoured to have claimed you as my father, however much I tease you. I have even fantasised about you being him, built on that special bond I detect between us. Could you not have got past my mother's chaste guard at least once? Somebody did, although they had to coldly rape her to do it, and that would never be you.

The moment Sam told me about you two was the moment I resolved to help you. I felt for your predicament. What do you do on a case where you do not have a clue? Where there is nothing? You stir things up—nothing. You wait—nothing. Nobody can give you any lead.

Your boss wants a solution. Your public demands a culprit to boo at. And each day you have nothing.

In the end, no doubt you seek a miracle, the left-field breakthrough, the deus ex machina. And, failing that, you hope for an informant who may have noticed something you have missed. I stepped forward as your accomplice, the one you also chose, and I swear that the situation is still as opaque to me as it was to you.

I look over at Mary. Is she still my accomplice, or is she someone just sitting in the car I have hired, numbed into unconsciousness?

❋   ❋   ❋

You fix me in the eye, Inspector, or you want me to believe that that is what you are doing, and you ask "Julia, what is going on? I know that you know more than you are telling, which is absolutely nothing, by the way." Your outburst is clumsy, but neither of us minds that.

"What makes you say that?"

"You know that we found George Knightly dead this morning?"

"Obviously not. Why would I know that?"

"He was lying strangled in Berringer's house."

"Do you think that Berringer did it?" I tapped your arm at the elbow. "Only joking."

"You have an interesting way of joking about the most appalling things."

"Appalling? George Knightly dead? A nondescript vicious bastard?"

"You didn't like him much?"

"I didn't ever really meet him, but I certainly knew him. I have *peered into his soul*." I smile ironically with over-emphasis. "Please acknowledge that it does not really matter whether he is dead or alive. He was Uriah Heep married to Lady Macbeth. Spare us the soliloquy."

By now you are seated at your ease on one of the two rather rectangular sofas in the sitting room, in front of the sash windows, with the sun streaming in behind you. "So what do you think is really going on?"

In line with the compact I have made with myself to help you in any way I can, I tell you absolutely everything I have learnt since my arrival, except for my partying with Sam at the Berringers' house a couple of weeks back.

"Are you being serious?" asks the Inspector.

"I thought I was. About what exactly?"

"All of it. You really think that an evil is lurking in this village?"

"In most villages, Inspector. It is just that I happen to be here."

"And you reckon that Berringer is at the core of all this?"

"Yes, I am sure of it."

"And that Samantha James and Mary Knightly are contaminated by him to the point of being totally evil themselves?"

"I think Sam may be redeemable, but Mary definitely not."

"Why do you think Mary's husband was killed?"

"George was a strange man. Unnaturally submissive. That suggests to me that he was hiding a lot. He always gave me the feeling that he was potentially quite dangerous. He had hugely angry thoughts."

"Oh, you can read people's minds now, can you?"

"No, of course I can't, Inspector, but I can read the expressions in people's eyes."

"And what are my eyes saying to you?"

"Well, your thoughts are saying that you wish to tease me playfully. Same old story. Beyond that, you can never really read the eyes of a policeman. They are always too well masked in order to keep the suspects guessing."

"Call me John, Julia, then try again."

What you start to think about is how hungry you are, and whether you could get a bite to eat at the Hanburgh Arms.

"You are wondering whether you should ask me out to lunch, John. I would love to. Thank you."

As this prospect is very far from your mind, you double-take, and add "Be my guest, by all means. I was thinking about dropping in at the Hanburgh Arms, but there is an excellent Ha! Ha! bistro in town. Would you like to try that?"

I always find it interesting when a relationship that starts in one paradigm slips into another. It is something I miss when I fall in love with somebody at first sight, like Mary. The source of thunder and lighting stays where it is, until it slips slowly down through the sky. There is no progression, only the inevitable dissipation. We begin on a high and, after a period of bliss, competitiveness, spitefulness, moral disagreements, disputes over money, and general lobbying for our own perspectives emerge and submerge us. Mary and I are still in the blissful phase. I can only guess at how long it will endure, and I fear our first real argument as deeply as tripping down a flight of steps. One day I will find myself at the bottom, laughing uproariously, but that is not my general experience.

Take you, Inspector John, here and now. You are transitioning from being a policeman about your duty into a colleague and an ally. That is not the direction you anticipated our relationship following, yet that is where it will go.

You may consider my attitude cynical, that I am using you ultimately to my own purposes. You would be right. However, at the same time, you are planning to use me in all the obvious ways—to solve your crime and get promoted, to scratch your itches, to stroke your ego. These are typical human interactions between Mr. Plod and the femme fatale. You just hope that you can get promoted and sated before you get embroiled in whatever I am up to. You'll have to be quick, you think.

As you surely do not know, I have promised to rid the world of little dictators without being caught. In this village, I mean to eradicate, or at least neutralise, Dr. Berringer and Mary Knightly. How do I do that without getting myself arrested and locked up for life?

This is the question the killers of Tom Willows and George Knightly also asked themselves. It is the only question you are ever going to ask yourself if you are planning to clinically remove someone from their lair. If you don't care whom you kill, you can join the army. If you do care, your options are more complex, tighter. You have no leeway. You cannot afford any mistakes, any bad luck, any loose words or even thoughts. You have to be perfect, and none of us is that over a protracted period. So, the window of opportunity is short, and ideally you need a fall guy, someone whom people will believe guilty before they ever consider you. I am currently that fall guy, aren't I, Inspector? But I shall continue to behave as a lady, which will buy us time until we stumble across the truth.

If I am the fall guy, who is the murderer?

✻   ✻   ✻

I have a theory, and it is an excellent one, that most human illness is an exaggeration of what is the normal healthy pattern of things.

So, for instance, cancer is a growth of the cells at a speed that they should not be growing. Our cells are always multiplying—that is the basis of our life. We would be soon dead if they didn't. Similarly, we are soon dead if they grow too much. To understand this, is also to understand how we best cure ourselves. It is not through the application of the venomous and incendiary duo of chemotherapy and radiotherapy. They are not only extremely unpleasant to undergo, they also destroy our immune systems and risk unbalancing our bodies further. We address our cancers by training our bodies through our minds and our immune systems to put themselves back on track, to return to their healthy pace of growth. This is what we never learnt for Louise's sake when she was alive. She took the full brunt of the medical profession's hyper-technophilia. She suffered, she deteriorated, she died. Her surgeon expressed surprise and regret, and no doubt proceeded to apply the same dark-age potions to others, expressing further surprise and regret in each's turn. To understand cancer's relationship with the body is also to understand that cancer does not spread beyond the immediate tumour. It erupts in more than one place independently of the existing tumour, yet dependently on the cancerous and unbalanced states of our bodies.

I have known people who have had the most advanced states of cancer, medically documented, who suddenly leapt off their death beds having shed all trace of their illness. I have known people who simply ignored it and it went away. The body can cure cancer more easily than many other illnesses because it is a disease generated by the body itself, albeit in the presence of external catalysts.

Take paranoia. If we did not become afraid in the presence of extreme danger, we would mostly not last long. Fear, flight or fight, is a healthy reaction to a life-threatening situation. However, to fear anything and everything, and to believe anything and everything is out to get us twenty-four hours in a day is not healthy.

Schizophrenia is similar. Our mind's ability to disaggregate and deconstruct ideas, to hold a series of thoughts, concepts and hypotheses in different parts of the brain simultaneously, and in competition with each other, is valuable in that it helps us view a situation from all sides, directly, laterally and metaphysically. It is partly why human beings are so clever. However, for the high-wire trick to work, we have also to be able to encompass these different thoughts within a common mesh, to link and gather them all up again. Schizophrenia is where the tight-rope walker falls off the high wire, where the mesh breaks under extreme stress, and each thought tumbles away into the weightless, gravity-free void all on its own, independent of, and unrelated to, any other thought.

The mere phrase "manic depression" tends to suggest that it is an overwrought form of depression. Things go well for us, and we are happy and elated. Things go badly, and we are sad and mildly depressed. When we are on a high, we cannot continue climbing forever. We have, at some point, to settle back into stasis, so a high will ultimately be followed by a low, as in the weather. Mild depression is a sensible and salutary reaction to fluctuations in our environment, contributing to the richness of our emotional landscape. Manic depression, is a Stuker-dive down, without ever stopping, a roller-coaster plunge into the eternal abyss.

And now to the bit I wanted to tell you about: sex again, I am afraid, and if you are Frank you will say "Heck! Has a fortnight gone by already? Is it duty night again?" I am afraid so, Frank. Buckle up, and get on down.

OK, would it be totally absurd of me to suggest that some men, and even the majority of them, get just a touch turned on by the sight of a beautiful naked girl coming towards them, there for the picking? My guess is that you would recognise that as normal enough. And if the man is fifty and the girl sixteen, is that still a reasonably normal reaction? Hell, yes, you say, especially if she is sixteen, and especially if you are a man of fifty. Big businessman, whopping great ego seeking inflation, teenage blonde trophy escort, the lemon tart. And if she were fifteen, with all the outward appearance of being twenty, and knowing thirty? Rape, we all shout at once, at least statutory rape. What a difference a day makes, as the song goes. And if he is sixteen, and he knows that she is fifteen? Technically statutory rape, we reply, but who is ever going to prosecute them? And if he is fifty, and she is ten? Gross perversion, prison, special section, the worst of criminals. Why? Because it is unheard of for a man to fancy a pretty young girl? No, because it is an entirely normal, healthy and indeed necessary urge taken to an extreme.

You have to feel sorry for paedophiles, don't you? No we don't, you say, eyes bulging, spit escaping from your lips. They are vile, predatory creatures, who abuse the innocence of our daughters and ruin their lives forever.

And that I grant you. Paedophiles do untold damage to those who are only starting out in life, to be destabilised forever by the experience. They should control their urges simply because of the damage they know they do, especially when they continue on to strangle their victim. Looking at Dr. Berringer, and knowing that he has sexually attacked, and frequently raped, nearly a score of under-age girls, with terrible consequences, what can you observe about him? He is a highly-respected doctor with a suave, sophisticated and educated manner; someone you would not suspect of harbouring demonic passions, never mind giving full rein to them in a relentlessly predatory stalking of the younger girls of the village. Is he emotionally vulnerable? He certainly gives not the slightest hint of it. Is he unbalanced? Almost certainly. Why is that? Well, partly, because he witnessed his own father sexually abusing his sisters. At one time it was quite common for the elder daughter to step in to satisfy her father's appetites while her mother was indisposed either through illness or childbirth. It may have been a highly undesirable and damaging state of affairs, but it was so usual as not even to constitute an extreme.

Dr. Berringer is fully aware that what he does is entirely immoral in that society condemns it, and his victims suffer from it. Indeed, he is the first to condemn paedophilia himself, loud and long, demanding castration and the death penalty for anyone caught indulging in it. "It is disgusting!" he snorts to his friends. "We should lock them up and throw away the keys!" Whether this is before or after castration, and before or after the death penalty is less evident.

At least he does not kill the girls. George Knightly did that, directly or indirectly, without Dr. Berringer's prior knowledge or approval. He was a great mopper-up, was George. A very angry man, with some very strange fetishist practices of his own, most of which he kept in his head, sublimated beneath the daily grind of financial audits.

❉　　❉　　❉

Sally Willows is magnificent. She has an enormous mane of straggly auburn hair, the flashing eyes of a Latino, and the directness of the knife that slices through butter.

It is no wonder that Henry Spence, and not a few of his contemporaries, were (and maybe still are) smitten by her. Dr. Berringer tried it on once with her when she was thirteen. Unluckily for him. She gave him an almighty belt across the head with a piece of broken piping that happened to be lying close by when he approached her, and subsequently used her abundant charms to persuade an underworld type to give her a revolver (yes, the Ruger) that she proceeded to carry round with her in her handbag. Dr. Berringer, never one to take a hint unless it was backed by military force, tried it on with Sally a second time a few months later. She shot him through the testicles, and told him that the other half of his brain would get it next time.

Today, though, she is magnificence saddened. She is examining Tom lying in his coffin, his scars barely disguised, wondering how she had strayed so far from her once-adored brother.

It was never a deliberate act of separation. She had moved away from the village because there was a wider world elsewhere, and they both gradually became caught up in their own separate activities. They phoned each other at least once a month, and even wrote to each other occasionally, but they have rarely actually seen each other over the last five years, and if Tom is seeing Sally too, it is not from this life.

Sally stands there with two tears dwelling in her eyes. They periodically interfere with her viewing of Tom. Inwardly, she swears revenge.

"Thank you, Henry," she says to Henry. "You are so sweet," and she sweeps off to visit the one woman of the village who can help her—Brenda. The villagers observe that she went straight to the pub after leaving the funeral parlour to get a stiff drink, thereby adding several shots of presumed vodka to her pure fruit juice.

After last orders, and the shepherding of the final rams remaining in the bar, Brenda and Sally sit in a corner and speak to each other earnestly for nearly an hour. Sally learns some critical information with which she returns home to Tom's house (and now hers) to ponder.

❉　　❉　　❉

The people of Hanburgh attend both the funerals of Tom Willows and of George Knightly. At Tom's funeral, everyone has a story to tell about him, most of them risqué and otherwise good-natured. It is a spontaneous celebration of his life. The vicar, Simon Stanley, stands up and says "It is the wish of Tom's family that we rather celebrate his life than mourn his death." That stops everyone talking, and buries some of the better stories. Watching Sally, the determined set to her face, and the thunder cloud of sorrow in her eyes, I would guess that revenge is far higher up her list of priorities.

We suffer the same exhortation at George's funeral the next day. Sadly, there are no stories to tell about him that match the manner of his death. There is great speculation. Was he murdered, or was he accidentally strangled as part of a near-death experiment to heighten sexual ecstasy? The notion of George in sexual ecstasy is so absurd that the idea catches on as an extended joke. There are fewer people at George's funeral than at Tom's, and the weather has turned cold and wet overnight.

The chilling sight is that of Mary Knightly. I hate her with all my passion, I want her destroyed, yet for once I also empathise with her. She looks already destroyed, lost among the rain and the people. She has truly lost a friend and ally that she rarely treated well, who nevertheless adored her. Now she realises what she will miss, and it has ripped her whole chest away. When she recovers her strength, she too will seek revenge with an unholy passion. Today she is bereft, down in the grave with George, holding him for the last time on this earth.

You, Inspector, parade the fringes of both funerals, watching for clues, listening for stray comments. You recognise that your work is to feed off cadavers and stray pickings. When you visualise yourself, it is as a vulture, hovering over the scene of the crime, poking your head intrusively through the windows seeking new flesh.

Currently you are concerned as much for the future as for the past. There is something going on in this village that threatens to be the source of extreme and continued violence. Hanburgh is becoming Sicily. There are interlocking vendettas and broken lives, sharp as jagged glass.

Looking round, Brenda is sympathetic, especially to those related to, or who have had relations with, Tom, which accounts for a significant proportion of the funeral party. Sally Willows is uncontrollably angry. Mary Knightly is devastated. Frank is nonchalant, but my Mary is agitated. Sam and Tony are floating above it all, more intimate with each other than usual. Brian and Kate, who have brought along their four children, are playing families. I am watchful. Henry and Hilary are circulating. Simon Stanley presides and hovers.

What next?

❋　　❋　　❋

This, Inspector, is a story I was told directly by Charlie, the fiancée of Tom Becker, Henry's assistant in the funeral parlour. I wasn't there at the time (otherwise I would not need to rely on Charlie's account). It goes something like this:

Mary Knightly is not at all happy with the way that Tom and Charlie have been looking after the house they rent off her. As far as she is concerned, people who are living in other people's houses never treat them the same way as they do their own. Besides, they are young, and youth is negligent.

She glances at the hedge. It has not been trimmed for months. The grass is too long. There are weeds in the driveway. Paint is peeling off the front door.

She knocks.

Charlie comes to the door. "Oh hello, Mrs Knightly. Do come in."

"Thank you."

"We are really sorry about Mr Knightly. It must have been a terrible blow." Charlie sent Mary flowers with a note immediately she heard of George's death.

"It was."

"Would you like some coffee?"

"Thank you."

Charlie leads her into the sitting room. There are magazines strewn across the floor, and it needs a good vacuuming and dusting.

"It's a bit of a mess, I am afraid. We are all caught up with the wedding arrangements."

She goes to make the coffee. Mary scrutinises the room. There is a crack in the ceiling she has not seen before. The table has been chipped. The windows have not been washed.

"Do you take milk and sugar?"

"I'll do it myself, thank you. Where is Tom?"

"He is at work."

"I was rather hoping to talk to both of you."

"Well, if you come back this evening, he will be here. We spend every evening now making final arrangements and writing thank you letters. I did not realise that so many people knew us. It's incredible."

Mary straightens up in abrupt formality. "I'll come to the point. I do not think that you should stay in this house. You are not looking after it properly."

Charlie meets her eyes. Mary is the first to disengage.

"What do you mean, Mrs Knightly?"

"Look at this sitting room. It is a mess."

"So?"

"Can't you use a vacuum cleaner?"

"When I want to. What has that got to do with you?"

"That ceiling is cracked."

"That ceiling was always cracked."

"Not to my recollection."

"We can show you the photographs we took when we arrived, if you wish."

"And that table has been chipped."

"Not by us."

"Assuredly by you."

"Not according to the photographs."

"And are these so-called photographs witnessed?"

"Of course. My dad and Tom's dad did the inventory with us."

"I am not sure that they count as witnesses."

"Why ever not?"

"They are your family."

"Well, you can argue that out with them."

"And the garden is a disgrace."

"You are meant to be sending Paul up here to tidy it up. You agreed on that when we moved in. We said that there was no way we would have time to sort out the garden which was pretty overgrown even then, and you said that Paul could lend a hand. We have never seen him here since."

"Show me where it says that in the lease."

"I don't know whether it is in the lease, but that is what you promised. My dad and Tom's dad were witnesses."

"I am sorry, but if it is not written in the lease, it does not count."

"Then you had better go off and do whatever you have to do, and we will use our photographs and call our witnesses to show that you are mistaken."

"Young lady, I do not take kindly to being called a liar . . . ."

"I said you were mistaken."

. . . . and I am sure that you would be much happier living elsewhere."

"We are very happy here, thank you."

Mary gets up. "Well, I mustn't keep you." She has resolved to make life very difficult for Tom and Charlie from now on. She does not appreciate being crossed by these disrespectful young people. "You should at least clean the house."

"And you should mind your own business."

"This is my house. It is my business."

"Then send Paul up to sort out the garden."

Tom and Charlie will answer for this, Mary decides. She has not been bettered by anyone yet, and she knows how to use the law.

And you cannot fault Mary's timing, planning to turf out her tenants just a few weeks before their wedding. Perhaps she believes that she will never get them out once they are married, and then she will not be able to live there herself.

❉　　❉　　❉

Chapter 13

Mary is more seriously agitated even than last time.

She is looking exhausted, and she says she feels tired and sick, especially in the mornings. "If I weren't in my forties, and if Frank and I had not tried for years to have children without success, I would think I was pregnant."

"Perhaps it is a phantom pregnancy. Perhaps your body desires to be pregnant by me."

Mary laughs. "Now that would be something. Caught out in my adultery, becoming pregnant by another woman!"

"The world works in mysterious ways."

"I just feel uptight and stressed all the time, and I cannot shake it off. It is a heavy load of lead pressing on my stomach. Maybe it's depression. Not wanting to eat, or drink, or get up. Buried in this deep, dark hole, with a great weight pressing down inside me."

"Let me cheer you up."

"If only you could."

I take hold of her and I kiss her, pressing my body into hers. I can sense a reluctance in her at first, not resistance, more a failure to engage. Gradually though, as I slide my hands around her body, she relaxes.

Naked, I have to say that she is beginning to look pregnant. She has been eating a lot, so she is overweight, but there is a definite curve to the stomach area. I rather like the idea that in sharing this time together she has become pregnant, although it would be disastrous for our relationship. I let my eyes roam around her chalky skin, the mole below her navel, her pubic hair. This is a body I want to keep in touch with.

"Now what?" asks Mary.

"Now what where?"

"Where does our relationship go from here?"

"That is a difficult question."

"So what is the easy answer?"

"There are no easy answers. I love you. I want to be with you, and to live with you. You are married to Frank, and I do not believe that you would put him behind you, especially if you were pregnant, but even if you weren't. He has meant too much to you for too long. It seems that we will coast along like this, until we don't, until Frank finds out, and then we will either be dead, separated or more together than ever."

"It's hard. It's hard for both of us, for all of us. I want to be with you, and with Frank. I want the two lives to be lived in parallel. I am intensely jealous of both of you. I am scared of how Frank will react when he finds out about us. Really scared. In my heart, I do not think he would hurt either of us, but he might. He is more likely to turn his back without a word and walk out. That scares me as much. He is a good man, and I need him. I need both a good man and a good woman. I want it all. I want you both."

"Maybe we will get there. How do we tell Frank so that he will listen? Do we cook him dinner together, play strip poker, compromise him, then suggest a solution?"

"I cannot imagine Frank playing strip poker, and certainly not with two women alone. He is far too shy."

"Well, I am not looking to crowd the room."

"Me neither."

"Yet we have to find some solution. We are in a Hanged Man situation, and that does not last forever. Either we tell Frank, or one day he will find out. Or we stop."

Mary starts slightly. "I do not wish us to stop."

"Nor do I. And maybe nor does Frank. Perhaps all this suits Frank fine. Maybe he knows about us already. Maybe it does not matter to him so long as you are here when he needs you, and you keep the books of your company up-to-date. He has his fishing, and you have me."

"I don't think so somehow. I cannot imagine Frank being as broadminded as that."

"Is he confrontative?"

"No, not if he can possibly help it, unless he is really riled."

"Well perhaps he does not want to confront the issue. I cannot believe that somebody has not told him what is going on, not with all the gossips, and spiteful ones at that, mentioning no names, in this village."

"I really do not think he knows. He would be worrying about it, tossing and turning at night, coughing. He usually coughs a lot when he is worried."

"So, let's start again. Frank finds out, however he finds out. He turns on you, and demands to be told how long it has been going on for, and what your intentions are. What do you say?"

"I don't know. I truly don't know."

"That is not an answer."

"It is the only answer I have."

"Then we have to create a better one. How long have we been seeing each other? Do you tell him the truth?"

"Yes, I will have to tell him the truth."

"Good. And do you intend to keep on seeing me?"

"Yes, I do. I have turned my back on you once, and that was disastrous. I am not doing that again."

"And if he gives you an ultimatum? It is him or me."

"Then I say that I cannot choose between you. You are both special to me."

"And if he insists?"

"The same."

"And if he goes upstairs and starts to pack his things?"

"That is still my answer."

"And if he walks out of the house?"

"Then I tell him that he is welcome back anytime. He probably will not be listening, though."

"And what about at work?"

"He will probably get someone else to do the books."

"They will still have to be briefed."

"Not when he is around."

"So you now have the house. Then what?"

"Then it will be up to Frank to decide whether to come back, or to divorce me."

"OK, that is one scenario. What about if Frank does not walk out? What about if he asks for your solution?"

"I still do not have one."

"What about if he suggests us carrying on as we are."

"Well, that would be perfect."

"What about if he suggests our living together, all three of us? We did discuss that once."

"I cannot imagine us all sitting in this room on a cold winter's night, chatting away cosily."

"Why not?"

"I just cannot imagine it."

"What about if he gets overheated and suggests that he share both of us? Alternate nights?"

"That is more a question for you. Would you be willing to do that?"

"Yes, I would. Could you cope with it?"

"It would certainly be bizarre. Imagine what the village would say!"

"Would you care?"

"No, actually not."

"Would I care? No. Would Frank care?"

"He would bloody belt them if they made any snide remarks within his earshot."

"And Mary Knightly would really care. With a bit of luck she would have a terminal bout of apoplexy and die on the spot."

"Not until after she has seen the music festival through. Mary is very selective about what upsets her when. Do you know who would be the most upset?"

"No."

"Jeff Berringer. He would be down on us like a ton of bricks."

"And maybe that would not be a bad thing. We could throw a few of them back." I pause. "So, to recap, unless Frank turns violent, there is no outcome we cannot cope with. The most unfortunate one would be if he walked out. Other than that, we either carry on as we are, or we carry on even better. It may be time to tell him."

"I think not. There is no need to put him on the spot. Let him find out in his own way, and come to terms with it himself. He will probably spend an inordinate amount of time by himself on the river bank. Then he will choose to do the sensible thing. Frank has his moments, but he is never vindictive or unkind. He is not a bigot either. And we have known each other a long, long time. We are like a pair of shoes together."

"That does not translate to a threesome too well. There are not many people about with three legs."

"You may have to be the socks then, or the laces."

I kiss Mary, and hug her close. "That is settled then. I hope that you are pregnant."

"Well, two mothers are always better than one, as my mother never said."

"And I can keep Frank occupied until you are fit to return to normal duties."

"I think he would rather enjoy that, and I am beginning to think that you would too."

"It sounds like I might get plenty of sleep."

"You haven't heard him snoring, although, if you open your windows at night up there at the House, you soon will, I promise you."

❇   ❇   ❇

Trying to unearth clues, takes me to some very strange places in my mind. I am currently on holiday with the Berringers in Malaga. Well, I am not really, but I want to think myself into that man's head.

"Can't we go out, Jeff?"

"In a minute."

"What are you looking at?"

Jeff is sitting on the patio, watching the sea. The clouds are gathering, the sea is threateningly still. There are several power boats out in the bay making their final runs. People on the beach are beginning to rustle, to pull their clothes on, to wash whatever is covered in sand, to collect their things.

Next door, Carla is playing in the garden. She is eight years old. Every now and again she smiles at Jeff. He smiles back, and tries out some of the phrases he has learnt in Spanish. She laughs at the mistakes he makes. He knows and does not care. He is making contact. He is on square one of the game, moving across to square two.

"Juice? Thirsty?" He mimes thirst and the quenching of it.

Eventually she understands.

"Ice."

"You want an ice-cream?"

"Ice."

"Ice-cream?"

Carla goes off, and comes back with an ice-cream stick.

"Ah, you have had an ice-cream."

Carla looks puzzled, then guesses that he is asking her whether she has had an ice-cream.

"Si."

"Jeff, let's go out."

"All right, Phyllis. Are you dressed?"

"Yes, Jeff."

"Have you got your make-up on?"

"Yes, Jeff."

"Are you wearing your dancing shoes?"

"Don't need them, Jeff."

"Then let's go!" Jeff puts on a wolfish expression and lunges at Phyllis, who swerves and giggles.

"You're not seventeen now, Jeff Berringer."

"I am up here." Jeff taps his head.

"That could be the problem."

"There is nothing wrong with feeling seventeen, Phyllis."

"I don't feel seventeen. I feel my age. Seventy-six. Would you believe that I am seventy-six?"

"Given that I am seventy-eight, yes. Still, we are not doing badly. We can still dance. I could probably even run a few yards. I can certainly swim. Life has been kind to us."

"So let's get going."

They climb into the Renault Twingo they are borrowing, and head towards the main part of the town. The streets are mid-touristy, not the squeezing mass of mid-summer, not the deserted streets of February. In a few weeks things will start to wind down. The street vendors are beginning to migrate. "Do you want to buy a genuine Rolex? Do you want some binoculars to view the bay? Do you want a donkey?" "No, no, no thank you."

The Berringers' favourite restaurant is in the corner of a square, and specialises in seafood. They go there are least twice a week, and are greeted as regulars. "Mr. Berringer, Mrs Berringer. Welcome! Your table is waiting for you."

"Thank you, Carlos."

"Your tan is coming on nicely, Mr. Berringer."

"This is my favourite time of year. Now and June."

"There can be storms in September. Everyone is tired. Shops start to close."

"And we get the town back to ourselves."

"Yes, Mr. Berringer."

They order paella between the two of them, as ever, and a bottle of Rioja. They watch the people on the streets, and wave at one or two, who come over and sit at their table for a while. They are very popular among the expats of the region.

"How long are you staying this time?" asks Walter.

"Oh probably a few weeks," replies Jeff. "We will get back mid to late October."

"What a lifestyle, eh? Who would have guessed when we were young that things would end up like this, living it up in the sun in our seventies, not a care in the world?"

"Yes, it's unbelievable, isn't it?"

"And some of the money the youngsters have nowadays. That is even more incredible. They don't even seem to have to work for it."

"Oh well, as long as we have what we want . . . ."

"You have to admit, Jeff, it is a bit galling nonetheless."

"No, it doesn't bother me. You can't take it with you. And I cannot imagine that I would be happier with more than I have now—the sea, the sun, Phyllis by my side, and a plate of paella in a charming restaurant where we are known and welcomed. All this and heaven too!"

"It's a good philosophy, Jeff."

"Jeff has always known what he wanted, and stopped when he got it," comments Phyllis. "We wanted a child of our own, but that was not to be. So we adopted Mary instead. What a wonderful child she has proved to be."

"Not such a child now. Fifty-two."

"She had a sister we considered adopting too, but Jeff said that one would be enough. No need to overdo it. So we left her behind. We felt guilty about it for quite a while. Really torn, but it was the right decision. It meant that we could pour all our love into Mary. Jeff did meet her sister once, just to make contact, however it was not a success. I am glad that we did not adopt her."

"She was pretty angry. Made all sorts of accusations. Most unpleasant business."

"Mary lost her husband last week under most unfortunate circumstances. He was found strangled."

"Oh, how terrible. Poor thing."

"Yes, she was devastated by it. We suggested that she come out here to take a few weeks off, but there has been the funeral to arrange first."

"Aren't you going back for it?"

"No. We thought about it. You cannot bring back the dead, can you? I don't know what he was mixed up in to come to that grizzly end. We are better off out of it. And Mary can come and have some peace and quiet out here. Besides, she knows everyone in the village, so she has lots of friends to comfort her. She doesn't need us. Parents cannot keep running every time when you are fifty and they are in their seventies. You have to be able to stand on your own two feet eventually, don't you?"

"Too right. Life's too short," Walter re-assures them. "Well must be getting on. See you around."

"And you too, Walter."

Walter rejoins his party. "You'll never guess what. Jeff and Phyllis' son-in-law was murdered last week, and they aren't even going home to the funeral."

"How uncaring can you get?"

"Some people get very selfish in their old age. I cannot imagine doing that to Frances. Heavens no!"

I often find weddings as miserable as funerals. What does the church know about marriage, and even more what does the Reverend Simon Stanley know about it? It feels like a whole tradition of blind monks discussing the colours and the nature of the sea in order to help two inexperienced sailors to cross it safely. Why does the church not recognise the depth of its ignorance and just throw a party—no moralising, no advice, just lashings of goodwill and great music. I am sure that the evangelicals do something like that.

Fortunately, the wedding between Charlene Brown and young Tom Becker has all the makings of a great event. Charlie knows everyone of course, and everything about everyone, including the stuff that did not happen. Her Maid of Honour is Brenda, so all are involved in the joyous arrangements.

The whole village has been pitching in. The florist is providing the flowers, the butcher the meat, the greengrocer the fruit and veg, the off licence the wine and soft drinks.

It is a wedding that will bring happiness and prosperity to all.

The Reverend Simon Stanley has his homily prepared around the theme of every cloud having a silver lining. Where there are showers, there must be sunshine. Where there is conflict, let there be harmony. Where there is hatred, let there be love. Where there is anger, let there be compassion. He knows just the passage he will be quoting from the Bible, an unusual text for a wedding, yet most apt under these circumstances. He is at least trying to provide some valuable input within traditional constraints.

Charlie's father, Harry, is very proud of his daughter. He is both honoured to give her away, and reluctant to do so. Still, young Becker is a good lad, and may end up running the funeral parlour one day. Henry Spence is very fond of him, and Henry's daughter, Kate, shows no interest in it at all.

The congregation starts to assemble outside the church, greeting each other with warmth on this most festive of days. The ushers, friends of Tom, are trying to shoo them into the church with little effect. Robin Marsden, the best man, marches up and down the path, checking the rings, and hoping to God that he will not lose them between now and then. He fears for his speech. He has never given a speech before.

Everyone greets Mary Knightly gently in deference to her recent bereavement and Sally Willows too, although Sally in contrast to Mary, is not giving any impression of requiring careful handling. She has the socially-detached air of a paid assassin who will gun down the person responsible for her brother's death on the steps of the church, before or after the service. Everyone who was around in those days remembers what Sally was like as a young girl, fiery and headstrong. Each one knows the story of what she did to Dr. Berringer.

I step up to introduce myself, somewhat apprehensively, but Sally smiles and shakes my hand. "My brother spoke very highly of you, Julia. I am sorry that your relationship was cut so short. You would have been very good for him, I am sure. You might even have rescued him from himself, the way that he talked about you. He said that you were somehow familiar, and that he felt he had known you for years."

We converse for a while, in fact. She describes, quite naturally, her devastation at the death of her brother, and her determination to get to the bottom of who killed him. Do I have any ideas? She has heard that Inspector Frampton and I are spending a great deal of time together. What is he thinking? How confident is he of finding out who did it? Can she rely on my help in the future?

"Of course you can, Sally. When whoever he is killed Tom, he killed a part of me too. He murdered a close and intimate friend of mine, and he threw me under suspicion so that I was arrested as a suspect and hounded by the press. Apart from my feelings for Tom, I have a direct stake in bringing this man to justice."

"Thank you, Julia. I get the strong impression that I can rely on you."

I admit here that I over-stated greatly my sentiments for Tom. They were not as pure, by any means, as I suggested to Sally. However, it seemed politic to get Sally on my side, and to commit myself to being indisputably on hers, which in fact I am. I have no desire to be shot by Sally as a result of her drawing the wrong conclusions about my involvement with Tom. On the other hand, what was she doing secretly in the village on the day of Tom's death?

Brian and Kate arrive, with their four children, followed by Frank and Mary, who greets me warmly, openly in public.

The ushers finally succeed in persuading us to move towards our allotted pews in the church. Shuffling, scraping and coughing ensues. Waving at people as they come in late. Lifting of eyebrows in greeting. Tom Becker and Robin Marsden stand side-by-side as if a terrifying ordeal awaits them. Will Charlie turn up? Will he be able to say the words? Will the rings still be there? Tom's parents and Charlie's mother are in opposite choir stalls, with their respective families, according them a good view of each other and of proceedings. Both mothers were barely sixteen when they had Tom and Charlie, so still in their mid-thirties now. Both their fathers are considerably older. Arnold and Pat Becker are notoriously happy together, but have never had any more children. Harry and Tessa Brown can be heard arguing across the entire village through the open windows of their home, altercations they continue into the local shops and the streets of the Hanburgh, and no doubt everywhere else beyond. Nevertheless, they have remained together for eighteen years. What got into them when they called their daughter Charlene, no-one knows. She has had to live down the name "Charlie Brown" all her life. Maybe it is the motivation for her bubbly nature.

Charlie pulls up on the other side of the beck from the church in the back of a Rolls Royce. She stumbles out, and the bridesmaids are assembled behind her to hold her train. She starts to process across the little humpbacked bridge over the beck, watched by several villagers and visitors who have not been invited to the wedding. One small boy, who is peering too intently at Charlie, over-extends himself and tumbles into the beck. He is frantically fished out by his mother. Jimmy Cuthbert drowned in that mill pond end of the beck.

They pass the gravestone of the seventy-year old man who had nine wives, a favourite tourist attraction. Someone has added RIP to the gravestone in chalk. Many of the gravestones have been flattened to make for easier mowing of the churchyard.

When Charlie and her father reach the porch, Simon does a thumbs-up to re-assure Tom that everything is OK.

"Are you ready, Charlie?"

"Yes, Dad."

"Good luck, Charlie, and all the best."

"Thank you, Dad. You have been the best Dad ever."

Harry squeezes her hand. "Off we go, then."

Left forward, feet together. Right forward, feet together. The bridesmaids are concentrating passionately in their attempts to hold their correct positions. Left forward, feet together. Right forward, feet together, all along the tiled squares of the aisle. People are turning to watch her, but Charlie keeps her mind on her progress down the aisle. They reach the altar, where Tom is waiting. She gives a huge, happy, nervous smile to Tom, who goes red. Simon Stanley ushers them together.

As the congregation wobbles into its first hymn, "Love divine, all love excelling," none of us conceive that things are about to go horribly wrong. The couple are standing there innocently aware of each other's proximity, anxiousness and fondness. Tessa Brown is close to tears. Harry has joined her, having delivered his daughter to the altar.

After the hymn, Simon plunges into his oration.

"It is so nice to see the church so packed today. I do hope that we will see you again tomorrow for Matins."

(Willing laughter from the congregation).

"It is always a joy to preside over a wedding, especially of such a popular young couple as Tom and Charlene here. With the recent terrible events in the village, we need a joyous occasion to celebrate. Even in life we are among death and, surrounded by death, life is renewed. Tom and Charlie are here today to celebrate their wedding, and to give us hope that a new generation will be born to revitalise the village. Where there is despair, let there be hope. Where there is strife, let there be harmony. When I came to Hanburgh eighteen years ago, one of the first things I remember was Charlene being born. She was a very beautiful baby, or so her mother, Tessa Brown, said."

(Dutiful laughter).

"And she has turned into a very beautiful young lady. Tom, you are a lucky man."

(Tom nods, and smiles at Charlie).

"Equally, Charlene, you are a very lucky young lady too, to have Tom so dearly in your life. As someone observed the other day, you two are just like brother and sister. Well, let's hope not exactly."

(Laughter).

"However, a marriage that is based first and foremost on friendship is a strong marriage. Marriage has its ups and downs. It moves between ecstasy and despair, between togetherness and dispute, between laughter and tears, between the highs and the lows. That is the natural rhythm of life, and it is magnified in marriage. Do not expect a marriage to be happy ever after. That is for the fairy tales. Marriage is tough and, if you weather the storms, ultimately the most rewarding investment of your lives, especially if you have children."

(The whole village knows that Charlie is pregnant. Tom and Charlie nod respectfully).

"Your marriage can mark the start of a new phase in the village, a healing phase. It is a great burden to place on your shoulders, but I am confident that you two are capable of bearing it. However, first the law and the liturgy demands that I ask a preliminary question. Does anyone in this congregation know of any reason why these two young people should not be joined together in holy matrimony today? Speak now, or forever remain silent."

(Silence).

"Good. I always like a silence at that moment. We can proceed."

(Dutiful laughter).

"I know a reason," says a voice.

Everyone in the church freezes. The voice, of indeterminate sex, comes from the loudspeakers that have been recently installed in the church.

"Excuse me," Simon orders. "Who said that?"

"They are brother and sister, well half-brother and half-sister."

"Please show yourself, whoever you are."

"They are both children of Tom Willows," continues the voice, then there is no more.

The congregation searches for the source of the voice. Simon hunts around for help. What does he do now? Does the objector have to show him or herself for the challenge to stand? He has never been in this situation before. He has never heard of this situation before. It seems impossible to stop proceedings now, yet he cannot legally marry a couple who are indeed brother and sister.

He turns to the parents. "What do we do from here?"

"I thought you would know that," Harry barks. "It is a ridiculous allegation, isn't it Tessa?"

Tessa is silent.

"Pat?"

Pat is silent too.

"Why do you two not say anything?"

"This is a very delicate topic," suggests Arnold. "We cannot discuss it in front of one hundred and fifty people."

Simon turns back to the congregation. "The parents and I will retire to the vestry for a few minutes. We will be back shortly. I hope that Mr. Johnson will entertain you with some of his excellent organ playing." Mr. Johnson nods his assent.

In the vestry there is a minute of settling, then Harry asks Tessa "Well?"

Tessa would prefer to avoid saying what she has to say, although she knows she has to say it. She pleads into Harry's eyes. "I had a brief affair with Tom Willows when I was fifteen, and became pregnant with Charlie."

"Oh my God," exclaims Pat spontaneously. "I had a fling with him too." Arnold is still holding her shoulder in consolation for the turning of events, and in solidarity against it. He looks bemused. Harry froths.

Simon summarises gingerly. "So Tom and Charlene could be brother and sister?"

Tessa nods. "I have always known, of course, that Charlie was Tom's child. It just never occurred to me that Tom was too. His name should have put me on my guard, at least to take the necessary precautions before it got to this. I am really, really sorry. I am overwhelmed, lost. It is a disaster. What do we do?"

"Yes, Tom is named after Tom. I had no idea that you were involved with Tom too, Tessa. It must have been about the same time. It's awful. How do we ever look them in the eye again? I want to crawl away and die"

"What a mess," growls Harry. "If Tom Willows were alive today, I would see that man in jail. I would see him strung up from the nearest lamppost." His face is alcoholic red, and he has tendencies in that direction. "I can't believe it."

"Those poor children," says Arnold. "And with a child on the way."

"What a disaster."

"What do we do now?" Pat asks.

"I am afraid that I cannot marry them, or even bless them," Simon confirms.

"What about the reception? Do we go on with it? Everything is ready and paid for."

"It is a complete and utter disaster." Harry paces the room.

"Well, there is no point in throwing all that food away," decides Pat. "We will just have to turn it into a party. The day that Tom and Charlie discovered that they are brother and sister. It is not what any of us expected, and it will take some adjusting to for everyone, and especially for Tom and Charlie. It is just the way things are."

"I can't for the life of me see it turning into a celebration," Tessa observes, "but we might as well carry on, and brace ourselves. It will be our act of penitence. We are going to be crucified, and we deserve to be."

"Are you agreed?" Simon searches each face for assent or dissent. He gets two yeses and two abstentions. "We had better call Tom and Charlie in," he decides.

"Yes."

Tom and Charlie enter the vestry apprehensively. Tom stoops as he crosses the threshold. They hold hands as they face Simon and their parents.

Simon clears his throat. "Tom," he takes Tom's spare hand. "Charlene," he takes Charlie's other hand. They make an intimate circle. "Something most unfortunate has happened. It appears that you are half-brother and half-sister to each other." He remembers the remark he made only a few minutes ago in the church about their behaving like brother and sister. He has never said that before at a wedding. He will never say it again.

Charlie bursts into tears. "What does that mean?"

"Well, it's obvious what it means," snaps Harry impatiently.

"Yes, Dad, but what does it *mean*?"

"I am sorry, Charlie," Harry apologises. "I shouldn't have said that. I am simply furious that this great day of yours has been ruined, perhaps your whole life, because of a couple of silly, irresponsible girls."

"So we are both Tom Willows' children?"

"Yes, I am afraid so."

"So you are not my dad?"

"No. I have always had my suspicions, mind . . . ."

"I haven't!" Charlie shouts.

"I should have told you, I know," Tessa breaks in. "I never saw the need."

"You do now!"

"Yes, we do now."

"And I am pregnant. Tom and I are having a child together. What will it turn out like? It might be hideously deformed. Tom and I have been together for ages. We did not know that we were related. How could we have known?" Charlie is despairing. Tom holds her hand tight. Charlie pulls it away momentarily from her lover, and immediately returns it to her brother.

Tessa breaks down into tears. "I am really, really sorry, my darling. It is a terrible thing we have done. I cannot imagine how to make it up to you."

"It's a disaster!" Harry proclaims again.

"What do we do? Can we live together? Will we go to prison?"

"No, no, there is no chance of that," Simon reassures them quickly. "It is absolutely not your fault."

"Will the baby be taken away from us? They are not having the baby, whatever state it turns out to be in. We are keeping the baby."

"These are things we can discuss later," Simon interjects, hoping to defer the discussion, fully aware that there is a large congregation outside in the church awaiting news.

"Yes, but they are questions that must be answered now," Arnold states firmly. "They are decisions we have to make to clear up our own mess, and to minimise the consequences as far as possible for these two unfortunate children of ours, so to speak, who happen to be our children, at least emotionally."

Tom raises his head. "I want to carry on living with Charlie. We want to keep the child, whatever. We want you to ensure that we are left in peace."

"You must not break the law though," Simon warns.

Tom smiles at him provocatively, angrily. "You will never know whether we have or haven't, unless there is another child. And that will never happen."

Charlie squeezes his hand. She is 100% beside him. They will have to live with the gossip, which in Hanburgh is mostly generated by her anyway. People will understand.

"You could have an abortion, if you two are worried about the baby," suggests Pat.

"We will not have an abortion," says Tom flatly, determinedly. "What is done is done. We are not going to add murder to the list."

"No we are not," Charlie adds. "The baby is ours. It will be our last one, but it will be ours. And you lot had better make it right for us."

"We will try," Harry promises, "however we can only do what we can do. And those responsible for this had better get started in earnest now, if you want my opinion."

Simon comes back into the church, followed by Tom, Charlie and their parents. They do not go back to their pews. They stand loosely behind Simon Stanley as he speaks.

"Ladies and gentleman, in the light of the anonymous allegations made just now, and I do wish the person making them would have the courage to step forward . . . ."

He waits. There is no movement.

"Obviously not. Anyway, in the light of these allegations, we have decided between us, and with the agreement of all . . . ." he turns to ensure that all are still agreed ". . . . that the marriage of Tom and Charlene cannot proceed as planned . . . ."

There is a gasp from the audience all along the aisle.

"However, Tom and Charlene and their parents have decided to continue with the festivities today anyway because even if Tom and Charlene cannot marry today, or possibly ever, they will always love each other dearly, and that is something to celebrate too."

The congregation is in uproar and so desperate to gossip with one another that it is barely listening. Everyone is whispering. Some are openly talking. Several have already abandoned their pews to leave the church and twitter outside. Robin Marsden fingers the rings that won't be needed any more.

"Please regroup at the village hall," Simon has to almost shout. "There will be no line of honour, but there will be champagne."

I am going to be really bitchy now, really reprehensible, and really truthful. I have to say that as weddings, or non-weddings, go, Tom and Charlie's is absolutely the best I have ever been invited to. The service turned out to be something worth attending, a drama, suspense, a near-riot, and only one hymn. I feel sorry for Simon. He made rather a good, honest speech, I thought. There are no photographs—the official photographer sheathed his camera sheepishly, as if he had been caught with his penis outside his trousers—and there is no great long queue to get to the champagne.

What would usually have been dutiful conversations between bored villagers who have been brought up with each other all their lives, is turning orgasmic with the scandal, and maybe the threat of more to come. Most of the children in Hanburgh marry locally, and who knows which of them are Tom's children?

I am trying to work out whether Tom would have been amused by developments, or embarrassed, or totally humbled. I cannot decide. He would certainly not have wanted the pain of the disclosure to be visited on his children. However, in the end, Tom and Charlie have found each other, they will have a child of their own which will probably be perfectly normal, they have every chance of being very happy together, and they can always adopt more children if they want to. A nice Vietnamese baby would be a welcome change in direction for Hanburgh, don't you think?

Sam James and her circle are whooping it up, over-heated with the excitement.

"So who was it who split on them?" asks Julie.

"Beats me."

"I cannot imagine anyone doing that. It is so unfair."

"Where's your husband then, Sam?" Mich asks.

"I haven't a clue," replies Sam, "but it wasn't him. I was sitting right next to him."

"The voice was probably a recording," Melody suggests, "activated remotely."

"Well, I am sure it was not him. He is never sneaky like that. I cannot imagine who it might have been. I didn't recognise the voice at all, did you?"

Everyone is agreed that the voice did not belong to anyone in Hanburgh whom they knew.

"Could it have been Sally?"

"What do you mean? It certainly wasn't Sally's voice."

"Yes, but she could have hired an actor, couldn't she?"

"Anyone could have hired an actor. Anyone could have done it."

"Except that it requires some knowledge of how to manage quite complex electronic equipment, and access to the belfry."

"Do you think it was Simon?"

"Not the way he tries to start his car in the morning. We are not talking Mr. Practical exactly, are we?"

"Does Sally know anything about electronics?"

"Tom did. He had his own PA system."

"That's true. Do you think it was his voice from beyond the grave, so to speak? That he and Sally set it up before he died? He knew that Charlie and young Tom were engaged. He knew that they were related. Perhaps he had decided to put a stop to it. Come to think of it, it was a bit like his voice, but disguised by raising the frequency, or something."

"Or it could have been Sally's voice slowed down."

"So Sally will have set it up. Shall we go and ask her?"

"We can't at the moment," Sam announces. "She is not here. She said she had to go briefly into town. She'll be back later."

"Do you think she will admit to it?" Mich asks.

"I doubt it, but we should ask anyway. It was really cowardly of her to go about it like that, sneakily. Shame on her. And I don't mind collaring her about it. I am not afraid of her, whatever her reputation," Melody declares. "Nobody shoots the piano player."

"You don't play that well, Mel," Sam retorts.

"Well enough not to get myself shot."

Frank comes up to me. "Mary has sent me on an errand. She says are you ignoring her?"

"Of course not, Frank."

"In that case, I have to drag you over."

I watch Frank as he leads the way across to Mary, and try to imagine what it would be like to go to bed with him. He is stocky in his suit. His trousers are noticeably askew and do not follow the swing of his buttocks. Something about his shoes tells me that his feet are probably smelly. That is the first thing I think about when I find someone physically unappealing, how they will smell, and especially their feet. I do not relish him inside me. I do not even relish him in the same sitting room night after night, but I do want Mary, and to get Mary I may have to be prepared to come to some sort of terms with Frank too. Life is not making choices easy for any of us. I sincerely hope that it does not come to that.

"Hello, Julia," Mary greets me radiantly. "I am glad Frank found you. I have been looking for you everywhere."

"Oh, I've been around."

"I was saying to Frank how we should invite you and Sam and Tony round for dinner sometime, wasn't I, Frank?"

"Yes, it would be very nice," Frank agrees honestly. "Mary is an astonishing cook."

"She is very gifted all round," I add.

"I am glad that you appreciate her as I do. We were childhood sweet-hearts, you know. Still are."

"I know."

"Wouldn't part with her for the world."

Mary laughs. "I should hope not, Frank."

I am trying to read whether there is a message behind Frank's words. He gives not the slightest hint, yet he has made a very definite proclamation.

"So you are not going fishing today, Frank?"

"Maybe later, Julia. I'll probably sneak off in an hour or so, before they cut the cake. If they cut the cake."

"Shouldn't think so."

"No, probably not. And what about you, Julia? You must have a fair number of men after you, if I may make so bold."

"Not that I have noticed."

"Surely there must be somebody in Hanburgh who attracts you."

"If there is, Frank, I am not saying."

"Well, I hope I will be one of the first to know when there is."

"But not the first, Frank."

Frank colours up. "No, not the first."

"What are you two on about?" Mary asks. "Are you talking in code?"

"No, I was only curious, that is all. With Julia's looks, I am surprised that there isn't a swarm of men buzzing around her."

"Maybe one day, Frank. I haven't been here in Hanburgh long."

"We will have to try to get you fixed up with someone, before you get into any mischief."

"Come on, Frank, ease up on the girl. Perhaps Julia is entirely happy as she is, without being pestered by unwelcome attentions."

"Maybe so. Oh well, you have to have some basis of conversation at a wedding, and I am not going to start gossiping about what happened in church just now, and dancing on graves."

"Wasn't that terrible, Julia?" says Mary. "I would never have guessed."

"Now what have I started after all?" Frank declares. "I am off in search of more champagne," and he wanders off.

"It must have been such an appalling shock for them. One minute they were worrying about whether they will get their words out right, and the next it is all off. It must be absolutely devastating. I cannot imagine who would be so unkind as to make the objection."

"It had to come out sooner or later. Talking of the which, do you think Frank knows about us? He was saying some very odd things."

"I was beginning to wonder myself," Mary agrees. "It would definitely be Frank's style to drop big hints before doing anything else, to try to extort a direct confirmation. He sees it as doing the decent thing."

"We had better be prepared for a showdown, then."

"I still cannot imagine how things will turn out."

"Nor can I, but we have to try, don't we?"

"We do."

❋ ❋ ❋

Tom and Charlie return home to come to terms with their new situation. They sit together in various rooms and console each other for a few hours, talking it all around indefatigably, until Charlie realises that there is a plane to catch.

"Should we even have a honeymoon?" asks Tom.

"You must be bloody joking," Charlie retorts. "You want us to cancel our trip to the U.S.? No chance. We go as brother and sister, or as husband and wife, or as two mates, but we are going!"

Tom jumps up from the sofa. "All right, then. What do we pack?"

"We? Me. I've already packed for both of us. You check we have all the documents we need."

"OK."

So they fly off to New York, and bounce around the city for a few days before driving up to Rhode Island, where they stay in an immaculate blue and white boarding house close to the harbour.

It is on the drive across to Rhode Island from New York that they talk themselves into a solution. We love each other. Better still, we are brother and sister. We have a child on the way. Nobody is going to do anything about us being together, anyway they can't except that they could take the baby away from us possibly, but they won't. What is the problem?

And they sleep together again, and after the initial shock of residual guilt it starts to feel great. Consanguinity meets co-linearity. Not only are they matched by birth, but also by voluntary lifetime partnership. If they had been brought up together, they would have had not the slightest interest in each other. Working it the other way around, they are very happy.

This is conjecture on my part of course, but this is how I hope it all went.

Chapter 14

Charlie, who has been feeling rather sick with her pregnancy, is having a few days off at home. She hopes that the sickness bares no relation to the health of the child. Everyone assures her that it doesn't. During some pregnancies you suffer terribly, during others you are on cloud nine much of the time. It is like the fact that some babies are really easy, and others scream the house down continuously and never sleep. You often get one of each, although Tom and Charlie will not be aiming for a second. They have discussed Tom having a vasectomy. They have not decided yet. He is very young, and what would happen if Charlie died suddenly, or they broke up? On the other hand, they daren't have Charlie being pregnant again, unless they leave the village for a while, and claim that their child is adopted. And then there is the risk of genetic malformation. You cannot take gambles like that.

The phone goes.

"Hello, Charlie here."

"Good morning, Charlene. This is Mary Knightly speaking."

"Good morning, Mary."

"How are things going?"

"Excellently, thank you, Mrs Knightly."

"You must call me Mary."

"OK."

"I am phoning to ask when you are planning to leave the house."

"Oh, about three to four years' time, I would guess, when Tom is earning more and we can afford to buy one of our own."

"I am afraid that I was talking about weeks, not years."

"Why would that be? We have no plans to leave at present, and you have no grounds for kicking us out."

"Would your perpetuating an incestuous relationship not be grounds? My lawyer says that it is immoral behaviour, and therefore that I have the right, and even the duty to ask you to leave forthwith."

"Forthwith, Mary? You must have a very old-fashioned lawyer."

"You can get as smart as you like, but that is the situation."

"No, it is not. We are not perpetuating any incestuous relationship, thank you very much indeed, so you have no right to kick us out."

"That is not what I hear."

"You obviously know the wrong sorts of people."

"Well, either way, I am afraid that I have asked my lawyer to serve notice on you to quit."

"We shall leave when we want to leave, Mary, and not before."

"We will see about that."

"Yes, we will."

"I am going over to Spain to visit my parents for a couple of weeks, and when I come back, I expect you to be gone, or to see you in court. Is that understood?"

"Would this be a good time to break it to you, Mary, that they are not your parents?"

"Of course they are not my real parents. They were killed in a car crash when I was four years old. How unkind of you to mention that."

"Just keeping the record straight, that you choose to acknowledge them as your parents whatever they have done."

"It is only natural, and none of your business, you little hussy. I cannot begin to understand where you think this tactic will get you."

"Nowhere. We are not leaving anyway, and you cannot make us, lawyer or no lawyer. It was just a spiteful comment from my side, meant to hurt you. And to continue, there is nothing natural about your relationship with Dr. Berringer, is there? Goodbye."

Charlie carefully replaces the phone, and wonders if Mary has done the same. She hopes she is shaking with remorse. There's a joke. Silly bitch.

❋   ❋   ❋

As I walk around the village, it strikes me as curious that there is no casual meeting place anywhere in Hanburgh. In most villages abroad, there will be a square where the villagers meet, free of charge, to ponder the enormities and trivialities of life. In an English village, this is rarely the case.

There is the pub, the Hanburgh Arms, but that is different. Most people never cross the threshold and, technically, children are not allowed to do so.

Still, there is much to appreciate about Hanburgh. A beck trickles down one side of the church towards the green, disappearing until it re-emerges in its second section, before flowing underground again into the estuary. A series of old-fashioned buildings house the greengrocer's, the post office, the baker's, and the florist's. Only the butcher's is situated apart, on a corner at the northern end of the church. There are several elegant houses in Hanburgh, seven large ones—Georgian or Victorian—and a few more modest ones. At one time the village was wealthy because of the passing trade it attracted. Now it is wealthy because of the people who come to live here, alongside those families who have occupied their place in the village for centuries.

Hanburgh is an apparently tranquil, picturesque, village that hides some right rum goings-on, as the older locals are no doubt describing them.

Mrs. Corbett is struggling down the street, the hair that grows widly out of her chin almost tickling her knees. She looks up at me sideways, and says "Hello, dear. Are you having a bit of a ponder?"

"You could say that."

"I did."

"Can I help you?"

"No-one can help me now, dear. I am old, and burdened, and awaiting the call of my maker. There is nothing that can be done about it."

"I could carry something for you, if you are going to the shops."

"You'll be the death of me, dear. It's carrying things all my life that has kept me going all these years, although it has made me rather bent along the way. You don't want to be helping old people like me, dear. You'll be helping us into our graves." She smiles at a very odd angle. "It was kind of you to offer." She fixes me with a rapier eye. "I knew your grandfather, and his father, and your grandmother, and your mother, and your father too, poor soul. Such a terrible thing to happen!"

"You did?"

"Yes. You cannot fool me, I'm afraid. I know who you are, and the best of luck to you. I always liked your family. I hope you find what you are looking for."

Just as I decide to talk about my family, and indeed myself, she shuffles off, and Brian appears.

"Hello, Julia. Chatting up the ladies, are you? A bit old even for you, isn't that one?"

"Thank you, Brian. There's life in those old bones yet, don't you think?"

"I would say so. She will see us all off, that's my guess. Anyway, where are you going?"

"To the post office." I wave some letters at him. "Letters."

"I was going there myself. Can I chat you up along the way?"

"Feel free, but you won't get anywhere I am afraid."

"Oh well."

❄　❄　❄

On the way back, I meet you, Inspector, pacing the village in your flat-footed, rocking way. I bet your feet are smelly too.

You always seem to undress me mentally for the first few seconds of each encounter. Ho, hum.

You are still getting nowhere with your investigations, and so you are frustrated, which you hide behind a faraway expression of distraction.

"Have you seen Henry Spence recently?" you ask me.

"Why on earth do you ask me that?"

"No reason. I was just wondering. Do you know him?"

"By sight, and to nod to."

"Best kept away from, I would say."

"Oh, is he a prime suspect of yours?"

"I was referring to his profession. No, he is not a prime suspect. No-one is, not even you. I am out of suspects altogether. I cannot get a single angle on this case. It is as if there is an invisible thread joining all the bits together, and making them all invisible in their turn. I shudder to think what is going on here, but I cannot believe it is healthy."

"You are probably right."

"Any ideas yet?"

"No. I am trying, though, I promise."

"And what if I told you I believed your life to be in danger?"

"Nothing. I don't believe it is for a second, at least not more than any life is. I could be run over by a bus," I add, watching the one of only two buses a day to come through the village drive past.

"Surely someone can give me a clue somewhere in this revolting village."

"It is a beautiful village."

"Yes, and it is beginning to stick in my craw."

There is a scream at the other end of the village, around the corner, up Beckside. Hilary Spence comes into view, flailing her arms and screeching without any of her accustomed reserve.

She comes racing up to us in an ungainly, almost threatening manner. "Inspector," she exclaims, gripping your arm. "Young Tom Becker is lying in the mortuary, covered in blood, with his throat cut open. Help him! Help him!"

You double-take. Hilary Spence works in a health centre. Why is she asking you? Then you rally yourself. Shock. It empties our brains sometimes.

We run to the mortuary. By the time we get there, young Tom's body has lurched around in its final death throes, and landed dead on the white ceramic tiles, blood washed away from him inexorably across the floor.

"Talk to Mrs. Corbett," I suggest.

"You think she did this?"

It is most unseemly, but we both laugh as Hilary Spence watches on flummoxed and outraged.

Sometimes when shock empties your mind, it tickles.

✳   ✳   ✳

I have had a short life, if thirty-three years can be considered short, and not a particularly happy one. In recent times it has been simply weird. I do not really know why I am still alive. I should have chosen to die after the car crash. My spirit outwitted my intelligence.

It is not worth living this life.

There is so much I did not expect after the accident. I did not even begin to imagine the insights into human nature I would develop by crossing the divide, by gaining the intuition to understand what people are thinking all around me. It is an extreme of data overload. A human being cannot process so much. I receive every thought from almost everyone around me, and I cannot cope with, or use, most of it. It frightens me, it shocks me, it infuriates me, it depresses me.

Human thought is at base so base. We do such trivial things with all that intelligence we have been lavished with. We could work towards a better world, towards making even the smallest of differences, and we waste our time worrying whether somebody of no importance likes us or not.

People are nicer than they fear they are, but we are also more futile, weaker, and lazier. We make only a minimal amount of effort to achieve things of lasting value, with the exception of those people in over-drive who work towards little else, much to their own vainglory.

We are not balanced. We go from peaceful intentions in peacetime to murderous ones in war. We are easily provoked to hatred by the simplest of cynical exploiters. We fall for the same trick a thousand times without recognising it. We, the wealthiest generation of all time, are more obsessed with the acquisition of yet more possessions than any generation in history. You would think that we would have reached satiety with all that we cram our homes with and later take to the dump. Apparently not. Rather than counsel ourselves that enough is enough, we carry on accelerating our desires, and cheering on people whose only intent is to profit from them.

We may be decent, but we are certainly stupid.

Sorry, I am feeling down today. I cannot say why. I woke up cheerful and optimistic, and then everything crashed around me because of nothing in particular. I cannot identify any incident that threw me into this state. It suddenly took over, and refused to be lifted off.

Things are going fine with Mary. We are in love again. There are complications, but those should not be depressing me.

Writing about these deaths, and about the shoddy little goings-on of the people in Hanburgh is beginning to burden me. Tom's death was catastrophic, shades of Louise. He was so young, he had just experienced terrible trauma with Charlie and bravely battled through it with her, there is a baby on the way, and now he is dead. Why?

I am beginning to believe that death is stalking me, waiting to strike me down too. I fear it at a time when perhaps I should be welcoming it. It is the anticipation of the jolt of it that scares me, suddenly coming face-to-face with someone with a coldly evil mind intent on doing me extreme harm.

Are all lives like mine, where apparent normality masks strange and ugly deeds?

We never consider ourselves to be wrong in our entirety. We may know that what we are doing is considered wrong by society or by a group within it, but we have the justification to argue that in this case everything is as it should be.

What can the killer, or killers, be thinking? What is their motive? How do they plan it? What goes through their minds just before they deal the final blow, while they are delivering it, after they have reduced their target to a bloodied or bloated heap? Do they stand and ruminate? Do they run away? Do they switch off and tidy up around the body? Do they dream about what they have done? Do they celebrate it? Do they relive it? Do they regret it beyond the remorse of being caught? I wish I understood these things.

I have never been able to hear what they are thinking. I can hear the victims insofar as they themselves realise what is going on. Tom did not. George knew for quite a while as he strangled to death. Young Becker had a fleeting intimation. I cannot hear the murderer or murderers. I have no better clues as to their identity than you have, Inspector.

❋   ❋   ❋

More guesses about Dr. Berringer, the creepy cockroach.

He is a living stereotype, sitting on his patio under the Spanish sun, waving his long warming cocktail around in its ice-clinking glass, the straw flopping around with the motion.

He is wearing sunglasses, a panama hat, and his face is tanning by the second.

He has persuaded Carla to come into the garden to claim her ice-cream. She is licking it uncertainly as he watches her intently.

Mary Knightly, who arrived yesterday from the UK, is sipping water under a large hat under a larger umbrella.

"You spoil these children, Daddy," she says.

"Children deserve to be spoilt," Dr. Berringer counters. "They are so rewarding, and so crucial to the future."

"You could at least look as if you are enjoying it," Mary admonishes Carla.

Carla looks at her. She can tell that this strange, rather ugly old foreign woman is cross, and neither knows or cares why. She does not like the man much, and she likes her less. She is only eating this ice-cream to please him, which it seems to do. She is content to ignore the bad-tempered woman.

A chunk of ice-cream falls onto her dress. "Here, let me help you with that," Dr. Berringer offers, leaning forward with a handkerchief. He smiles straight into her face up close. She does not appreciate either his movements or his breath, yet she does not flinch, and lets him wipe the ice-cream off her front. It must have slid a long way down, as he is rubbing her below her tummy button. She steps back. "All off!" he declares. Carla says nothing. She will not bother having an ice-cream here again.

"Let me show you something," Dr. Berringer offers. Carla sees his finger beckoning her, and feels disinclined to obey its presumption. "Have you ever seen English money? It is different from your euros."

Carla can see him attempting to hand her money, and does not understand why. What must she do for it?

"Go on, have a look at it," Mary choruses impatiently. "Daddy is trying to educate you. Heaven knows, you need it."

Carla decides she is going to return to her garden. She is bored here. "Adios." She waves cheerfully, even at Mary. Jeff waves back in exaggerated child-friendly gestures.

"Sweet little thing."

"What was I like as a child, Daddy?"

"You? Rather shy. Watchful. Always concerned about what people's reaction to you would be. Hurt if they rejected you. Exploitative if they humoured you. Is that what you wanted to know?"

Mary is used to her father's dispassionate clinical analyses of people and situations. He does not allow sentimentality to distract his thoughts. He says it as it is, as he would with a patient.

"Do you remember me as a baby?"

"Naturally. I was there when you were born."

Mary glances up suddenly.

"What was I like?"

"All babies are much of a muchness at that age, except to their mothers. You cried, you fed, you mostly slept. There wasn't much to take notice of really."

"What do you most remember about me as a baby?"

Dr. Berringer pauses while he reflects. "You always had nappy rash. Your mother was always making appointments to see me to try to cure your nappy rash."

Mary winces. "Did I?"

"Yes. We got rid of it in the end."

Mary looks away into the distance. "I certainly don't have it now."

Dr. Berringer watches her. She is a strange, strained, nervy creature. "Is it hard without George?"

Mary's attention returns. "Harder than you might think. Certainly harder than I thought."

"He was devoted to you."

"And to you. I am not sure which I found the more appealing. He would have done anything for you. He did do a lot for you." Mary is watching him intently again.

"I never asked him to. Like what?"

Instead, Mary's thoughts wander to the times when her father used to come to her room, and settle down beside her. She knew he should not be doing what he was doing, sliding his hand down her body, stroking the inside of her thighs. Yet, she loved the attention and the affection between them. At that time, she felt that her father was totally devoted to her, wanted to participate in her every breath. Perhaps her mother would leave them, or die, then they could be together, just the two of them. She has to admit to herself that those moments were intensely pleasurable, if fringed with stirrings of guilt. She used to make some token, cursory gestures to resist him, "Daddy, don't do that," but he did and she permitted him to continue. His fingered exploration excited her down from the depth of her stomach. Sometimes she would quiver uncontrollably with what she later learnt to be an orgasm, although she had rarely encountered them with George. George did not have the edge of danger her father had and has. He was a good man, at least good to her, but not at all thrilling. Hesitant, always seeking approval, always consulting her. He found it hard to act spontaneously, on a hunch, and to take a risk. He was always mortified if he did something she disapproved of. He would instantly become sulky and defensive.

Mary smiles in recollection of that expression George used to pull when hurt. The shake of the head bound up with a grimace. Suddenly, she misses that. In fact, she misses a lot about George. There will never be anyone she will be close to again. She will be lonely, wasting her time organising village events and having coffee with people who really do not matter to her. There is no-one who matters to her to the extent that she would suffer from their absence for more than a few hours, except George, and her father. George was always a reassuring presence in the room, like a loyal dog.

Who had killed him, and in that horrible way? Did they have to be that brutal? It had taken Mary some time to come to terms with sharing her life, her drawing room, her bedroom with George. She used to wonder whether he would ever turn on her. She did not treat him particularly well, and she knew it. Sometimes she was loathsome towards him, and shamelessly cruel, just to see how far she could go. She could not stop herself. It was a desperate need, a headlong, repetitive urge. George never resisted, and never retaliated. He would smile behind his dark-framed spectacles and offer her some tea, or some other kindness. How could he have been so tolerant of her, without ever once giving her any cause to miss a beat?

And now someone had killed him. Was it simply a failed burglary at her parents' house? Not with a wire. No burglar would walk into a house with an electric cord intending to garrotte anyone who got in their way. It was a premeditated killing from someone who knew he would be there. They had slowly watched him die as he flailed and they maintained the pressure. They must have been strong, although if you are caught off balance it is sometimes impossible to recover unless you are thinking straight, and George was not someone who adapted well to situations. Maybe there was more than one of them. "George, I miss you." She imagines him, his face bulging, his eyes popping, swallowing as if parched, helpless. This is not the way she wants to think of him, but it is a recurring image, almost the only image she now retains of him, one that is not even real as she never saw it. It is an imaginary self-torture, persistent and remorseless.

One night, her father eased himself onto her, parting her legs first with his hands and then with his own legs. He did it slowly, careful not to frighten her. She was scared nonetheless. What was this? Why was this? She felt his fingers open her up, and his penis ram hurtfully inside her. She had screamed momentarily with the shock, so that he had feverishly covered her mouth with his hand, bearing down his full weight upon her. The breath was crushed out of her. She could no longer scream if she had wanted to which, in any case, she hadn't. It had only been that it had hurt. He took his hand away again after he had whispered that she must not make a noise and assured himself that she wouldn't, and lifted up his weight so that she could breathe again. He rocked himself backward and forward on top of her, breathing heavily. She was mesmerised by what was happening. It was bizarre what he was doing, and his body hair tickled and prickled. He was becoming more and more feverish in his wriggling and in his breathing. She could smell is underarm sweat that she usually found reassuring. It was sore and she felt bruised where his bones were rubbing hard against her. Suddenly, he stopped rigid, and she felt a warm sensation flow up her body and fill her stomach. Without a word or a gesture, he removed himself from her, got up, and left the room.

This was not how it was with George. He would stay inside her, and kiss her, and say how much he loved her. He would not want to let go of her, saying how pleasurable it was to remain inside her, how safe he felt. Then when they finally separated, he would go to the bathroom straightaway to bring her a towel and a warm wet face cloth to clean herself.

Her father walked out, leaving his sperm to leak out of her onto the bottom sheet so it was always cold, damp and sticky for the remainder of the night. She would get up and wash herself, and sometimes cry herself to sleep, not for his act of defilement, but for the fact that he left her so absolutely each time, which she took to be a cruel rejection and criticism of her. She had not performed her duty in a way she did not understand. He was disappointed in her. He wanted to punish her.

Now she realises that it was more that he wanted to punish himself. That he was degradedly ashamed of what he had done to her. Ashamed, partly repentant, but intent on returning for more soon.

Chapter 15

I am sitting here trying to re-create my mother. She was once someone other than I knew her. She was beautiful, and fierce, and courageous and savage. She frightened people with her intensity, and allured them with it too.

I lived with the intensity, each hour of each day I was around her, but I never met her spirit head on. Occasionally I caught momentary hints of it. They lasted nanoseconds. By the time I knew her, she had mellowed, she had saddened, and she had been crushed.

I used to ask her to tell me about her childhood. She always changed the subject. I used to beg her, telling her that I was asking for myself, not for her. She made it clear to me that her past was closed.

She revealed only four facts about her life. That she had been raped at the age of sixteen, and that I was the beloved product of that rape. That she hated Mary Knightly more than anyone had ever hated on this earth. That Dr. Berringer was right next to Mary on the list. And that she had been orphaned when she was very young, and she never got on with her foster parents. That is it. That was her life before I came along, and there was very little afterwards.

I never knew who Louise's father was, and I am not sure that she did. She may have been drugged out of her mind at the time, another rape producing another baby.

Recreating my mother as she was is rather like working from the bones of dinosaurs to design a verisimilitude of their actual appearance. How can you ever be sure that you are even remotely correct? The only thing you can reassure yourself with is if others are prepared to swallow your truth. That is what truth is—the belief of others. If you say that the cosmos is 15 billion years old, and weight of opinion agrees with you plus-or-minus, then that is how old it is until that belief coalesces around other data. Truth is data under-pinned by a shared belief. That is how shallow is the basis of our lives. Everything we honour can be founded on a plausible lie and a touchstone of fact.

I imagine my mother at the age of fifteen, wiry-haired, wiry-framed, wired up, challenging the boys to come and get her, to dare to get close to her, offering them an emotional fry-up, great to devour and risky for your health long-term. Somehow I see her at a fairground, on a November evening, teasing the boys, living dangerously.

Strangely this image seems to fit the way the people of Hanburgh describe her, although they appear to have been barely more acquainted with her in her youth than I. She was impossible, then she disappeared, and later they heard that she was dead.

I miss my mother. I wonder if she misses me. I want to believe that she is beside me in this library at Hanburgh House. Toss me some data, and I will turn them into truth. But the mother I want to be with is the woman of before my birth, the one who had at least a one part in a millionth possibility of living a different life. I doubt that anyone ever accorded her a greater chance than that.

There is something that has been troubling me, Inspector. I should have discussed it with you a long time ago, but for some reason I didn't.

A few days before my mother died, a man came round to our house to talk to my mother. I was upstairs listening to music, so I wasn't paying that much attention. When the front door bell rang, I glanced outside the window and got a glimpse of her visitor. I saw him for less than a second and, as he had turned away from the door waiting for it to be answered, I only caught the back of him. I could not possibly prove it, but I am convinced he was George Knightly.

❈　　❈　　❈

"Hello. It is Dave Cheveley here, The Sun."

"Hello, Dave. I have missed you."

"Yeah, right. How well did you know George Knightly?"

"I met him once at his house when I briefly joined the music festival organising committee."

"Is that all?"

"Yes, Dave."

"How well did you know Tom Becker?"

"I never even talked to him, Dave."

"Well, you're not much use to me, then, are you, Julia."

"I am afraid not."

"Happy hunting. 'Bye."

❈　　❈　　❈

It was about this time, Inspector, when we started spending our evenings together in the Hanburgh Arms. Not all our evenings, by any means, but two nights a week, at least.

I don't really know why. We just seemed drawn to each other. Ostensibly, you were pumping me for information, perhaps with a lingering suspicion that I might have been a busy lady. I had time on my hands. It was that moment of limbo when Mary and I suspected that Frank knew all about us, but we were not sure, and Mary was unwilling to confront the issue. So Mary spent her evenings at home and, ironically, Frank and I spent them in the pub, Frank with his cronies, and especially Tony James, me with you.

Our conversation was desultory and pitted with holes. After all, we were not lovers, yet we passed many pleasant hours nonetheless. To be honest, I would rather have been with Mary, and that was not possible. I am not sure where you would rather have been. You ended up with me.

"If you two spend any more time in this pub together, you had better get married, or at least buy the pub," Brenda chided us.

"Is this how you treat your best clients?" you asked. "We keep this place populated."

"Shouldn't you be out there catching criminals?"

"If you tell me who they are, I'll gladly catch them."

"Well, just about everybody in here is drinking and driving."

"Yes," you replied, "but I only catch real criminals."

"And then not."

"I will, Brenda, I will. I promise you. Just tell me who it is."

"I know, I know. I can tell you, it is really bugging me too. Perhaps I should sit down here with you, and Julia can cover for me behind the bar."

"I wouldn't know where to start," I said.

"You're right, Julia, it is not your scene. Come back when you need the money."

❋　　❋　　❋

And finally Frank admits to Mary that he knows all about us. Not all about us. Enough to be concerned.

He holds Mary by the shoulders. "It is all right, Mary. We go far deeper than this."

"Are you sure?"

"Of course I am bloody sure."

They hold each other for a long time, while the washing machine swishes out a mechanical beat.

"Do you want me to leave, my love?" Frank asks her.

"No."

"Do you want to run off with her, up to the House? Move in with her?"

"No."

"Do you want her to come and live here?"

"No, not really. I like it here with just you."

"You must have discussed it."

"We did."

"And . . . .?"

"We couldn't work out a solution either."

Frank laughs. "This is crazy. Isn't there a single unreasonable person around here anywhere?"

"No. We all want a perfect answer."

Frank sits down in his favourite chair, and holds his head in one hand.

"I couldn't believe it when I realised what was happening, although it was obviously true. Strangely, it wasn't really a shock either. It was simply a question. What do we do now? I have so much faith in you, so much love for you, I can not believe that we can ever go wrong."

"We won't."

"We had better get Julia round and thrash it out then, man to woman to woman to man."

"You must have been practising that line, darling."

"Funnily enough, not. It just occurred to me as I said it. Give Julia a call now."

When I ring at the front door, Frank quickly answers it. "Come in Julia. It is nice to see you."

I search his eyes for sarcasm or malice. There isn't any that I can detect. "Come and sit down. Let me get you a drink. Vodka and coke, I assume. I have sat there watching you drinking it enough times, or do you fancy a change?"

"No, that is good for me. Hello, Mary."

Mary smiles wanly at me, and points me towards a single chair, what we used to call a "comfy chair", although it isn't at this moment.

Frank comes back into the sitting room. "Here you are, Julia. Cheers."

"Cheers."

"Can I say one thing?" Frank begins.

"Of course."

"Well, two actually. The first is that I feel no animosity towards you whatsoever, Julia. You love Mary, I can see that, and why shouldn't you? I love her too."

"OK."

"And the second one is that we are going to sort this thing out somehow. No-one here is going to get hurt any more than they choose to be."

"That is very generous, Frank."

"I am being honest, Julia, and pragmatic, and I would ask you to be the same."

"I will."

"Good, then we understand each other. So, Julia, the big question is what do we do from here?"

"I don't know, Frank."

"Even better. Then there are no foregone conclusions."

"No."

"No," repeats Mary.

"Can we carry on as before?" Frank inquires. "As if I didn't know?"

"You do know."

"All right. Does it have to be any issue at all? Do we just play it by ear?"

"Yes, we could do that."

"No," Frank contradicts me, "we can't. If we do that, things will drift. There will be misunderstandings. There will be jealousies. Things will get ugly. We need to agree a solution we are all entirely comfortable with."

"But what is it?"

"I'm buggered if I know."

Mary leans forward. "Julia, will you stay the night?"

Frank looks startled.

Mary continues. "Let's try it."

"Try what?" asks Frank.

"Let's try it," Mary repeats.

"You mean a three-some?" Frank challenges.

"I mean a relationship between the three of us, however it works out."

"I am not sure I can cope with that," Franks admits.

"None of us are, Frank. This is new territory for all of us," Mary consoles him. "So get your kit off!"

"You have got to be bloody joking."

Mary fixes him with a straight look. "No."

So we try it. Mary undresses me. I have never seen eyes on stalks, but those are Frank's eyes. Then we undress Frank. He protests ineffectually. Naked, his feet actually do not smell. He is more attractive that I would have guessed. He stands there, exposed. There is a hesitation between Mary and me. How do we relax him? After a few seconds, I drop to my knees and start to pleasure him. He is literally sucked into our relationship. From there it is easier. The peace treaty is sealed. It is not what he would have voted for, but it is what we can all accept. All of us. We are not exactly home, but we are past the hotel room.

❋   ❋   ❋

And then there is the miscarriage. I am excluded again. Frank and Mary close ranks. It is their grief. They have been trying to have a child for many years. That opportunity eludes them in a slurry of blood and despair.

They refuse to answer my calls. Frank bars the door on me. Mary must be left to rest. It is a grief I am not allowed to share in. I was only an intruder after all.

Back to the pub, and to you, Inspector.

Back to my empty house, and to rooms that absorb my thoughts. Back to an empty diary, and no Tom to talk to, no Mary. Back to the beginning, and you, Inspector, do not count. You are only making weight.

Eventually, Mary comes to my front door with a suitcase in her hands. "Julia, I have to go away. Will you come with me?"

"What about Frank?"

"He will stay here. He will hold the fort. We will all be back together, but, for now, I need to escape. Save me."

Well, I already have my assignment from you. I have to write about everything I have seen. "Come in, Mary. I will only be a few minutes."

I search the Internet, and find the house in Bézier. I try to book it from tomorrow. It takes. I search Ryanair. £423 for two one-way tickets. "Your payment has been accepted. Your confirmation is XYC4RC." We leave immediately.

❉　　❉　　❉

We drive out to the lake about 20 minutes away from the mill. Su and David, who own the mill, have told us it is worth visiting, and that there is a community of Brits who live out there. They have under-played it. I don't know why.

We approach it down a road which is returning to the rough track whence it started. Some signs went up the other day, saying "Beware. Poor road surface." We wonder what they thought it was like three months ago. We worry whether we will need a four-by-four to complete the journey.

There is deep gorge to our left, and then, unannounced, a stunning, shy, elegant viaduct with a track running across it. A couple of tourists are standing midway. Entering the village, having branched onto the main road, there is a second one, its brasher, blowsier elder sister, curvaceous, colonnaded, and the lake, the deepest of turquoise.

There is a beach all around the lake, and an island that even small children can almost walk to through the water. The wind is gusting hard and warm on this bright October day. There is a sparse population of families spread across the shore and into the water in cheerful groups. Several of the women could raise the water level by several inches if they were ever to join their hippopotami relatives. Instead, two of them are dancing, without music.

"I am suddenly feeling slim again," Mary remarks.

We lie on the beach and watch. We, too, are being surveyed surreptitiously but not intrusively. Our emotions together are still for the first time since we left England, maybe even for the first time.

"What a wonderful place," Mary adds.

"I wasn't expecting anything like this."

We hug up, and the locals seem entirely comfortable with our behaviour.

Back in Su and David's restaurant, El Almendro, we castigate them for not selling us the lake properly. "Yes, it is beautiful," they say. "It is excellent for children." I glance at Mary. She steals herself not to react, and continues to smile.

"Nice place you have here."

"Thanks."

The chef is on show in that the kitchen is only separated from the dining area by a long, low counter. He looks to be enjoying himself. He is obviously not the sort of chef who throws pans around when things get tense. Alternatively, the diners are the sorts of people who know how to dive under the tables at the sight of trouble.

"It hasn't happened yet," Su remarks. "We did have some trouble before the restaurant opened, though. There was a dispute with the plasterers over money, and one of them picked up a hammer and threatened to smash the place up if we did not pay him what he was demanding. Our partner, Paul, grabbed hold of a wrench, and threatened to trade damage to the man's head blow-for-blow."

"Now *that* is more like a real chef," I observe.

We move to eat outside on the square. There are tables dotted around under candlelight.

Mary fixes me with a gaze of oblique intensity. "Julia, why do I always get the impression that most of you travels separately? There is a third person missing from this table—the rest of you."

"What do you mean exactly?"

"Who are you exactly?"

"Please, Mary, let's not fight."

"I am not trying to fight, Julia. I am trying to get access to the greater part of you which you deprive me of, which never shows up."

"What part is that?"

"I really wish I knew."

"There is nothing to say. You know everything about me, about my mother, about my childhood, about my sister, about my car crash, about my life as a City trader, about what I like to eat, and what I like to do. Please tell me, Mary, what you need to know."

"I need to know the bit I don't know. The bit you hide from me, and therefore almost certainly from everyone."

"And maybe from myself."

"No, not from yourself. You are extremely aware of it. That is why you hide it. What do you think? That if I knew everything about you, I would hate you? That I would be ashamed of you? That I would love you any the less?"

"Undoubtedly."

"You are wrong, Julia. It is more that we cannot love each other completely until all of us is here, at this table, in this square, infront of this restaurant, in this village, in Andalucia, now."

"I am not sure that he is free tonight."

"He?"

"A slip of the tongue. A manner of speaking."

"Now that is interesting."

"You think it is a Freudian slip."

"No, I think it is a confession."

"How, exactly?"

"You once said that you could not technically be a lesbian. What did you mean?"

"Only that I have also slept with men."

"With how many men?"

"Well, you know about Tom, and about Frank."

"Yes."

"Do you really want a list? Do we have to talk about this?"

"Only if I matter to you."

"Of course you matter to me."

"Then how many other men have you slept with?"

"Not many."

"Not many, or not any?"

"You are being very persistent, Mary."

"And you are refusing to be truthful."

"I have not lied to you. I don't think I have ever lied to you."

"And even less have you told me anything like the truth."

"So you suspect I am hiding a deep dark secret somewhere."

"I suspect that you think it is dark."

I try to listen to Mary's thoughts. They are steely. Focused.

"We all have things we are ashamed of."

"And now is the moment to talk about them."

"So what are yours?"

"Uh-uh! We are discussing you, Julia. We can do me tomorrow."

"I look forward to it."

"So . . . . why did you really come to Hanburgh?"

"To meet you."

"Charming, but 100% untrue."

"You are discounting destiny. That may well have been the purpose."

"I am not really talking about the cosmos, Julia. What was your purpose?"

"To take revenge?"

"To take revenge on whom?"

"On those people who made my mother's life hell when she lived there."

"Who was your mother?"

"Lucy Benson."

"Oh my God! I knew she had one daughter, but I thought she died of cancer or something when she was only a small child."

"Leukaemia."

"So she had two daughters?"

"No, she only had the one."

Mary tugs at her hair in frustration. "Julia, I am totally lost here. Who are you?"

"She also had a son."

"Had?"

"Yes. He died too."

"And?"

"And he was reborn as me."

"As you?"

"Yes."

"You used to be a man?"

"Quite a man, actually."

"You mean that I am really in love with a man?"

"Hard to say." I grin. "I hate to categorise."

Mary takes my right hand, and ostentatiously and deliberately strokes it.

"That is truly extraordinary."

"Now I may have to kill you."

"Is that what people do when they return from the dead?"

"It does make things easier. They are harder to trace."

"Are you really planning on killing me?"

"No, of course not, Mary."

"Are you planning on killing anyone?"

"Yes." I sit back. "And I think it is the time."

❄   ❄   ❄

Chapter 16

I am home. There is that usual thrill of expectation as I re-enter my house after my holiday, and that immediate disappointment as I realise that it is just the same as I left it, only filled with dead air.

Having checked into each room to ensure that there has been no interference in my belongings (there hasn't been), I go to collect Gargoyle from the kennels.

He is so pleased to see me, he is all wags, licks and leaps for over 15 minutes. It is horrible in its way. I abandon him for months, and he is so grateful for my return. If I were him, I would bite me, and I, being me, would respect him for it.

I have to wait a further twenty minutes before I drive off because I am terrified that he will leap the seats and get under my feet.

He is even more excited once he is let into the house. He is everywhere, scrabbling, snuffling and barking.

I have to leave him there and get out. I must announce my arrival to Hanburgh, and where better than the pub? It will be an ordeal. Just another one. I will be swamped with questions about Mary I cannot answer. So be it. I will face them down (Frank will be the worst), and no doubt I will live to tell another tale.

I enter the Hanburgh Arms. Brenda is behind the bar, and immediately says "Hi, Julia! What a surprise! Where's Mary?" Jeff Berringer is standing at the bar with Mary Knightly. Jeff does not bother with me at all. Mary notices me, and looks away.

I hug Brenda. "I'll be back in a minute, Brenda," I stall her. "There is something I forgot to bring in from the car."

"A present?" she asks.

"And certainly thoroughly deserved," I reply. "I hope that the recipient learns to understand the significance."

Brenda looks puzzled. "I'll try."

I go to the boot of the car, and retrieve my "present". Entering the lounge, I am holding the petrol can, with its cap removed, in my left hand, slightly behind me so that it cannot easily be seen in the time I need to do this. In my right hand, the cheap non-refillable lighter is at the ready. I only have a few seconds of opportunity and I have never done this before. I have never even practised it.

Jeff is ignoring me naturally—he does not know who I am, and if he did he wouldn't care. Mary is ignoring me studiously, not even attempting to hide the sour expression besmirching her face.

I march smartly forward, lift the can, and glug the contents all over Jeff's silver head. It takes so long to pour out. I needed another air hole in the can, ideally. Too late. Fortunately, Jeff is slow to react. Eventually, he throws his left arm up in the air, drops his pint against the top of the bar, from which it crashes to the floor spilling beer everywhere but not breaking, and swears "What the hell?"

I flick the lighter, and he immediately conflagrates ingloriously in the flames of hell fire. What the hell indeed!

Mary Knightly hurls herself into the corner of the room and crouches there. I smile at her graciously. It is almost fun standing over her as she anticipates pitifully that I will do the same to her. Instead, I prefer to kill her with condescension. "I am sorry, Mary," I declare. "You are evil, but not evil enough for that. I forgive you."

Brenda is squirting Jeff with the soda siphon, trying desperately to dowse the flames. She looks at me with horror and dread. "Take your time, Brenda," I advise her. "There is no rush. I love you. Bye." Dr. Berringer, I am pleased to see, is writhing around in frantic anguish, aflame from head to toe. Soda siphons are useless in that sort of emergency.

I am off to find you, Inspector. There is nobody I would rather meet up with now in my moment of vengeful triumph.

Hurrah for Julia! Hurrah for Julian!

✳ ✳ ✳

An Inspector's Tale

Chapter 17

"Julia, Julia, what have you done?"

She faces me calmly, her dark, sharp eyes almost twinkling at me. "Is he dead?"

"It's touch and go."

"Well, I hope that the touch is painful."

"No remorse then?"

"No remorse, Inspector. You know what he has being doing over many years. You know the lives he has ruined. You have never tried to stop him. Who is the guiltier, I or you?"

"Taking the law into your own hands is never right."

"Not applying the law when it is your job to is never right either, John."

"We couldn't pin him down. There were never any credible witnesses. Most of his victims refused to talk. Those who would were so distraught as to be unreliable. We would never have succeeded in obtaining a conviction."

"Don't you think it was your duty to stop him, whatever the price, because the price others have been paying for your lapse has been so much higher?"

"We cannot waste public funds going after people on whom we could never secure a conviction. The Crown Prosecution Service would never let us proceed."

"I admire your courage, John."

"And I regret yours."

"So be it."

"So, will you confess?"

"Of course I will confess. There is no question that I poured petrol all over Jeff Berringer while the state of my mind was temporarily disturbed. I shall tell the story in court of how many people in Hanburgh knew exactly what was happening, of how many victims there have been of his paedophilia, of the depths of their suffering and of their many suicides, of the extent to which the police were fully aware of his filthy activities and chose to do nothing to stop him. I only set fire to Jeff. I am now going to blow this whole village apart."

"I never realised you were quite so angry. So can you explain why you killed Tom Willows, George Knightly and Tom Becker?"

"I never killed any of those people, as you well know. It was at best a coincidence that I was near them at the times of their deaths, and at worst a plot to incriminate me."

"And whose plot was that then, in your far from humble opinion?"

"I keep saying that I really haven't got a clue. I do not know who hated them. If it was intended to incriminate me, I don't know who hated me. I have certainly pissed off a few people around here, but I have not actually made an enemy out of them, as far as I am aware. Except perhaps Mary Knightly, and she hates everyone. If she were the killer, she would be stitching up the entire village, and maybe anyone she has ever met."

"So you will not be confessing to the murders?"

"As you well know, Inspector, a false confession not only puts an innocent person in gaol, it also leaves the guilty one free and, from the look of things, you have a serial killer on your hands. He may well kill again."

"He, or she, seems to have stopped for the moment. Since you left the country, in fact."

"Console yourself with that, then, Inspector. I will not compound your complacency."

❊   ❊   ❊

I have had three appalling shocks today. They are to be expected when, like me, you investigate the ugliest corners of our existence, yet I have never, ever, had a day like this.

I am reeling. Rather, I was reeling. I am now lying on my back on these cold tiles, my head resting on my pinched hands, the knuckles frozen and bruised against the floor, gazing intently at the ceiling, examining the cracks, the chips, the paint slopped over the plastic of the light fitting, the caked dust of the bulb hanging there. Hanging there.

Julia was found in her cell this morning, hanging there. Her throat was strangled blue and raw, her face bloated over its sharp structure. For the size of her personality, her frame was surprisingly slight as it hung like a pepper from a bush.

My darling Julia, did either of us deserve this? You were so special to me, and I think that you were fond of me too behind your teasing, mocking ways. You had such a blighted life, hurt, battered, angry, crazed. I suppose that it was an inevitable end, and maybe better than the alternative—many long years of imprisonment.

They took your body away for an autopsy four hours ago. I have rarely seen any personally sadder sight.

And the repercussions! A woman dowses a renowned paedophile at large with petrol and sets fire to him because no-one will do anything about him. The villagers have done nothing to stop him over twenty to thirty years, and nor have the police. She is arrested, and shortly afterwards is found hanging in a police cell, having apparently committed suicide. What a gift to the conspiracy theorists! A suspect who is denouncing the police for their gross negligence is found dead in her cell. The newspapers are already phoning in a thousand at a time. Somehow Dave Cheveley of The Sun got through to me but, generally, it is a wonderful day for any petty criminals to go about their rounds. Nobody could report them, even if they wanted to. All the lines are jammed. And I bet you that somebody will do just that. I know human nature, or at least I sometimes believe that I do.

The second shock that happened two hours ago was when Joey, one of our French-speaking team, phoned l'Inspecteur Herbert in Béziers. Scanning through Julia's narrative, it seemed opportune to try to contact him.

"You have found her?" he exclaimed.

"Found her? Well, we know where she is. We didn't know you were looking for her."

"Half of France is looking for her. Half of the rest of Europe is supposedly looking for her too. We want her in connection with the murder of Mlle. Alice Picard, although we have yet to find her body. If you have her, we would like to extradite her without any delay."

"She is dead."

"Oh."

"She died this morning. She killed herself."

"Are you sure?"

"You think someone killed her?"

"No. I want to make sure that she is dead."

"Yes, she is definitely dead."

"Oh, I am sorry."

"Yes, so are we"

"It is an odd thing to say, perhaps. We need her for trial here."

"Too late, I am afraid."

"Yes, that is the end of our hopes. How did she die?"

"She hanged herself."

"How did she manage to do that?"

"With a rope. We don't know how she got hold of it."

"Ah. We don't have the death penalty in France."

"Nor in Britain, I assure you."

"Not officially, anyway."

"Not at all."

"Well, thank you for contacting me. We will need to talk again. I must make a formal statement to the press here. I assume that I will be in a position to provide copies of all your paperwork to my superiors."

"We will be pleased to co-operate with you."

"When will that be?"

"I am not sure. Possibly three to four weeks, maximum two months."

"That is not acceptable. This is a case of national importance."

"For us, too. We will do our best."

"I will have our Ministry of the Interior contact yours."

"You do that."

"Thank you."

The third shock came an hour ago. We had an e-mail from Records as they could not get through by phone. There is only one record of a Julia Blackburn. Two years ago, she formally changed her name from Julian Benson. He never officially changed his sex.

Julian Benson. I knew his mother, Lucy Benson, very well. I was madly in love with her. I adored her. No wonder I was so fond of Julia. That is the link—invisible but detectable. That energy between us, that genetic affection.

Lucy was magnificent, untouchable. She was considered too wild to be handled as a child, too hot to be handled as a teenager, and too tragic to be handled as an adult. She drove Tom Willows mad with the desire of the unattainable, and me.

"I realise what I do to people," she once told me, "and there is nothing I can do about it. After what happened to me, I cannot stand anyone anywhere near me. If you want me, John, you will have to rape me. Maybe I will forgive you. Maybe it will cure me, but I will fight you, and bite you, and scratch you, and kick you, and do anything to stop you all the same."

The savage laser expression was quite enough to scare me off at the time. She kept her nails more like talons, and she had already bitten me once. It hurt like hell while she told me that she felt a lot for me, that I was very special to her. Love hurts.

"And Tom?"

"Tom? Tom? Tom is a dog!" and she shook her hair in disgust.

What had happened to her was Jeff Berringer, of course. And it was Mary Knightly, her sister, who betrayed her to him. She came rushing round to Lucy's foster parents' house one night, begging to speak to Lucy. It was so urgent, it was a matter of life or death.

"Lucy, are you up there?"

"Yes."

"Can you come down? Your sister, Mary, has something urgent she needs to talk to you about."

"I'll be down in a few minutes. There is just something I have to finish off."

When she finally came down, Mary grabbed her arm. "You have got to come and talk to them. I am desperate. You have got to help me." Mary's beseeching brown eyes are still very persuasive.

"OK."

Lucy rushed round with Mary to where she lived. They ran into the house. Only Jeff was there, in the sitting room, waiting for her. He grabbed her coldly, and meticulously raped her, while Mary watched, exultant. Mary was ten. Lucy was twelve.

But that is not how Julian was born. Well, it sort of was, I suppose.

❄   ❄   ❄

Another day, and another shock. The French police have told us that they have never heard of Mary Maloney.

We have started our search for her body in the garden of Hanburgh House. Nothing yet.

❄   ❄   ❄

I must take some fresh air. With the renewed press attention, it is difficult to decide where to go. I would naturally head for the pub, and have a couple of pints and maybe something to eat, but I wouldn't get a moment to myself in there. The reporters would pile in on me first, then the good people of Hanburgh would descend for the late pickings.

I decide to walk up the dale. It is getting rather late, so I will not be going very far, but it is peaceful climbing up the hill accompanied by the clacking of my footsteps. I am passing Hanburgh House. From the road I can see a light through the branches of the trees. There should be nobody there that I know of. Forensics must have left hours ago. Who else would be there?

I enter the driveway, trying to step quietly over the gravel. As soon as I can, I transfer to the grass which means tangling with the large conifer tree that dominates the top part of the garden. The light is in the hallway. There is no obvious sign of movement.

I peer up close to the window. There is someone there. I can see a shadow. Suddenly, a face looms up right opposite mine through the glass. It is deathly pale, and yet totally recognisable. My brain screams "Julia" at me, as I turn and run, and do not let up until I reach the bottom of the hill and the heart of the village.

Maybe I was wrong. Perhaps a car's headlights sweeping up the hill showed me my own reflection. Sometimes, thinking back, it could have been Lucy. In my memory, she seemed to be trying to kiss me through the glass. That is the sort of thing Lucy would have done, Julia never. However, on balance, and trying to lay all prejudices and expectations aside, I am convinced it was Julia. I will swear it to my dying day.

It was a cowardly response to run away, a betrayal. I had been so close to her over recent months, and yet also so far, as I am discovering. However, when your survival instincts take over, and the danger appears immediate and acute, you just leg it, don't you?

I went back the next morning in the safer light of day. I have to admit that I was, if not terrified, nervous to the extent of a trembling body and icy skin. The light was still on in the hallway, and there was not the slightest possibility of my going inside to turn it off. I marched straight up the driveway this time, and peered sharply at the window, ready to run, and initially from a much greater distance. The sun glinted on the window. I had to move obliquely to my left to slip the reflection, which also meant I had to edge closer and closer to the window. I kept glancing into the sitting room, daring another face to appear. Nothing yet, a step further, nothing yet. At last, I had a clear view. The reflection had edged into the corner. And there, in the middle of the window, at human height, was some lipstick in the shape of a kiss.

❋　　❋　　❋

Mary Knightly phones me at the station. The lines are clear now.

"Is it correct that Julia Blackburn was really Julian Benson, my nephew?"

"Yes, Mary, that is correct. What a sad story. What a sorry waste of so many lives."

"That makes me her next of kin," she ruminates.

I cannot fucking believe it. In the midst of all this human misery, Mary is counting her inheritance, creating it almost.

I chuckle. I have never enjoyed saying anything as much as I enjoyed telling Mary Knightly this. "Not exactly, Mary. I was his father. So, as I say to all my clients, I'll see you in court."

The protracted silence at the other end of the line is most gratifying. I can almost see her speechless face, her peevish eyes as she settles down to concoct another plan.

❋　　❋　　❋

Julia, it is your funeral today. It is turning into the usual media circus witch hunt. The press knows it has discovered a perfect story of sex and death, steeped with lashings of shame and degradation, to be unearthed, like open-caste diamonds, with a minimum of digging. The dust is stirring. I am about to be torn apart.

As a policeman of over thirty years, I have experienced these atavistic rituals before, where morality is deliberately outraged to stoke money. There is so much cash to be made here, so many ephemeral reputations that will ultimately only survive in career reminiscences around a rowdy old codgers' beer-soaked table, so much popular anger to unleash.

Barely constrained below the surface of us all, lies the magma of outrage against the world and its failure to deliver on its promises to us. We complain about the injustices suffered by others, but only as a reflection, as a star to a moon, of our own grievous disappointments. Everything, but everything, we are told by our parents, by school, by the media, by the church, and by politicians is a lie, or at least an extreme over-sell, designed to make us want to carry on.

I don't know where we should start the cycle of life, but let us say that two teenagers meet each other, as I met your mother. The promise is that they will fall in love, albeit after a tense and complicated act of courtship, have a fairy-tale marriage where they are the stars and everyone smiles all the time, especially at key moments of the ceremony such as the "I do", the "I now declare you man and wife", the speeches, and the cutting of the cake. They go on to have perfect little babies who will be brought up in wondrous familial harmony to become handsome, exciting, professional achievers, and renew the cycle with their own lives. The promise rather glosses over our twilight years, except as supporting players to the new generation.

I think that it is a safe bet to assume that no-one has ever experienced this, but we all peddle it, first and foremost to ourselves. We determinedly suspend disbelief in order to build the energy and optimism to remain in the game.

Many criminals are just sad and unfortunate individuals, even more stupid, and bungling, and shambolic than I am. Some, however, are true masters of deception. I have often observed that in everyday life we tell many lies. We tell other people lies, or fashioned versions of our truth. However, we tell many more lies to ourselves. A successful liar is someone who has told himself the lie before he attempts to convince anyone else, and he has believed it. We are all adept at deceiving ourselves first and foremost, which is why we cling to life.

And what is the truth? The truth is like taking out a bunch of OAPs with cataracts, and asking them to describe the world. Through the fog, they earnestly attempt to tell you what they believe they are seeing, but their observations are viewed through the lenses of their experiences, and they are heavily influenced by both the passionate and the sceptical commentators heckling and contesting from the side.

So, life is the same for all of us, Julia. You are not unique. In truth, it is not worth living for any of us, but we persuade ourselves to bear with its continuous worry, stresses, daily insults and oppressions in the bleak, unfounded, optimism that tomorrow the promise will be delivered. We have deserved it for coming so far. We have paid our dues, now give us the pension.

Every time until now, I have been an onlooker, or even a ring-master, for the broil of the crime story of the moment. Safe behind my barrier of microphones, I have been the man doggedly tracking down the wrong-doers. Occasionally, the press has turned on me in frustration at my slow process, but it has attacked my competence not my integrity.

This time, I am the story. Despite being brought up in Hanburgh, despite being fully aware of Dr. Berringer's antics, why did I do nothing? What happened to you in that cell? Was it suicide, or was it an execution to cover our tracks, perhaps ordered by the Home Office? So far, the newspapers have focused more on the moral corruption of the police than on my personal responsibility, but the police committee is clearly trying to edge it that way, the "rotten apple in the barrel" defence.

They obviously know nothing about our relationship and, for my sins, I am toying with the idea of using it to regain an element of human sympathy—"the tortured discovery of Inspector Plod: his long-lost son became a woman and a serial murderess, and died tragically in his arms in a lonely police cell, having confessed all." I'll only use it if the police commission succeed in frying me, if then. It will be a tricky, double-edged line of defence.

And so to you, Julia, on the day of your bodily release from this earth, the day when you are reduced to dust so that you can fly away. I need to return the compliment, and write a shorter love letter to you, for that is how I interpret your submission, as a love letter to your father despite being overtly unaware of my identity. Subconsciously, I think you realised who I was, and that I recognised you too through your disguise. You designed your writings to be an oblique confession, secreted, as with much of your life, behind an elaborately woven miasma of lies—a confession that only I would be capable of interpreting, a private bond between us.

What can I say?

My first impression of you too was as a shadow through the glass, which was fairly appropriate given that I was there to arrest you for one of the most gruesome murders I have ever investigated. My one concern was that I could not understand how a woman would have the strength to deliver such a blow. It was a man's blow.

The minute I caught a glimpse of your face, you captured my interest. I hid it. I walked straight past you into the sitting room. You were right, I already knew the house. I used to attend Robert Markham's birthday parties as a child. They used to be great parties. I wasn't used to being invited to houses like that. It was wonderful to have so many rooms to hide in when it came to playing sardines. The Markhams are an exceptionally friendly family too, fallen on harder times, I am afraid.

So, at that stage, I was probably more at ease in your house than you were. I do not know whether your mother ever went to those parties. I cannot remember her there, and she tended to be resolutely memorable wherever she was. Mary Knightly was there at least once or twice, though, I recall.

It is strange walking into a house you are familiar with only to discover it to have been totally disguised, and betrayed, by the new occupants. Not only are most of the fixtures and furnishings apparently out of place, the whole atmosphere changes. Luckily, when I visited Hanburgh House that day, you had barely moved in, so it more resembled an empty house being worked upon.

The first time that you meet someone whom you believe may be the one responsible for the crime, you are asking yourself all the time "Is it him/her?", "Is it him/her?", "Is it him/her?", especially for more important cases, and even more especially if you are me (a very committed tracking angel, even after all these years). I could name a whole roomful of police professionals who probably don't do anything of the sort. They simply stand there and listen. That may even be the better way, but I am a hyperactive questioner. I need to provoke a reaction. You can metaphorically wait in ambush for the criminal to mix up his facts and disclose himself. I attack to drive people off-balance. Sometimes they fall over, as you did literally. I play it pretty rough.

I couldn't work out at all where you were as I was questioning you. I could not settle on a clear view. I thought you were dangerous, perhaps a little unhinged. Mary Knightly later described you this way, and I agreed with her. You were self-evidently extremely clever, and trying to use your intelligence to unnerve me. This made you a potential serial killer. Psychopaths and sociopaths enjoy toying with their pursuers like that, teasing them, provoking them, proving to themselves that they can outwit them. However, they go out of their way to create opportunities to humiliate us, and you did not do that. Your approach was more defensive. Where I attacked you, you snapped back, to hurt. And I still could not understand how a woman could have split Tom Willows in two.

Anyway, you were clearly not going to crack, and there was no evidence that you were any danger to anyone else, so I had to let you go. But I did still keep coming back to you, partly because you never escaped my suspect list, partly because I became increasingly fascinated by you. I am glad now that I did. It was to honour you.

You claimed in your account of events that I was fantasising about you sexually, that all I wanted to do was to talk you into removing your clothes so that I could enjoy you bodily. I can honestly say that this was never the case. My interest in you was emotional, and indeed intuitive. There was something between us, and I never discovered what it was while you were still alive. Through my cataracts, I could perceive that there was a truth, but I could not decode it. It never occurred to me that I was spending all this time in the presence of my son. Equally, I assume, you never realised that I was your father, although I am convinced that you too were experiencing the same pull towards me.

And no, I did not think you had any sexual designs upon me. I have never inspired that. Late into a drunken party, I once told a girl that I fancied her, as did the rest of the amateur football team I played with.

"Really?" she said. "They all fancy me?"

"Every single one of us," I confessed, exaggerating somewhat.

"Oh." She seemed appropriately flattered, and bemused that I was telling her, although she will no doubt have guessed why. "And where do you play in the team?"

"Do you know anything about football?" I asked.

"Enough."

"I play right back."

She smirked, and disconnected from me, as if she had been insulted. "I only go with centre forwards and goalkeepers," she announced, and sidled off.

So there you are, in the mating game I play right back. If I score, it will be a once in a lifetime achievement.

So how did I become your father, you would have been asking yourself (if you weren't already dead)? Well, that was sort of scoring, and sort of striking, I suppose.

Your mother, Lucy, and I had a strange, tugging relationship, similar to us in fact. We were tied to each other, but never together. We struggled with the ropes, to be free of them, or to be closer to each other.

Lucy was a very dangerous girl, and then woman, when I knew her. She unnerved everyone. She was the village's rock star, burning towards an early death, capable of great fun and brutal rebuffs. The one thing she would absolutely not surrender up willingly to anyone was her body. Yet she wanted to. She temperamentally couldn't, and she was increasingly desperate to have the experience. She went out of everyone's way to experience everything.

I can almost remember Lucy and her sister, Mary, as very small children, as I almost still was, before their parents died. While I am not absolutely sure that it is a true memory, I recall that Mary was the sweet one, and Lucy was already wild. That is why the Berringers only adopted Mary. Lucy would already have ripped him to pieces.

Lucy made a terrible confession to me that day, just before we made love. Mary begged her many times to help her against Dr. Berringer, without exactly telling Lucy why. Lucy was envious of Mary, who was living in a nice house with a respectable family, whereas Lucy's situation was what it had always been, except in the additional absence of her parents. Lucy simply ignored Mary, and let her rot. This is no doubt why one day Mary got her revenge, enticing Lucy to suffer just once what was probably a daily ritual for her (as you also imagined it), to make her understand at last. Mary became a very bitter woman, and Lucy subsequently exploded.

"I hate Mary," she shouted. "I loathe that little scum. Smirking as she tricked me into it. A real sneaky little rat. Vermin." She glared at me, challenging me to imply that she may have been partly to blame. "Do you know what it is like when you go through a door, and it shuts behind you, and you absolutely know that you are about to be torn apart, fouled throughout, head to toe, and possibly destroyed? And there was Mary, watching me out of the corner of her face, measuring the pleasure of her spite. That man coming towards me like an executioner. The shock as he slips your clothes undone before you realise he has even touched them. His cold, deliberate hand. Your freezing, frozen soul. Unable to move. The fear in your bum, the panic. I watched everything he did to me in great detail, and from a safe distance. I am sure that he did the same. It was so precise, so practiced. Mary, over his shoulder, was scared and happy, and even jealous, I think. Can you imagine that? She was actually jealous and angry with me. She hated me, just in case he preferred me. And I think he did. I taunted Mary with that afterwards. I told her he craved me, but he would settle for her because at least she was always available. It was a horrible thing to say, but I think it stopped her procuring anyone else for him. She couldn't take the competition, silly cow." She stared me out again. "So what do you think?"

"I think it is horrific." I said dutifully, trying to fill my voice with shock, although I must admit that I was more turned on by the story.

"Does it excite you?"

I stood back. "Of course not."

"If I said he took a film of it all, would you watch it with me?"

"He took a film?"

"Yes."

"Have you got it?"

"Do you want to watch it?"

"No, I don't."

"Everybody else wants to see me naked."

I waited. Lucy was grabbing my shoulders. "You don't?"

"Not like that."

"And like this?"

"Not at this moment," I declared chivalrously, hoping that she would not let it go at that. "Not after that story."

"It's not so bad," she laughed. "At least I am not still a virgin, unlike some. Are you still a virgin, John?" She usually called me "Johnny". The switching of my name was significant.

"Yes," I admitted.

"Are you ashamed?"

"A bit. I think I am being left behind."

"You are a very honest boy, John."

"I try to be."

"Do you still want to be a policeman?"

"Yes."

"Do you want to experience what it is like to be a criminal? A really bad criminal. One of the worst. Totally safely?"

"I don't understand."

"It's OK. Relax." She stroked my face. "Rape me!"

I must have swallowed loud enough to wake up the whole village. The phlegm got in the way of my voice, and falsettoed it. "What?"

"Get on with it. But don't expect it to be easy. I am going to give you two black eyes while you do it, and I'll never tell anyone why."

"This is crazy."

"That's me. Get on with it. It's your only chance, ever."

She turned to walk away. "Stop."

"That's better," she smiled triumphantly, and slapped me as hard as she could across my face.

I grabbed her. She pushed me away, although I could tell that it was not with her full strength. She punched me in the eye. That did it. That really angered me, and I went for her. Somehow her clothes became successively ripped. She punched me in the other eye, and I knocked her to the ground, wrestled with her for minutes, then finally shoved myself into her and rode her. It was just like riding a cantering horse that is much more powerful than you, and yet is tolerating you. After I foamed inside her, which did not take me long, we lay quietly together.

"How do I explain my eyes?" I said. I could barely see through them, and they were watery and aching.

"You'll think of something. You can lie on top of me for a bit, John, while you figure it out."

That is when we had you. I am sure that Lucy was planning to have you. I doubt she really wanted a baby as a human being. I think she wanted you more as an act of revolt. When she discovered that her rebellion resulted in a mundane routine of child care, I think it destroyed her. It dragged her down. I don't mean you. She absolutely adored you, but having you finished her life. She could no longer convince herself that she could be brilliant. She was just a sad, lonely single mother with a baby.

She didn't have to be. I offered to marry her. I loved her. She was not remotely interested. She barely talked to me after that. And she broke Tom Willows' heart too. That was deliberate. She wanted to hurt men in general, and Tom in particular. I am not sure why, beyond that fact that he really did love her.

I suppose you thought he was your father, did you? That must have hurt. You didn't like Tom much, did you? What were you doing, going round there and seducing him, the man you thought was your father? It must have been your mother inside you. How could you let him undress you, and take you, and play along with him, planning all the time, I assume, to murder him? Was it sheer anger at Mary, Mary Maloney, that you wanted to hurt your father that much? When did you realise that he wasn't your dad, or did you always believe he was? That was a sick mind you had that day, my son. Sick, warped, crazy, dangerous. And I do not even get the impression that it touched you. His death was simply something you had to lie about to survive, which you did consummately, scattering clues around all the while, like an extended, high stakes session of "Call my bluff." Did she, didn't she, how could she? Repeat. Repeat.

And no doubt you dropped in the fact that Sally Willows was around that day to implicate her, yet the strange thing is that she really was. That totally threw me. I suppose that you thought I had picked up the bait, yet it was in fact the live fish. Why she disappeared again, I have never been able to work out. I have sometimes wondered whether there was something happening between them, and she could not afford to have the whole thing surface. Anyway, she was on the trail of the murderer like a possessed creature, yet she never believed it was you. Why? Everyone thought it was you, except I who should have arrested you, and Sally who should have killed you. We were the only two who were 100% convinced of your innocence. Perhaps we were both totally hooked on its being a man's crime. Sally did say to me "I can be incredibly violent sometimes, but I would never have had the physical strength to have done that. And Henry Spence thinks he has done such a brilliant job disguising it all. Ridiculous man! Complete wanker!" And she laughed in that Sally way of hers.

❄   ❄   ❄

We tracked down Dr. Georg Eckardt in Grenoble, thanks to the book that Julia wrote for me, and we got an interview logged into his busy schedule, at eight o'clock at night.

"Good evening, Doctor. My name is Inspector John Frampton of the Greater Manchester Police in the United Kingdom . . . ."

"Good evening, Inspector."

"It is very generous of you to find the time to talk to me."

"That is no problem."

"I am phoning to talk about the late Mr. Julian Benson, whom you treated several years ago, whom you helped to become Miss Julia Blackburn."

"I remember him well, of course, although I am afraid that I cannot discuss his case with you."

"I understand, Doctor. I am afraid Mr. Benson/Miss Blackburn is now dead."

There was a pause at the other end of the phone. "I am very, very sorry to hear that."

"He or she committed suicide."

"That very much surprises me, Inspector. Anyone who went through the operations, and the pain and suffering, and indeed the trauma that we experienced together during all those weeks must have had an enormous appetite for life, a giant's refusal to give in. It would have been far, far easier to have died."

"Am I allowed to ask you about your impressions of his character during that period?"

"No, I am sorry, Inspector, I really cannot comment. After a formal application through the proper authorities, and with their approval, I am allowed to confirm that I treated Mr. Benson, and to provide you with the full details of the procedures we followed. I am not allowed to, and would not wish to, add any personal commentary or private impressions."

"Would it help if I were to tell you that I was also his father?"

"My every sympathy for you, Inspector. No, I regret not."

"I will ask you one question anyway. You can choose to answer it, or not. Did Mr. Benson strike you as being mentally stable during that period?"

"Extraordinarily. One of the sanest and most courageous people I have ever met. A clear-thinking visionary, brave almost beyond belief."

"Are you sure?"

"Inspector, I regret that a patient has just arrived to see me. I must end this conversation. If you require to know more from me, please follow the formal procedures and I will co-operate as best I can."

"Thank you, Doctor."

❀   ❀   ❀

I read Julia's account yet again, and at the end realised that I had better contact the owners of the mill she was staying in to inform them that she would not be returning.

I found it immediately on the Internet ("Cacin Mill"), and picked out their contact details.

"Hello."

"Is that Mr. David Erhardt?" (remarkable coincidence).

"It is."

"I am phoning about Miss Julia Benson."

"I am afraid Julia is in England at the moment. Would you like me to get Mary to phone you?"

"Mary?"

"Yes, Mary. I do not remember her surname I am afraid."

"Is she blonde, around forty, pretty, and homely looking?"

"Yes, that would be about right. If she phones you, you can make sure. Or I can give you her direct number and you can call her now."

"Yes, I would like the number please. I will not contact her immediately, but you can say that I called, if you don't mind. Inspector John Frampton."

"OK. I'll pass on your message. I will be seeing her later, if that is soon enough."

"That is perfect."

I immediately got hold of Joey. "Could you check your facts with the French police? I have reason to believe that Mary Maloney is still alive and living near Granada."

"Really? Wow!"

Joey came back half-an-hour later. "I got straight through. They again denied any knowledge of the existence of Mrs. Mary Maloney. Then suddenly he said 'We did talk to a Mrs. Malanny, though.'"

"You're joking."

"Nope. They knew Mrs. Malanny. She disappeared at the same time as Julia Benson. That is why they were so keen to get hold of Julia. They thought she had killed her, and the other girl . . . ." Joey refers to his notes ". . . . Alice Picard. I must say, he sounded rather embarrassed. Well, aggressive, actually."

"Figures."

❊   ❊   ❊

Which meant that I had to read that damn book again. I began to hate it. I began to feel that it was personally torturing me, that Julia was deliberately holding back the key information.

Then suddenly a sentence grabbed me. It is funny how you can skate over something numerous times and then, in a new context, you gain a completely different understanding of what is being said.

I knew exactly who the killer was, and it would not take me more than half-an-hour to get myself the evidence I needed. Even though it was 11:30 at night, Sally Willows answered her phone.

I phoned the station. I needed four officers at 6:00 that morning. Could it be arranged?

"They are going to love you for that. It had better be worth it."

"It is to arrest Henry Spence for the three murders in Hanburgh."

"Oh, yes, that is definitely worth it. You are not going to wait for a warrant?"

"No, I will sort all that out later."

"Okie-dokie, John. Consider it done."

Henry was not at all amused to be called to the door at 6:30 in the morning.

"Are you Henry Adam Spence?" I demanded.

"You know damn well I am, John." He eyed the accompanying officers.

"In that case, Mr. Henry Adam Spence, as the officer in charge I arrest you for the wilful murder of Mr. Tom Willows, of Mr. George Knightly, and of Mr. Tom Becker. You do not have to say anything now, but I must warn you that anything you do choose to say may be taken down and used in evidence at your trial."

"This is absolutely ridiculous, John. Wait until Hilary hears about this!"

"You may, of course, tell Mrs. Spence where you are going, to Hanburgh police station initially, and that you are being taken in for questioning. I regret that the conversation will have to be kept brief, Sir, and that an officer will have to be present at all times."

"My wife is in bed. I am not having one of your officers in our bedroom."

"Then please call Mrs. Spence, and ask her to get dressed and come downstairs."

"That will not take only five minutes, John. Hilary always takes a long time to get dressed."

"It takes what it takes, Sir. It is the conversation which must be kept brief."

❋   ❋   ❋

"Hello, Inspector."

Julia was looking calm, pre-occupied, and pleased to see me.

"I have been reading your book, Julia. Although it is not exactly what I was expecting, it has given me some excellent insights into all that has been happening here. It must have taken you a great deal of time and effort, not to mention pain to complete."

"I am glad that you have found it useful, John. Has it helped you solve the case?"

"I still get the impression that you are holding a lot back. I doubt that you were being entirely honest."

"I did hold back the last section. I wanted that to remain private between Mary and me."

"So it wasn't included in what you gave me?"

"No."

"What was in that section?"

"That is what will remain private, John. Mary has a print-out. It is her choice too as to whether, and when, we release it."

I sat down on the end of the bed, next to Julia. "Off the record, Julia, why did you kill Tom Willows? Did you think he was your father when you decided to sleep with him? Were you, in some perverted way, taking revenge on him and the way you believed he had raped and abandoned your mother? How could you do that?"

"I did think it was a possibility that he was my father, but only the slightest of ones. I slept with him because I was getting my own back on Mary for her betrayal, showing her that I could replace our warm, loving, apparently homosexual relationship with a cold, clinical, heterosexual quickie. I was challenging her to take a stance for her own values, not just to accept the dumb customs of the village which almost celebrated Tom's behaviour and morality. And, John, I did not kill Tom. Either Tom."

"I find that very, very hard to believe."

"I know you do, John. Try. Listen to your intuition. Did you always think I was the killer?"

"No."

"Did your intuition tell you I was not the killer, despite appearances, and despite the absence of any alternative explanations?"

"Yes."

"Do you have the slightest hard evidence that I killed any of those people?"

"Only what you have just done to Jeff Berringer."

"I did that in broad daylight in front of witnesses. It was hardly the same modus operandi."

"That is true. He is pulling through, by the way. He will be horrifically scarred for life . . . ."

"Which seems appropriate . . . ."

"He will have to go through years of surgery to try to hide the scars . . . ."

"Many of us have been there, John. Put there by him, in fact. There can indeed be true poetry in justice, if you plan it carefully enough, much more so than there is justice in the law most of the time."

"Don't you feel any pity for him, Julia?"

"Yes, I do. You know I do, John. You have read about it. However, just because I empathise with his situation does not preclude me from acting, and this was the only course that you and your kind left me with. You wouldn't stop him, you wouldn't arrest him, you wouldn't even confront him. You could have stopped all this years and years ago. You chose not to. I chose to."

"It wasn't as simple as that . . . ."

"It doesn't matter now. The deed is done, and justice has been served. Can I ask you one favour?"

"You can ask. Doing you favours is a little tricky at the moment."

"Have I tried to help you?"

"I think so. I am not terribly sure. I cannot decide whether you have mostly sought to clarify or obfuscate the facts."

"Believe me, John, I have really tried to help you. I have really tried to do what you asked of me, the enormous task you asked of me, in my own way, of course."

"Let us say, for the moment, that I believe you."

"I will go to prison for what I did to Jeff Berringer."

"Undoubtedly."

"What am I looking at—15, 20 years?"

"About that, unless your lawyer can put together a really compelling mitigation plea."

"And then what—ten?"

"I would say so."

"I do not want to go to prison for 10 years."

"Maybe you should have thought about that before you set fire to him."

"I did, John, I did. Why do you think I took so long to do it, left the country to get a distance on it . . . ."

"And you still did it."

"In the end, as a moral human being, there was no choice."

"You absolutely had a choice."

"Anyway, the favour I was going to ask you was for you to help me escape from here."

I froze. "Julia, you have got to be joking. Apart from any considerations of justice, I would get ten years myself if I were to do that. Give me one good reason why I should even remember that you have asked me."

"Because, John, I did what you did not have the courage to do. I did your work."

"It never occurred to me to set fire to Jeff Berringer."

"I don't believe you."

"I wouldn't have been as subtle as that."

"I am not sure that anyone would call it subtle."

"You said yourself it was poetic, branding the hidden scars of his victims visibly onto his face and head. I think that many will understand the significance. You may yet become a heroine."

"It is not an age of heroism, John."

"And yet you are asking me to be heroic?"

"Yes. A small act of heroism. You will get away with it. Six metres of rope, and a knife."

"Is that all? Why on earth do you need rope? You are on the ground floor here."

"It may depend on how many people I have to tie up. At least one, I should think."

"Meaning me?"

"It is possible."

"How do I get six metres of rope in here?"

"Easy. A change of clothes, a bag of evidence, under your coat."

"I'll think about it, Julia. That is the most that I can promise. Do you still have the gun you took from me?"

"Yes, in Cacin."

"So long as it is not here."

Author's Note

The reason Sally Willows was in the village on the day of Tom Willows' murder was that she had been summoned by Tom to discuss an issue that had been disturbing him.

Two of his children—Tom Becker and Charlene Brown—were planning to marry each other, neither knowing that Tom Willows was their father.

What should he do about it?

Having talked the problem over with Sally, Tom decided to raise it with his best friend, Henry Spence.

Henry was absolutely furious. Tom Becker was his protégé in the funeral parlour business, and virtually his adoptive son. Tom Willows' decadence and irresponsibility threatened to ruin Tom Becker's life, and that of Charlene, of whom Henry was extremely fond.

Henry also bore a deep, hidden, grudge against Tom Willows for the humiliation of his early adult years when Tom could pick up any girl he wanted, and made no effort whatsoever to help Henry hook up with the girls he fancied. Worse, Tom was adamantly opposed to any relationship between Sally and Henry, and not only expressly forbade Sally from getting involved with him, but actually ran Henry down in front of Sally, and spread false rumours to render him unpalatable to her.

Henry knew about the secret tunnel into Tom's house from his friendships with Tom and Sally when they were young, and decided to act before Tom could intervene in Tom Becker and Charlene Brown's marriage. He sneaked into the house via the secret passageway, found the double-shafted axe outside the back door, picked up the towel from where Tom had let it drop, and attacked him at his desk from behind, cleaving his head in two.

After the collapse of the proposed marriage between Tom Becker and Charlene Brown, in saying how sorry he was for what had happened, Henry accidentally provided Tom with enough information for him to realise that Henry had murdered Tom Willows. Despite his affection for Henry, Tom Becker made it clear that it was his duty to go directly to the police. Perhaps the courts would be lenient when they understood the full circumstances of the killing, and would find Henry guilty of manslaughter rather than of murder. Henry panicked, had a heated argument with Tom, and slit his throat with a knife which Tom had just been using. As both were wearing gloves as part of their standard working practices, no fingerprints were left on the handle. He then fled the scene of the crime just before his wife, Hilary, arrived to find Tom in his death throes.

George Knightly was not murdered by Henry, but by Julia who was outraged at his self-appointed role in warning off Dr. Berringer's victims from exposing him, and maybe even of killing them. Julia had seen George visit her own mother only days before her eventual suicide.

In her usual poetic style, she used an electric cord because George "shocked" Dr. Berringer's victims into silence. From her recent foray into the Berringer's home with Sam, Julia knew George's schedule and routine, and lay in wait for him, catching him off-balance from behind, and preventing him from regaining his balance while she choked him to death. Indeed, George's desperate struggling only served to ensure his death, as it forced the cable tighter around his throat, and made it easier for Julia to execute him.

About the author—
Tim Roux

Born near Hull in the UK in 1954, Tim was called to the Bar before working for over 20 years in business strategy and strategic brand marketing for a major multinational corporation.

With degrees in both law and social sciences/psychology, and having worked as a volunteer for Amnesty International for several years, he is fascinated by the complex issues surrounding personal rights (human, civil and animal), and much of his writing has and will address these themes.

Tim has a wife and two children, and lives between the UK, France and Belgium running Valley Strategies Ltd. which leads a community of expert consultancies in bullet-proofing business strategies.

Other books by Tim Roux, to be released in 2007 are:

Shade + Shadows, which is about Alan Harding, an alternative healer with a particularly unusual basis for his therapies, who marries the former wife of a controversial ambassador who survived an assassination attempt by Muslim terrorists. When his wife, Jane, is kidnapped as retribution for her husband's crimes, everyone assumes that the kidnappers are referring to the ambassador's activities. However, the good doctor has his own dark secrets . . . .

Blood & Marriage, a factional account which explores the strained relationship of a couple moving country, against the backdrop of the histories of their respective families, who were both forced to leave the German States in the late nineteenth century, and who were both linked to events in Southern Africa, including the first genocide of the 20th century, of the Herero Peoples of German South-West Afrika/Namibia, which took place in 1904.

About the artist—

Sharon Hudson

I first came across the work of Sharon Hudson, the San Francisco Bay artist, when I was looking for an e-card to send as a commiseration for the death of a young girl, Clare, after half a lifetime of chronic illness.

I was immediately struck by the warm immediacy of her paintings. She herself uses the word "sensual" to describe them; I would prefer the words "intimate" and "private", although I find "Sheherazade", which is to be found on the cover of this book, extremely sensual. It was also an inspiration for the final version of this story.

Many of Sharon's paintings are nude portraits, yet it is the serenity and ease of their subjects that strike you more than their naked bodies.

Searching for a front cover for "Little Fingers!", I thought Sharon might just have something appropriate and, sure enough, there was "Sheherazade".

As you probably know, the tale of Sheherazade is of a young girl who is due to be executed by King Schariar of Samarkand as a sacrifice for the adultery of his wife, and who tells the king the enlightening stories of the 1,001 Arabian nights to save both her life and the lives of others, in the same way that Julia Blackburn tells her life story to Inspector Frampton in "Little Fingers!", almost as a confessional, in an attempt to earn her own liberty.

The presentation of Sharon Hudson's "Sheherazade" is of a beautiful, sensual woman of strong, ambivalent character, with a touch of the tomboy about her, again a perfect match for Julia Blackburn.

If you would like to see more of Sharon's work, and I strongly recommend that you do, you can visit her virtual gallery at http://www.byhudson.com. I would give you a list of my personal favourites, but it would be a very long list, and what is the point? You will have your own.

Tim Roux, July 2006.

Printed in the United Kingdom
by Lightning Source UK Ltd.
135643UK00001B/293/A

9 781425 745134